Rain Song

ALICE J. WISLER

Rain Song

BETHANY HOUSE PUBLISHERS

Minneapolis, Minnesota

Published by Bethany House Publishers
11400 Hampshire Avenue South
Bloomington, Minnesota 55438

Bethany House Publishers is a division of
Baker Publishing Group, Grand Rapids, Michigan.

Printed in the United States of America

Library of Congress Cataloging-in-Publication Data
Wisler, Alice J.
    Rain song / Alice J. Wisler.
        p.   cm.
    ISBN 978-0-7642-0477-7 (pbk.)
    1. Young women—Fiction. 2. North Carolina—Fiction. I. Title.
    PS3623.I846R35   2008
    813'.6—dc22

2366   2008028123

*For Rachel, Benjamin, and Elizabeth, and in
memory of Daniel, my reason for waving to heaven.*

"Life is either a daring adventure or nothing."

—HELEN KELLER

AME, AME

FURE, FURE

KAASANGA

JANOME DE

OMUKAE

URESHIINA

—A Japanese children's song
about a mother who comes in the rain
to pick up her child

Chapter One

MOUNT OLIVE, NORTH CAROLINA
1999

When they suggest changing the location of the family reunion, I am first to speak. I clear my throat a few times—something that irritates me when anyone else does it—and then, with my eyes focused on the crystal vase of scarlet roses centered on Ducee's kitchen table, I begin. I remind them that we've always had the reunion in North Carolina; why break tradition? Tradition is big in the McCormick family.

I see Ducee nod, which gives me courage to continue. Since there are more family members in this region, I add, making all of us fly to Wyoming would be senseless. Wouldn't it be easier and much more logical for the Wyoming group to fly here? They are younger. I mean, should Ducee really fly at her age? And her heart condition, don't forget that.

Cheyenne, Wyoming, residents Aunt Betty and Uncle Jarvis, who are spending the weekend with Ducee, look uncomfortably across the table at each other. In unison they blurt, "Oh, Nicole, of course Ducee shouldn't fly." Then they apologize to Ducee for even making the suggestion.

"Oh my, what were we thinking?" Aunt Betty reaches her round pink arm across the table toward Ducee, tipping the flower arrangement; Uncle Jarvis grabs the vase just in time. Aunt Betty croons, "Oh, Mother, I don't know what came over me."

I gnaw on a thumbnail and stand to wash the dishes. They don't need to be apologetic about their idea; they just don't need to give it any more consideration.

So nothing has changed, and once again, this July, the family reunion will be here in Mount Olive. We'll make the usual food—potato salad, chicken salad, honey-baked ham, corn on the cob dripping with butter, green bean casserole, delicate egg salad sandwiches on white bread, and of course, traditional homemade pineapple chutney. We'll spread the checkered tablecloths over the rickety picnic tables in my grandmother Ducee's backyard and cover ourselves with insect repellent and eat until the stars flicker out one by one. Great-Uncle Clive will swing the great-grandkids in the tire swing as Maggie, Ducee's white-pawed donkey, brays and nibbles at ripe blackberries growing over the edge of the wooden fence.

The Wyoming group—Aunt Betty and Uncle Jarvis, Kate, Linda, and their spouses and children—will inevitably wonder how we handle the humidity and tell us a few dozen times that the air is less sticky in Cheyenne, until Cousin Aaron drives them in the church van to the coast. Then, after splashing in the salty waves as they watch the sun set over the Atlantic, they will smile and say how lovely the ocean is and what a blessing it is for us in Mount Olive to be so close to this spectacular view. For a moment, they will envy us, their bodies not at all bothered by southern summer stickiness.

Ducee knows, though. She lifts her chin and adjusts her bifocals and I know she knows. She's thinking that Nicole doesn't care if we have Japanese squid and octopus at the reunion, as long as it means keeping the gathering here in Mount Olive. Just don't make her get on an airplane. That's what Ducee is thinking as she nods and wipes her pale lips with a pastel linen napkin.

No plane ride for me. Ever.

Last time I was on a plane I threw up three times. I was only two and don't remember it, but I'm sure things haven't changed. Just the sound of planes racing overhead is enough to pump fear into my veins and churn my stomach.

Great-Aunt Iva says that everyone is entitled to at least one phobia. She adds that if you have any Irish McCormick blood in you, you are most certainly entitled to even a few more.

————

On a crisp February afternoon, Iva, Ducee, and I sit around the kitchen table with bone china cups of tea. They ask how I am. We've just made three gallons of pineapple chutney and we're still in Mount Olive pickle green aprons. We're pretty wiped out; that's what this chutney-making tradition does to you. Hours and hours of slicing pineapple and adding spices while standing over a simmering pot can really sap your energy. That's why, after the chutney is sealed in jars, we allow for plenty of time to relax with hot ginger tea.

Ducee adds black tea leaves to freshly ground ginger root and seasons the mixture with lemon juice and sugar. She boils this concoction with distilled water because she is convinced that distilled water creates the best tea. She says it's common southern knowledge.

"I'm fine," I reply. Quickly, I take a long drink. The tea scalds my tongue.

Ducee glances at me, raises an eyebrow, and waits.

She can wait all afternoon; I am not about to tell her anything more. I reach for a grape from the fruit bowl and admire the carnations in the crystal vase.

"You've been in another world," Ducee says. Her greenish-blue eyes soften as she studies my face.

I force a smile. "Really, I'm okay." Sticking my thumb into my mouth, I chew a ragged nail. Nail-biting and fear of flying are my two known weaknesses. The other ones I work at hiding from everyone else.

Iva lights up a Virginia Slims, stretches her long, slender legs, and crosses her ankles. When she does this, it's as though she thinks she's the original Ms. Virginia Slims. She says she hopes we can have cucumber sandwiches at the reunion. "You know how much I like cucumbers thinly sliced on white bread." She exhales and adds, "Peeled, of course. Never did like the skin of a cucumber, not even the ones we grew growing up on our farm."

Ducee shakes her head, causing her gray curls to bounce. "Not at all proper." She enunciates each word as I do when teaching. "I told you before, Iva. It isn't done."

Iva asks, "And why not?"

"You can't have both egg salad and cucumber sandwiches at the same party." Ducee states this as though it's a fact, like the population of Mount Olive, which happens to be 4,427.

Iva's hazel eyes widen behind her silver-rimmed glasses. "Says who?"

"It's common etiquette. All southerners know this. Take

pimento cheese, for example. Our southern classic. However, it cannot be eaten with egg salad, either."

"I've never heard any of this before and I've lived in North Carolina all my life," Iva says, her voice laced with aggravation.

I roll my eyes at Iva. There is no point in my aunt continuing with her desire to have cucumber sandwiches. When Ducee mentions etiquette, it's useless to argue. My grandmother thinks she is the queen of etiquette, at least southern etiquette.

Once, as a young girl visiting her during summer vacation, I asked Ducee what the name of her book was. Puzzled, she questioned what I meant.

"Your book you wrote," I said. "The one about how to wipe your mouth on a cloth napkin and how to kiss cheeks."

Ducee played along. "Oh, my book of important Southern Truths." She patted my arm. "Yes, that's it, yes. They are written somewhere, I'm sure. Emily Post or Mrs. Vanderbilt."

I was nine before I realized Ducee had not written a book on etiquette; she just liked to talk about certain ways one should conduct oneself—her renowned Southern Truths. I do admit I was disappointed and couldn't bear to tell my classmates at my elementary school in Richmond, Virginia, that my grandmother in Mount Olive, North Carolina, had not authored a book, even though, yes, one day in third-grade show-and-tell I proudly shared she had.

As the afternoon sun shifts behind a cloud and darkens the kitchen, Iva takes a slow puff on her cigarette. She exchanges the cucumber-sandwiches topic for her grandson-in-law. "I just don't know what Grable is going to do about Dennis. She's having to live the life of the single parent." Grable is Iva's granddaughter who is thirty-five, four years older than I am.

I know nothing about marriage, since I've never been married. I would like to be married, I think. But some nights, I watch my aquarium of saltwater fish swimming in their tranquil patterns and wonder why I'd want to bring chaos to our home. My fish and I are doing quite well without a human male mate.

Iva inhales, blows out a smoke ring, and says, "I knew Dennis was no good from the get-go."

"Yes, yes," Ducee chimes, a frown encompassing her brow. "We all know that he reminds you of Harlowe."

Harlowe, named after the river in North Carolina, was my great-aunt Iva's third husband. He was known for a temper that caused him to throw cans at the kitchen walls. When he threw six cans of pork and beans in one afternoon, Iva marched out of her house for the lawyer's office. The divorce was final twelve months later. Iva, known for always having a man by her side, has yet to remarry. After Harlowe's frenzy, she's decided gratitude for being alive—not six feet under due to an accident caused by tin cans—is enough reason to be content.

Iva slides the cardinal ashtray closer and twists the butt of her cigarette into the body of the red bird. "Harlowe was impossible." She lets go of the butt like she let go of him.

Right when I think we're going to hear a pathetic Harlowe story, my aunt sighs, cups her chin in the crevices of her palms, and lets silence take over.

After a moment she cries, "Why has Grable followed in my footsteps? Sure as the sun, she married a man who doesn't appreciate her."

"She was in love," Ducee tells her younger sister brightly. "Grable saw the moon rise and set in his smile. Remember their wedding day?"

I don't. I was invited—Grable is my second cousin, or

something like that—but I didn't make the wedding. Three days prior to the event, I came up with the brilliant idea to free my backyard from overgrown weeds. I must have pulled the wrong weeds because I ended up with the worst case of poison ivy ever. Grable was covered in white and delicate flowers. I covered my body with prescribed triamcinolone acetonide and sat in a tub of Aveeno, trying to ease the constant desire to scratch.

"It rained." Iva's face is covered by a sour expression. "It was cold and wet. I must have stepped in six puddles before I even got inside the church. My feet were soaked the whole day. My red dress has a mud stain that to this day hasn't come out."

I did see the pictures of the wedding. Everyone looked happy, except for Iva. It is hard to smile, I guess, when your feet are wet.

Ducee smiles. "Oh yes, yes, it was a beautiful ceremony. The church looked exceptionally pretty with all those tulips. I'd never seen so many colors in one place." She shifts in her chair to look Iva in the eye, but Iva turns away from her sister. Her sigh fills the kitchen. I can hear it lift out of her lungs and span the ceiling and the lemon-colored walls.

Ducee traces the rim of her teacup with a bony finger. Slowly she says, "You aren't in control of everything or anybody. Remember that, Iva."

If I ever compile a list of my grandmother's sayings, this one will be at the top.

We know she will add another part to her thought, and she does. "Good things happen in fleeting moments. Enjoy what you can—those moments are sometimes all we get." She focuses on both of our faces and then, "Yes." There is a long pause as though she is remembering something almost lost, like one of those long-gone fleeting moments she wants to recapture in her mind. "Yes, that's it, yes."

Iva finishes her tea, pushes her cup and saucer toward the middle of the table, and smacks her lips. "Well, Grable's not having any good things happening these days. Having to do it all alone and then when Dennis does decide to come home, he has no patience for Monet. She *is* his daughter." She lights another cigarette and coughs.

I think of Grable and Dennis's three-year-old, Monet, the child no doctor at Duke or UNC hospitals can figure out. The child is wild, and my patience for her runs thin. The last time she overfed my fish, I screamed at her. Then I felt awful and bought her a coloring book and pack of Crayolas. Grable has aspirations that Monet will live up to her name and be able to paint like Claude Monet.

Grable also thinks Dennis will cut back his hours at the law firm, take some time off, and fly with her to an exotic country, preferably Costa Rica.

"Monet is a treasure," Ducee says with feeling. "Trying, but if you listen to her heart, she is charming."

Both Iva and I give Ducee looks as if she's lost her mind.

Iva crumples her empty cigarette pack. "Don't know why God made her the way she is."

Ducee starts to speak, but Iva interrupts. "I know, I know, you're going to say His ways are not our ways. And to trust Him and not doubt. Birds of the air." She waves her cigarette in front of her face. "I know, I know." She clears her raspy throat. That action always makes me quiver.

"Actually," Ducee says, "I was going to ask if you wanted more tea."

Iva places the end of the Virginia Slims in the ashtray and stands. "No, got to get to the Friendly Mart."

We know why. She just smoked her last cigarette. We watch her untie her apron and fold it on the back of the chair. She ruffles her dyed-platinum hair by running fingers through the roots. Her smile shows her gold molar. She thanks her sister for the day, extending her arm so that Ducee can touch it with her lips.

"See you tomorrow at church," Ducee says as Iva pulls on her short fur coat and fastens the pearl buttons.

Iva coughs. "The Good Lord willing and the creek don't rise." She squeezes my shoulder before striding for the front door. Iva is tall—close to six feet—and she has a way of easing across floors when she walks, like a waterbug skimming the river's surface.

Ducee tilts her head and looks at me through smudged bifocals. "Is it Richard?" she asks after Iva leaves the house.

I sigh. "Richard and I broke up last night." There, I've told her. Why does my grandmother always win?

She nods as though she already knew. That woman knows me like her famous family chutney recipe. When she looks at me, I swear she can see the missing ingredient.

"Why don't you come over for dinner after church tomorrow, then?" She pats my hand. Her hand is tiny, the skin thin with age spots and protruding purple veins. "I'll make barbeque chicken." She smiles, adding, "With the Smithfield sauce you like so much."

A moment passes and the silence eats at her. "Nicole, dear? You okay? Anything else you need to tell me?"

Can she see into my mind?

"No." I can't tell her that I've received a beautiful poem from a carp owner in Japan. Surely when she looks at me she doesn't know that, does she? I have also dreamed of him, although I have no idea what he looks like in real life.

Since the death of my mother, Ducee has practically raised me. Although I lived with Father until I graduated from high school, during those years, my summers and school breaks were always spent at Ducee's house. She knows I have a mole the shape of an apple on my lower back and that even at age thirty-one, I continue to sleep with a cloth kimono doll.

But there are still lines I draw. She doesn't get to know every-thing.

Sometimes, though, on chilly, dark nights when the only sound in my house is the humming fish tank, it would be nice to sit in Aunt Lucy's wingback chair, curl my legs up under me, and just spill it out.

Chapter Two

I stop at the Friendly Mart on the way home and buy a pint of Chewy Caramel Chunk. At the local park, I eat the ice cream with a plastic spoon, running the heat in my car as high as it will go. I shiver, warm my hands on the blowing air vent, and dig in the carton for another spoonful. The ice cream melts on my tongue as I taste the chocolate bits and the thick caramel syrup.

Two children in matching plaid jackets take turns racing down the slide. An elderly man in a Durham Bulls ball cap watches. When they sail off the slide, he catches them in his broad arms. Even though the heat is raging through my car's vents and the windows are up, I can hear the children giggle. They break from his arms and rush again to the slide. For a moment I ache with a longing to join them.

The last time I was here was after three of my students failed an English test on Hemingway. I couldn't believe they did so poorly when I'd gone over almost every single question two days prior to the written test. I was in a slump—it did something to me to see those low scores. I questioned my ability to teach and their desire to learn. Had I not been enthusiastic enough; had I omitted passion in my instruction? What was wrong with me?

Seated in my car that day, I ate a pint of Raspberry Almond Delight, watched a pudgy toddler play peek-a-boo with his mother, and heard Ducee's familiar line, *"You aren't in control of everything or anybody. Remember that."*

An hour later, when I left the park, I concluded that things weren't so bad.

Sometimes all you need is ice cream and a little time. And Ducee's sayings, whether I want to admit it or not, do make sense. *Yes, that's it, yes.*

The sun sinks lower in the sky, and I know I must leave the park soon, go home, and feed my aquarium of hungry fish. They're probably at the top of the tank, opening their miniature mouths along the water's surface, tasting only wisps of air.

I'm baffled because I can't remember ever going to a park as a child. Father never took me. Maybe he thought I'd throw up on the swings like I did on my plane trip coming back from Japan. But I do recall sitting in his car on a winter's day, eating ice cream from the container, with the heater blasting warm air throughout the musty Buick.

Father said that this was life—cold, warm, and hot. I laughed because that sounded funny to me, an impossibility for something to hold the characteristics of all three adjectives. I threw my head back and laughed like Uncle Jarvis. Swing your head back, open your mouth, and let laughter flow like a rushing waterfall in the North Carolina mountains. It sounds like sunshine in your ears. I eagerly waited to be joined, but Father has never been one for laughter, or even a good chuckle.

Richard said he heard Father laugh once. But I can't trust Richard. He said we would be together *always.* Funny how

Richard decided to end *always* last night at the Lucky Golden Chinese restaurant. I understood his reasoning too well. We'd been over his list, written on the back of a sales receipt from the shoe store he manages, about fifty times.

Last night he crumpled the list, as Aunt Iva does with her empty pack of Virginia Slims, and said, "It's over, Nic. It's over this time."

I stared at my congealed plate of Hunan beef.

With obvious frustration, he bellowed, "Do you even know what you want?"

It's all Mama's fault. It all goes back to her. If she'd lived, I'd be normal. Married, with two or three kids and a husband fiercely in love with me. We'd live in that old Victorian house off East Maple Street. I would get my nails painted at Lady Claws each Saturday like Grable does because I wouldn't be ashamed of my short, bitten nails. My tapered long nails would be glamorous, and the envy of all. I'd also be graceful, full of poise. I wouldn't snort when I laugh loudly. I'd probably be a piano player like Mama; she would have taught me to play. If Mama were here, I wouldn't be anxious, wondering what went wrong and why she had to die. I would have had a proper mother to raise me and teach me about pantyhose, makeup, and shaving my legs.

I finish the ice cream and wait for tears. None come. I stare into the empty container and then toss it on the floor by the passenger seat. Opening the glove compartment, I push the plastic spoon between a crumpled map of North Carolina and the car's owner's manual. I like to keep a spoon in my car—like a spare tire—because you never know when you just might need it.

As darkness starts to pull its heavy blanket across the sky, I shiver in spite of the warmth blowing through the car vent. I guess I'll just go on home. Everyone else has left the park.

———

At home there are English papers to grade. One of my pet peeves is the frequent improper usage of the English language. *Your* for *you are*. *It's* for *its*. *There* when it should be *their*. My middle school students like to groan, "Aw, Ms. Michelin, you're too hard on us."

That's when I tell them rules were made to follow and the best way not to repeat my English class is to follow those rules.

When they laugh and say I can't make them take the class again, I look into their eyes and without a grin tell them, "Oh yes. Yes, I can."

They squirm in their seats, study my serious face, grip their pencils tightly, and look as if they're going to concentrate.

It is then that I know just how young and impressionable they are. They believe me still. One day, they will look upon me as they do their own parents, doubting nearly everything I tell them.

When the room becomes too dark to see, instead of turning on a light, I abandon the papers, leave my antique desk—one of the items I inherited from Great-Aunt Lucy—and check my email messages.

My desk chair is an overstuffed swivel, purchased for a bargain at the Raleigh flea market. Ducee got the vendor to accept ten dollars instead of the sticker price of thirty.

She went on and on about how the chair was flawed a little on the back, looked a bit threadbare on the seat, and didn't swivel as well as it should. "My, is one of the wheels on the bottom bent? Look here, Iva, what do you think?" I think the vendor was so glad to get rid of her that he accepted the wrinkled ten-dollar bill she withdrew from her bra and even helped us lift the chair into Ducee's red truck.

The chair, unfortunately, has never been comfortable. I've added a yellow cushion for padding, but I still feel as though I'm sitting in an object about to topple over. But it was a bargain, so what can I say?

Ducee says that a real southerner knows the value of a bargain, just like Robert E. Lee knew. I've studied American history and never read anything about Lee enjoying bargains. I suppose that tidbit of information is only in Ducee's mind, in the file she keeps of her Southern Truths.

There is nothing new in my email inbox, not even spam, so I read the familiar messages from Harrison, the carp owner. This is getting to be a ritual for me. I am creating a new habit. Ducee says she read somewhere that a new pattern only takes thirty days to become a habit.

It was three weeks ago, right after my newest column at the Pretty Fishy Web site was posted, that I heard from this stranger. My column was on plants to stock in an outdoor pond so that larger fish, especially koi, won't eat them. As usual, I'd researched the topic at the library and also consulted my own collection of books on tropical and saltwater fish. The editor of Pretty Fishy had my column on the site within two days of my sending it in. And the next day, I heard from a reader. His letter was simple and the closest I've ever had to fan mail.

Dear Ms. Michelin,

I read your interesting and helpful article on plant life at the Pretty Fishy website. I have a pond with six koi and am having trouble with the plants. What kind of plant life do you think does best in an outdoor pond with koi? Mine seem to eat everything. It's costing me a fortune.

Harrison Michaels

I responded the next day after school while eating a bowl of hot grits loaded with butter. I believe grits is one of God's finer creations.

Harrison,

Thank you for reading my column at the Pretty Fishy site. You are right; koi love to eat the roots of lots of plants. As for the answer to your question, maybe your local pet store might have a better response, but mine would have to be to get some water lilies. I like the Colorado and Pink Sensation.

Cattails are nice, too. Some fish owners have built underwater fences to separate the plant life from the fish so that the plant life can stand a chance. Perhaps you will just have to expect to replace your plants often. Good luck!

Nicole

I finished the grits, read what I'd written, used spell check, and when no spelling mistakes were detected, pressed the send button.

Three mornings later, there were two new messages.

The first was from Uncle Jarvis with a joke about how many teachers it takes to change a light bulb. Uncle Jarvis has a large supply of jokes he circulates around the Internet. Ever since he dressed up in a clown suit as the entertainment for one of his daughter's birthday parties, he's felt he should continue being funny, always ready with a joke. No one laughs as loudly at his own jokes as my uncle.

The second message was from Harrison. To my fish I read,

Nicole,

I took your advice and went to my local pet store. The guy there said if I just bought all my plants at the temple at the foot of the mountain, I wouldn't have to worry because the plants sold at the shops there are protected from all ailments including destructive koi in ponds. This is just a common belief among Japanese based on superstition.

I think your comments about just being willing to replace plants often or separate the fish from the plants are really good ones. I will opt for the first and in time may realize the second is well worth the hassle.

Thank you for taking time to write to me.

Harrison

That night, as light snow fell, I dreamed about a carp named Harrison.

Chapter Three

In the dream, I was in the warm ocean, swimming in a sapphire one-piece suit. Bright coral and fat pagodas sat at the bottom of the waters. I was a child, about two years old, and my frizzy red hair stuck straight out from my ears, dancing with the strands of seaweed beside me.

Suddenly fish joined me, large as fully grown humans. Koi—red bellies glistening in the seawaters. One of them, the shiniest one, directed me over to a garden with rows of purple and yellow irises and trees with pink blossoms, the color of my cotton doll Sazae's kimono sash. This fish even spoke. "Hi, I'm Harrison. Harrison Michaels."

I watched him swim, his strokes gliding his body through the water. I was amazed at the beauty of the garden, grateful he had taken me there. This was a tranquil place; I even wondered if it was a taste of heaven.

Even though the garden was bright from the sunshine, I kept anticipating that something horrible was going to happen. Since I was a child, dreams haven't been kind to me. I've had some ferocious nightmares; Ducee knows about those.

But when I woke, it was morning, just minutes before my

alarm clock was set to ring. And I felt light and excited, a rare combination for me.

At school that morning, Kristine Buxy, the science teacher, talked to me for fifteen minutes in the teachers' lounge about the new gym teacher, Salvador. She asked if I'd noticed his long eyelashes and smooth skin. "He's from Puerto Rico," she told me. "I'd love to go there, wouldn't you?"

On most days, even good ones, Kristine's voice bothers me. Beautiful as she is with her endowed chest and tiny waist, her southern twang is an annoyance. Generally, I find southern accents like Iva's, Grable's, and Ducee's to be quaint and comforting. Kristine's has a whiny, nasal tone.

However, I listened this particular day, or gave the impression that I was following her every word. Yet my mind was still in that carefree ocean, replaying the dream of a human carp named Harrison. Would I dream of him tonight? More importantly, why was I dreaming of him? Surely, at last, I was headed off the deep end and ready to join Aunt Lucy, about whom everyone said—*"The craziest of the relatives. Oh, yes, absolutely crazy!"*

It was a week later that Harrison sent a poem.

> Cherry blossoms scatter over warmed pond
> abundant like God's generous grace
> Koi and I eager to view open lilies
> beauty handmade each spring
> by a Creator whose face is hidden
> yet whose love abounds.

He added that every spring he wrote a new poem and this was last year's production. I read the poem aloud to my tank of five fish and one black eel. It sounded serene as the words fell over the surface of my aquarium.

I've told no one, but I've printed his poem, and I read it each day. I guess I'm hopeful that by reading it, I'll know how to respond. Of course, I could easily reply with something like, "It's a beautiful poem." But does that mean he'll write back again? How long will this correspondence continue? Who sends a poem to a stranger? Who is he?

I suspect he lives in Japan.

Tonight, after I eat two boiled eggs for dinner, an idea of what I could write to Harrison pops into my head. Finally, a logical way to respond. But as I walk toward my computer to compose an email reply, the phone rings and my thoughts are scattered.

"Nicki?" Iva coughs and sputters like a faulty vehicle.

"Hi, Iva." I carry the cordless phone from the kitchen into the living room and sit on Aunt Lucy's chair. When Iva calls, the conversation is never short, and comfort is vital for listening to her. Aunt Lucy's wingback chair is the epitome of comfort. I've taken many naps in this chair of peach velvet fabric.

"Ducee seems to be slowing down, don't you think?"

We were just with her this afternoon making chutney. She seemed healthy to me—lifting the ladle, spooning the mixture into mason jars, singing a few off-key lines from her favorite Irish ballads.

Before I can answer, Iva carries on. "She's looking pale and lacking her zestiness. She was short of breath, I could tell. You could tell, too, couldn't you?"

I settle into the chair, resting one hand on the armrest. I hear Aunt Lucy's skin was once as soft as this velvet. Imagine having skin like that. I say, "I think she's doing really well for eighty-one."

"Oh, Nicki." Iva's sigh is loud. "What will I do?"

"She's fine, Iva."

"Why won't she stop being so stubborn and go to the doctor?" Iva coughs, clears her throat, and inhales. I know she has a Virginia Slims in her right hand. "Do you know why she won't see a doctor?"

"She has her prescriptions. That's all she says she needs."

"No, you know what it is. She hates going to the doctor. She flat out told me that. I can't blame her. All they ever do is complain about me. Telling me I shouldn't smoke." She inhales loudly. "Why would they take away a girl's only pleasure?" I wait as she coughs. When she gains control again, she says, "Nicki."

"Yeah?"

"Do you know that of all my siblings, she's my favorite?"

My voice becomes soft. "Yes, Iva. I know."

"How do you know?"

"You've told me."

"I have?"

"Only about a hundred times."

"If she dies before me, I'll kill her."

When I laugh, Iva joins in and sputters, which makes me laugh even more until I let out a snort. After telling her good night, I place the phone in its cradle. As I run my fingers through my hair like Iva does, I ask God to keep Ducee strong and well. If she dies before I do, what will I do?

Chapter Four

Putting on my short brown suede coat, I head outside to sit on the brick step by my front door. Sitting outside calms me. Some folks do yoga or listen to music; I watch the stars. Tonight they are out—shiny, glittering, beckoning, and so far away.

As a child, I used to watch the stars and try to determine which one was heaven's doorknob. I'd usually pick the brightest, focus on it, and then wave. I hoped my mama could see me waving. Sometime around the age of eleven, I thought waving at the stars in hopes that Mama would look down from heaven's perfection to see little ol' me was ridiculous. That phase of my life didn't last too long. It was sad to break my habit. What was wrong with waving, just in case? How did I know Mama couldn't see me? Perhaps she could just feel me wave and the love from my heart would travel up through the air and meet her in heaven. Tonight, I lift my hand and give a small wave. And again I ask God to keep Ducee here on earth awhile longer. Like until after I die.

I've prayed this prayer for a long time. We may grow older, but our desires often stay the same.

My attention strays from the sky to across my lawn, where

I hear noises from my neighbor Hilda's garage. Hilda has never, to my knowledge, been seen without pink curlers rolled around her grayish brown hair and black boots on her size five feet. Through her lit garage windows, I watch the foamy curlers bobbing up and down as she putters in the large area, no doubt moving boxes and making decisions.

Hilda is known for supporting causes. Trucks, vans, and cars stop by her house at all hours of the day, bringing boxes of donated items for her to give away to whichever cause she feels is worthy. The community trusts Hilda to choose where the needs are—the homeless shelters, children's wards of hospitals, boys' and girls' clubs—and to meet them. And willingly, Hilda loads her own vehicle, a spruce-colored minivan with the personalized license plate SHARE, and drives these items to organizations and individuals across our state.

The *Mount Olive Tribune* likes to write articles about Hilda; one editor named her a saint. Her tireless work gives us that ol' hometown pride.

———

When my hands feel like ice, I come inside.

Suddenly I know why I haven't commented to Harrison on his poem. I haven't written back to him because it is clear he lives in Japan. The temple, the superstition, the outdoor pond with koi—it all adds up. Japan is where Mama died. Japan has been nothing but a mystery to me, producing eerie emotions and fear. All my life I've avoided anything that has to do with Japan. It's decided, then: whatever idea I came up with earlier of a potential reply to Harrison, I won't use. Because I'm not writing to Harrison again.

It's okay, I think, as I peel off my jeans and sweatshirt and put on my flannel nightgown for bed. Chances are he doesn't care to hear from me. He's probably dating a petite Asian girl with almond-shaped eyes and silky black hair.

As I brush my teeth and eye my red hair in the bathroom mirror, I wonder who Richard will date next. The librarian with the tattoo of two crimson roses on her ankle? Last year at the annual Pickle Festival, he said he liked her tattoo. Just out of the blue while we were eating corndogs, he glanced at the librarian—who was standing by a banner that read, "Welcome to the Mount Olive Pickle Festival!"—and nudged me. "Wow, what a nice tattoo."

I looked around and couldn't see a tattoo. "Oh yeah," I said, pretending I saw it, and finished my corndog.

At the library a week later, I actually got a view of her tattoo. I spent that Saturday morning doing research on domino damsels for an article for the Pretty Fishy Web site. The librarian was there stocking books on poets. Her tattoo was two delicate roses the color of Red Delicious apples. It looked okay—nothing special.

Now I can't get that tattoo out of my mind. Why would a man leave a woman for another because of a tattoo? Where is the loyalty?

Before snuggling into bed with Sazae, my childhood doll, I look at Richard's picture. I haven't taken the framed color photo off my bedside table. I study his brown hair and matching eyes. I recall the first time he told me I was pretty. These same eyes I am looking at now were filled with life as he held my hand and said, "Nicole, you are so pretty." The sky was a dismal gray, the wind scattered damp leaves over the sidewalk, and my heart wanted to leap out of my skin.

Now I feel nothing for him but foolish. I take the frame and throw it into the top drawer of my dresser. Facedown. I slam the drawer shut and listen to the noisy echo. I hope the glass broke, but I don't check to see.

I think it's time to give up on men.

Even so, I hope I dream of Harrison again tonight.

———

I dream of Harrison again, which makes it all the more difficult not to send a reply to his email. The school day has ended, and I'm in Aunt Lucy's chair, watching from my window as two cardinals dart around the front oak tree. I've often wanted to be an angelfish or a regal demoiselle so I could swim in soothing waters. I've never desired to be a bird; flying is just too dangerous.

Drawing my knees to my chest, I loudly breathe in and out like my cousin Grable did hours prior to giving birth to the terror-child, Monet. In and out. Steady.

We timed Grable's contractions with a stopwatch—laughing, smiling, as if it was a party—around Ducee's kitchen table. Of course, after Grable's water broke, the fancy breathing she learned was tossed out the window—somewhere between the Mount Olive post office and the door to Wayne Memorial Hospital. I remember her begging God for mercy, pleading with Him not to take her life before her child's birth. Lying on the bed in the maternity ward, she screamed for Dennis. A Hispanic woman down the hall, also about to give birth, and those in the waiting room on the second floor heard, but Dennis didn't hear a sound. He was at a lawyers' convention in Seattle.

I sink my bare toes into the soft fabric of the chair and wonder what would possess me to dream in such vivid color about someone I've never met. One email message from him and the dreams started like ocean waves. I take a long breath in. Harrison Michaels. Slowly out. I've repeated his name over and over to my fish, using different intonations, and each gives me the same sensation—he has a name like a movie star.

I've never known anyone with the first name of Harrison. There was a freckly kid in my third-grade class in Richmond named Joey Harrison. He was the only child I knew with more freckles than I had. In seventh grade, I had a friend named Katrina Harrison. We used to take turns bringing oatmeal cookies and sharing them at lunchtime. She ended up liking the same boy I did—Leon Perdusky. He wrote her name on the cover of his math notebook, and after that I didn't share oatmeal cookies with Katrina anymore.

Letting out a breath, I calculate. What I know about this first-name Harrison is little. He lives somewhere in Japan. He has an outdoor pond with koi. He wrote a poem that I can't get out of my mind.

Why did he do that?

"Perhaps," I say aloud as I pause from the steady breaths, "I could reply to him, and that'll be the end of this correspondence. Just a short thank-you for the poem." I run my tongue over a rough thumbnail.

When the phone rings, I prepare to talk with Iva. I expect to hear about Ducee's failing health and how we must have cucumber sandwiches at the reunion. Only the voice on the other end is not raspy but firm—Grable's.

"Nicole? I'm at McGuire's."

McGuire's Pet World must be having a carnival, because I can barely hear Grable over the shrill ruckus of wild chimpanzees. At least it sounds like chimpanzees. Until I decipher a distinct shriek—Monet. Her voice is matched by another and that one does belong to an animal—McGuire's one-legged green Macaw, kept in a cage by the shop's front door. He squawks between Monet's peals of laughter and high-pitched cries.

Grable's voice rises in my ear as she says, "Monet won't leave the store unless she can come see your fish."

My fish. I carry the phone to my fifty-five-gallon tank sitting in the middle of my dining room table as the screaming from across the phone lines blares. I watch my aquarium of peaceful beauties sail through the water. I remember the time Monet stuck her hand into the tank, trying to grasp a clownfish with her small fingers. Then there was the Saturday she poured an entire container of fish food into the water. Once she tossed in a graham cracker. Another time a purple jelly bean. And now Grable is asking if this child can come to my house to see my fish—a ploy to get her to leave McGuire's.

"Well . . ." I watch my eel bury his head in the gravel under the green-and-red ceramic pagoda. One of the angelfish glides over his head. If only I could bury my head in the sand.

"Nicole?" A familiar man's voice is on the phone.

"Mr. McGuire! What's going on?"

"The little lass wants to see you." Joseph McGuire, even after all these years in North Carolina, still keeps his thick Irish accent. "She will only leave my store if promised a visit to your house."

More shrill screams cause me to hold the receiver at a distance to spare my eardrums.

One thing is for sure: Monet at the store can't be good for business. If the noise is sounding this loud over the telephone lines, it has to be twice as loud within the four corners of McGuire's.

There is a rattling on the other end and then, in a thin voice, Mr. McGuire says to someone else, "Careful now, careful. Hold the phone like this."

Suddenly Monet is talking to me in her slow, mumbled style. She asks, "Niccc hows? Pleeez. Nicc fisssz? Pleeezz. Pleeezz."

And before I know it, with all the sincerity I can muster, I tell the terror child she can come to my house to see my fish.

There is shrieking and clapping of hands. My stomach knots. Then the phone is dead.

I begin to prepare for a visit from the wild one.

I turn off my computer, place students' papers in my tote bag, and stick the bag in my bedroom closet. In the kitchen I check to make sure each cabinet is shut. Tightly. I stand over my fish tank and pray my three clownfish, two angelfish, and eel will live to see tomorrow. Then I hide the nearly empty container of fish food in my underwear drawer. There is no way she'll be able to find it and overfeed my fish today.

Monet's piercing screams still ring in my ears. Moments after her birth, her great-grandmother Iva reached out to embrace the newly arrived baby. Above the screams Iva cooed with joy, "Ah, you are a loud one. No doubt you belong to us."

Now, three years later, her great-grandma's pride has shifted to sheer annoyance. "Oh, God," she will mutter, "please help me tolerate that child."

To which Ducee will comment, "Monet is a treasure. You have to dig deeper, Iva, to see what beauty lies within."

I groan as my front doorbell rings. I think the Beauty Within has arrived.

Chapter Five

We watch Monet closely as she stands by my lit aquarium. In low tones, Grable tells me she is tired. She doesn't need to tell me this. I can see *tired* written on my cousin's face—under her blue eyes in the form of smudged circles and in her voice, which is slow and lacking its usual lightness. Her nails are still painted though, a creamy light pink today. They are like ten jewels, glistening, especially when she stands near the fish tank and the fluorescent light dances on them. I am afraid she will break into tears any moment, but she just keeps her eyes on Monet.

Monet, dressed in a denim skirt and green shirt, presses her nose against the aquarium and in intervals squeals, "Fiszzzzz!" Then she tilts her head full of brown curls to the left and to the right, stops, laughs, and says nothing. She jumps on one foot, lets out a "Niccc fiszz!" and then squeals again. Between her outbursts, I focus on Grable's words.

"Dennis is going to Boston this weekend. Some lawyers' thing. This means it'll be me and Monet all alone." Her words *all alone* sound hollow. She stiffly moves toward the aquarium and places a hand on her daughter's shoulder. "Monet, please speak softer."

Monet, with her mouth on the tank's glass side, says, "Okaaa, Maaam." Then she laughs.

I think of all the glass cleaner and paper towels it is going to take to clean the outside of the tank after she is gone.

"I don't want my mama to know about Dennis. Not yet."

"Have you told anyone?"

Grable whispers, "No, but Iva . . ."

"Iva?"

"She suspects. You know, guesses something is wrong."

I nod, because I know she does and I know that she's running with her suspicion. I don't tell Grable that Grandmother Iva's guesswork was blurted out to both Ducee and me recently. That she stated Dennis was no good from the get-go, just as Clarisa Jo, Grable's mom, states. I wouldn't be surprised if the whole staff at the *Mount Olive Tribune* already knows about how Dennis is never home.

Grable studies her shiny nails. "Mama didn't ever approve of Dennis," she says as though to all ten of them. I see her diamond on her left hand, the diamond that once had all the relatives talking because it is two carats and all the way from South Africa. "Mama just thought Dennis was a playboy, you know. Still thinks it."

"Oh." It sounds like such a dumb thing to say. The alternative would be, "I know." And how much dumber would that be? I could gush that Dennis is great, but that would be lying.

He did, at one point, seem good to me. Tall, broad shoulders, eyes that sparkle, and hair the color of coal. I must admit I was jealous of Grable the first time she introduced me to Dennis. He was too handsome. His eyes could melt butter. His smile showed rows of perfectly shaped teeth, an orthodontist's dream. Then it happened. I turned my gaze away from those two beams of light and those flashing teeth to notice Dennis's ears. They point at the tips. Not just a little, but a lot, like triangles. At first you don't see beyond his face, but once you do, you can't help wondering if he could wear a green cap and double as one of Santa's elves.

Suddenly we are aware of the quiet. Grable speaks first. "Where's Monet?"

"She's probably on the floor." Sometimes Monet likes to sit cross-legged on my dining room floor, rock back and forth, and try to whistle. My eyes scan the floor. When I don't see her, I look at my aquarium, as though maybe she fell in there. All I see are the smudged glass sides. Every single side has been finger-painted by Monet. This is the type of art the child enjoys.

I'll have to buy more Windex.

I count; the fish are all there, even the eel, poking his tail out near the clump of swaying seaweed.

"Monet!" How could we have lost her? I stride to the front door and open it. Surely, she didn't venture outside into the cold.

"Monet!" I glance around my lawn, even look up at the branches of the gnarled oak tree. Those branches are high up there, but part of me wouldn't be shocked to see Monet swinging from one of the limbs, waving one hand, and honking like a flock of geese on an autumn day.

Grable is by my elbow. "She never leaves the house to go outside without her jacket," she informs me.

Oh. Well, this is fascinating. The child will dump a whole container of fish flakes into my aquarium, but she doesn't go outside on a winter's day without her jacket?

———

Grable holds Monet's violet jacket as though walking around the house with it in her hands will make her daughter appear from wherever she's hiding. "Monet!" She uses her harsh voice, even though the doctors tell her she must always deal with her daughter calmly. "Monet, come here! Come here right now!"

I wonder if Monet can hear her mother. A year ago the child had a hearing aid attached to her left ear. But I didn't notice it on her today.

Entering the kitchen, I look around, but it appears the same as it did an hour ago. The teakettle is on the stove. Next to it is a pan I boil eggs in. Boiled eggs with salt are another one of God's finer creations. Pantry and cabinets are shut. I listen and hear nothing except for a neighborhood woodpecker that spends time in a tree across the street.

I join Grable in the hall. She checks the bathroom and spare bedroom. She opens closets and cabinets, but there is no three-year-old in any of them.

There's a light shining from under my closed bedroom door. I push the door open as Grable stands beside me. The door swings open to show us a small figure standing by my antique dresser, looking at her reflection in the mirror. In her arms is my cloth doll, Sazae, snuggled against her chest.

Grable sweeps into the room. "Monet!" Her voice holds relief.

Monet smiles at herself and turns from the mirror to say in a slow, yet loud tone, "Heellooo Maamm."

"Come on. We need to get home."

She squeezes the doll. "Okaaaa, Maaamm."

Grable attempts to put her daughter's jacket on as Monet grasps tightly to Sazae. "Put the doll down."

"No!" Her teeth are clenched and her eyes narrow slits. Her

hands clutch Sazae's torso, and I am ready to grab my doll from her. She's going to rip Sazae.

Grable tries again. Her voice is calmer this time. "Monet, put the doll down."

"No!" Monet sinks her face into Sazae's stomach. "My, my, my!" She lets out a monotone moan that evaporates into Sazae's body.

Slowly, it dawns on me that this wild child thinks the doll belongs to her, or wants it to be hers. It's a doll and she's a three-year-old girl. The two go together. It doesn't take a team of Duke doctors to figure this out. I hear myself thinking above my fear for the doll's safety: Give the doll to Monet. Any other adult would let the child take the doll. Keep it. After all, why would a thirty-one-year-old woman need a doll in her room?

My throat clamps as I try to swallow the urge to rush over and snatch the doll from Monet's little hands. Instead, I shoot a look at Grable. She's the mom; she'll handle this. She'd better.

Grable crouches down to her daughter's level. Her polished nails rest against Sazae's black hair. "We must leave the doll here." She looks at her daughter, although Monet's face is still covered by Sazae's body.

There's a muffled voice, and then tears. Screams follow, each one piercing. There's movement—a kick and a stomp. And then Sazae is flung across the bedroom floor, her arm hitting the wall. She lands at the foot of my double bed.

I gasp. Twice.

In a heap in her mother's arms, Monet sobs. Her face is now buried in Grable's coat collar. Grable embraces Monet and stokes the child's curls.

I step back, using the wall to support my body. Aware of my rapid breathing, I suddenly pretend I'm not here, not in this scenario. Instead, I wonder how Claude Monet would paint this scene and what he would title the portrait. *Peace After the Storm? Terror Child Breaks Down?* Perhaps just a one-word title— *Surrender.*

Monet's wails subside and change into words, words I have to stretch my ears to comprehend. "Ma . . . Mammm." She wipes her red nose against Grable's hair. "Homm. Pleeeze. Go go homm."

Grable's hands are steady as they ease her daughter's arms into the sleeves of her jacket. "We will go home, Monet." She zips the jacket and plants a kiss on Monet's flushed, wet cheek. Taking the child by the hand, she glances my way and says with sincerity, "I'm sorry, Nicole."

Words won't form, so I just nod.

As they leave my house, I hear Monet calling for her doll. I watch from the living room window as Grable puts Monet in her car seat.

I lean against the wall and hope it will hold me. "Oh, Mama. Oh, Mama."

If Mama were alive, I'd be normal. Instead, she's gone and all I have from her is an old Japanese kimono doll. Mama gave Sazae to me way before I can remember. I have no idea why she chose this doll or why one of the silky kimono sleeves is shorter than the other. Most likely, I took scissors to it as a child. In the one photo I own of my mother and me—a black-and-white, wrinkled from the hands of time—only Sazae's face shows. The doll's kimono sleeves can't be seen, but the doll is the same, only newer, for Sazae's lips and eyes aren't as faded as they've become over the years.

This photo sits in a silver frame on my bedside table. Mama's in a kimono with flowers. I sit beside her, also in a kimono with matching cherry blossom print, and my hair is pulled back in a bun. Sazae's face is snug against my left shoulder. Mama is to the right, her hair curled around her cheeks, one strand drooping under her chin. Both our smiles are as wide as dill pickles at a family reunion.

One summer day on the porch swing, I asked Ducee, "How do I know she was my mother?" I'd recently been given the photo of Mama and me. Ducee had found it in a ragged photo album and asked if I would like to have it as my very own.

Ducee stopped swinging and faced me. There was a sparkle in her eyes. "My dear," she said to me, "she is you." With richness in her voice she added, "You are her."

"But how do I know she is my mama?" Exasperated, I cried, "I don't remember anything!"

"You think you don't," Ducee said softly as she caressed my arm with her opened hand. "But the memory is there." She nodded. Then she took my right hand and lifted it carefully so that it rested against my chest. "Inside your heart. Oh, yes. It is always there. Yes."

Over the years I wonder what good it does to know that memories are there within my heart if they are so well hidden that I can't recall any—not even one. I have no idea what Mama's voice sounded like or what she smelled like. Did Mama bathe in lilac like Ducee always does? And what about pineapple chutney? Did she really make this family dish in Japan as Ducee claims she did?

Evening settles across my front lawn, and I am standing in the dark. The hum of my fish tank is like a steady procession ushering in the day's end. I turn on a lamp, and its light melts the darkness.

A truck filled with boxes, children's bikes, and other items I can't decipher in the dark is being unloaded in front of Hilda's. Hilda helps the drivers carry the goods into her lit garage. I see her bright pink curlers under the streetlight and, yes, her feet are, as usual, encased in black boots.

In my bedroom, I carefully head over to Sazae, now a pink and black ball on my floor. When I pick her up, I check to make sure she's still intact. Black eyes, thin red lips, two white cotton arms, pink kimono with a sash, two white legs—all accounted for. Yes, still with that faint smell of moldy oranges. I embrace my doll. You see, Monet, I'm sorry, but she is *my, my, my*.

Sazae's spot is on the right pillow of my bed. I set her there, pat her left cheek twice, run my finger over the left *geta* with the damaged heel, and trace the shortened kimono sleeve with my knuckle. Why is one sleeve shorter? Neither Father nor Ducee have ever been able to tell me why. The damaged heel of her shoe holds no mystery. It's due to my teeth. I used to sink my teeth into it as a child, after dreams about burning buildings. I went through a phase of dreaming about fire and being chased by something that resembled Godzilla. When I asked Father why he thought my dreams were so violent, he shook his head and told me not to drink sugared drinks before bedtime.

No wonder I am enjoying my recent peaceful dreams of Harrison and tranquil waters. Perhaps if I want these dreams to continue, I'd better write back to him.

Tentatively, I sit at my computer. What should I say? I start by thanking him for the poem. Then I ask him about life in Japan. Which city does he live in? What does he do there? How long has he lived there? I give him plenty of questions to respond to. Of course, I do not tell him I have any connection to Japan. I certainly won't let him know that Sazae, my kimono doll, is my prized possession. Or that my mother died in Kyoto. Or that I have a scar the shape of a polka dot in the middle of my forehead that Father says I got in Japan.

One has to be careful. And over the years, I've taught myself just how much to say and what to keep locked, buried, secret. Unlike my great-aunt Iva, early on I learned the value of secrecy.

Chapter Six

I'm not sure about modern technology. It took me five years to finally give in and get a computer. Mr. Vickers, our principal at Mount Olive Middle School, continued to tell me that owning a computer would enhance my life. I'd be on the way to my classroom, the soles of my shoes flapping down the hallway, not at all graceful like Iva's glide, and he'd stop me. Certain he'd ask how I managed to always be late to class, the palms of my hands would sweat. I fought against biting every nail. But instead of issuing a reprimand, he'd smile and talk about an educational Web site he'd just visited or ask if I was aware that the Internet holds a world of knowledge "at our very fingertips."

"That's amazing," I'd say.

"Do you own a computer?"

I'd tell him I really didn't think I was the emailing type. He'd look seriously into my eyes and, with his coffee-stained breath just inches away from my face, say, "Nicole, emailing is only one aspect of the savvy computer. There are more ways it enhances one's life."

Whenever I have to call technical help because the monitor

freezes or I get a virus, I wonder how I am being enhanced by my *savvy* computer.

A year ago I got an answering machine because Iva said I needed it in case she couldn't reach me at school and had to leave me a message about Ducee. But that's about it for me. I refuse to get a cell phone. I don't think I need any more enhancing in my life.

When I get home from school on Thursday afternoon, there are three messages on my answering machine. One is from Bonnie, my stepmom, asking when I'm going to make the trip to Richmond to visit her and Father. She lets me know that Richard is welcome, too. I delete it, as I did the one she left three weeks ago.

Iva's message is about the reunion. She wonders if I'll create the same centerpiece I made last year. "It was the talk of the reunion," she says.

All I did was stick olives in a large fresh pineapple. The piece was to represent Mount Olive—the pineapple was the mountain and the green olives spoke for themselves. Of course, everyone knows that Mount Olive has no mountains or olives. Just a company famous for its Mount Olive brand-name pickles.

The final message surprises me. It's from Richard. I play his message six times just to hear his tenor voice, even though he has called only to ask that I return his Michael Bolton CD. "I know you borrowed it. Please give it back."

I search my house by looking in the desk drawer where I keep my CDs. I shuffle through my meager collection: The Eagles, Sandi Patty, Stevie Wonder, Michael W. Smith, a local group called Jason's Gospel Band, Brooklyn Tabernacle Choir, but no Michael Bolton. I feed my fish, watch their little mouths bubble open to consume the flakes, and it dawns on me that I don't like Michael Bolton, so why would I have borrowed his CD? In fact, I don't think I ever borrowed any CD from Richard. As usual, you are mistaken, Richard. I delete Richard from the machine.

It gives me a great sense of power to be able to delete with one touch of a button. Effortless.

Suddenly I start to feel an ache tugging my insides. A moment from my past crosses the lens of my memory—Richard and I are making snow angels outside his apartment as large flakes spiral from the evening sky. Later we go inside and drink hot chocolate with miniature marshmallows. He takes a sip from his mug and then kisses me with lips of chocolate.

I push away the growing ache by rubbing the palm of my hand over my heart. I will not cry. Not today.

Quickly, I make some Earl Grey tea and sit in Aunt Lucy's chair, steadying the mug on the right armrest. I run my free hand over the chair's soft fabric. Aunt Lucy had skin as smooth as this fabric, and yet this afternoon all I feel for her is sadness. Poor Aunt Lucy. Poor crazy Aunt Lucy. I was told she died the day before her forty-first birthday from some sort of liver disease because she drank bourbon with her morning orange juice and with her evening iced tea. Pretty soon she forgot the orange juice and the tea and just drank straight from the dark bottle. Ducee says she was trying to forget.

Lucy had a baby at the age of sixteen and her parents, my great-grandparents, made her give it up for adoption. She wasn't even allowed to look at it or hold it after it was born. The baby was whisked away minutes after Aunt Lucy nearly died giving birth to it. And, Ducee tells me, that day when the baby entered the world was the day Aunt Lucy lost a part of herself, a part never to be restored again. Maybe that's why she bought the haunted house on James Street and turned its basement into her art studio, where she drew dozens of oil paintings of mother and infant.

Ducee can never tell Aunt Lucy's story without tears forming in her eyes. She's told the story over a hundred times and each time has to blot her eyes with a tissue. I know she loved her crazy baby sister. I can see the love in every tear.

Aunt Lucy—whom I never met—was trying to forget. I am the opposite of her—trying to remember. Sometimes on rainy nights I shut my eyes to recall a smell or sound that will take me back to a memory of my early childhood with Mama. Although I've spent countless moments believing I can remember, I have yet to do so.

I force myself to do some lesson planning for my middle school students before I check my new email messages. But I have trouble concentrating because I remember last night's beautiful dream where I swear fish were dancing in the ocean to Beethoven's "Ode to Joy." Harrison was swimming under a tall, shady palm tree. I didn't want to wake up, and even after my alarm sounded, I closed my eyes to continue the dream. It didn't work. I pulled the fabric-softener-scented sheet over my head and waited, hopeful. No peaceful ocean; instead, I saw a classroom filled with rowdy students. It was time to get out of bed to teach them.

With one finger in my mouth, I check to see if any new messages were deposited into my computer while I was at school. I hold my breath, the finger still in my mouth. Sure as the sun, I have new mail, and yes, one of those messages is from Harrison.

The dreams, the email messages—maybe even the cold weather and the breakup with Richard. I can stack this all up as my own rationale for what I do that night when Grable calls to apologize for Monet's throwing Sazae. "I know that doll is priceless to you," Grable says.

This is true. Sazae is no ordinary cotton doll. She is the only gift I have from Mama. "She is."

"I'm sorry." Her voice is weak, strained. "Remember that doctor I told you about at UNC?"

There have been so many doctors, I wonder which one she's referring to this time. I don't ask that, just simply say, "Yes."

"Well, last week he changed Monet's medicine. He says he thinks she has trouble concentrating along with hyperactivity. I don't know if the new medication is doing a bit of good." She speaks so slowly I fear she might fall asleep in midsentence. "He also says she's autistic."

"But I thought they ruled that out last year."

"She's only three. Sometimes it takes a while to diagnose."

"Really?"

"I don't know. I'm no medical professional. People tell me to go on the Internet and search." Her voice trails off.

I know she can't go on a computer. As simple as it might sound to the people encouraging her to do so, my cousin, like most of my relatives, doesn't own a computer.

I've invited her to use mine, but whenever I do, she just murmurs, "It's a tad confusing," and dashes my hope for any further discussion.

Dennis should be more proactive in regard to his daughter's condition, all the relatives feel, but none of us ever tells Grable that. It's amazing how we can talk about someone we love behind his or her back, so certain of what he or she should do to make his or her life more manageable, yet we don't ever tell that person. Wisdom, we think we have so much. Yet why can't we freely disclose our ideas? Instead, we smile and nod and cringe inside. Never showing how we really feel.

I wonder if Dennis has left for his business trip. This question I can freely ask.

"Not yet," says Grable. "He leaves early tomorrow morning."

"And what are you and Monet going to do?" I wonder why I care.

She sighs—one of those that lifts up from the very depths of her lungs. "I guess we'll make do."

"Eat ice cream," I suggest. I know my cousin is fond of Chocolate Nutty Chocolate.

"Oh, I don't know." She pauses. "I don't think I have any in the house." She sounds so tired, as if she couldn't possibly go out to the Friendly Mart and pick up a carton herself.

And so I say, "Why don't you come here for ice cream."

Silence. Then, "Really?" There is a brightness in her tone. "Really?"

"Sure."

Slowly, she adds, "I'd have to bring Monet."

"Of course," I tell her with too much enthusiasm.

"Are you sure?"

Never. "Yeah."

"When?" Eagerness fills her voice.

When? When? I look at my kitchen clock as if that will help me decide. "How about tomorrow night?"

"Okay. Okay."

"Great! See you then."

I am about to hang up when she asks, "Nicole, what time?"

Time? "Seven, eight."

"Monet goes to bed at eight."

Suddenly I know I have lost my mind because I suggest she and Monet spend the night. "I have the spare bedroom with the double bed."

I feel sunshine pouring through the receiver. "Oh, Nicole. Really? That would be wonderful. Are you sure?"

"Yes." I try to match her happiness. "Of course. Come over at seven. We'll have pizza first. And hot dogs for Monet."

Monet hates pizza but loves hot dogs, another lesson I learned the hard way. The first time I served her pizza, she took the gooey slice covered in cheese and smashed it onto the tabletop. "Hooot doooo!" she demanded about fifty times until I caught on. *Hooot dooo* means hot dog. She likes them sliced with a little pool of ketchup on the plate. Using a fork, she submerges each slice into the ketchup, laughs, and then, quicker than a crocodile swallows a pesky fly, pops the hot dog into her waiting mouth. She chews about a dozen times, swallows, opens her mouth, and repeats the entire experience again.

When I place the receiver in its cradle, I hear the pounding shrieks of Monet in my mind. I have just invited the wild one over. Voluntarily. I think I'd better stop spending so much time sitting in Aunt Lucy's wingback chair. Her crazy behavior is rubbing off on me.

I have no hot dogs or ice cream or even a bottle of ketchup. I jot down these items on a slip of paper with plans to head to the store tomorrow after school. I add fish food. Naturally, with Monet around, I will keep the container of flakes hidden. And this time I will also secure Sazae inside my closet.

Chapter Seven

The next day, while Kristine and I are standing in the teachers' lounge, she flips back her dark brown hair that smells of peaches and coconut and asks if I'm still dating Richard. Kristine reminds me of being at a slumber party. She doesn't talk about the science classes she teaches or her students; guys are the only topic she cares to address.

I tell her Richard and I broke up. I don't let her know that he wanted someone committed to marriage and that I am not ready to have a ring on my finger and pick out a wedding dress. Kristine, longing for marriage, would drop her mouth wide open and let her pretty eyes bulge. She might even faint if she knew I had a prospect of marriage and refused it.

"Well," she begins, "I know this guy." Kristine knows many guys. I can tell by her tone of voice that this particular one is from the lineup of men that are either skipping out on child support or running from the law. I am not surprised at what she asks next. "How about me setting you up with Eduardo? He's cute. We could double-date."

"Double-what?"

"Double-date." She smiles, flashing her pearly whites.

"Didn't I tell you?" Edging closer to me, she says, "Salvador asked me out last weekend. We rode his motorcycle to an Italian restaurant in New Bern. He has a red Harley."

Motorcycles! I need to add motorcycles to my list of fears. I hate planes and motorcycles, especially those large Harleys.

"We had the best time. Did you know Salvador collects pottery?" She fingers a strand of hair. "Salvador, me, you, and Eduardo." She peers at my eyes, expecting a response. When I give her nothing but a blank stare, she tosses her head, giggles. "It'll be fun."

My mind wanders to Harrison's latest email message. He answered my questions, every single one. He lives in an old traditional Japanese house in Kyoto with a rock garden that surrounds his outdoor pond. One bonsai he keeps in a ceramic pot and, during the winter months, brings it into the warmth of his house. He hopes it will live to see spring, but it's looking a little *peaked* lately. For eight years he's been an English professor at a local university. His parents, former medical missionaries, are coming for a visit in a few days, and he may get his dad to help build a retaining fence under the pond's surface to separate the lilies from the fish, just as I suggested in my message to him. Harrison says that his best friend Jurgen, from Germany, might even help with the task. Jurgen is in love with Tomiko, but there is no future in this relationship because she refuses to marry a foreigner. Her father says he'll disown her if she does.

There is no mention of Harrison having a girlfriend or wife.

"Want me to get Eduardo to ask you out?" Kristine's question breaks into my thoughts of Harrison.

"Uh . . . no."

"You don't like Hispanic men?" She frowns.

"No. I mean, it's not that."

"I know!" Her frown now becomes the widest smile. "You're still getting over Richard!"

"Well. . . ." I doubt Harrison is married. He would have said he was. Some line like, "My wife and I have lived here in Kyoto for eight years."

Kristine nods with sympathy. "I understand." When she leaves the lounge as the bell for the last period rings, a faint trail of coconut and peaches stays in the air.

I breathe it in. Maybe when I get home there will be another message from Harrison.

———

As I shop for hot dogs, ketchup, and ice cream, a smile does find my lips. This could be a nice night—once Monet goes to bed, that is. Grable and me, girl talk. I toss in a brownie mix and a bag of peanut M&Ms. After reading the directions for the brownie mix, I gently add a carton of eggs to my shopping cart. We can sit in the living room, and I'll let Grable have Aunt Lucy's chair. I'll light the vanilla candles Iva gave me for Christmas. She gave everyone candles as gifts—I think to cover the odor of her cigarettes. Over the years, she's grown tired of the way some of the relatives complain about "that nasty smell."

I make a mental note that pint-sized Bell mason jars are on sale. If I had a cell phone I could call Ducee and ask if she'd like me to buy some for her next chutney-making event. But even if I could call, I wouldn't be able to talk with my grandmother. Ducee doesn't answer her phone. She hears it ring; at least I think she does. She just doesn't ever pick it up. I don't know why she owns a phone. Iva says it is in case one of us walks into her house, finds her having a heart attack, and needs to call 911.

That did happen once. Mrs. McCready, Ducee's neighbor with the streak of silver hair, entered my grandmother's house one autumn afternoon, bringing over her renowned apple-cinnamon-walnut pie. She dropped the pie onto the hard-wood when she found Ducee slumped over in her La-Z-Boy recliner. After calling Ducee's name and patting her face, Mrs. McCready dialed 911. The ambulance whisked Ducee away, and Mrs. McCready sat in the recliner to catch her breath. Then she called Iva, who panted all the way to Wayne Memorial. That was eighteen months ago. Ducee says she's fine now. Iva isn't so sure.

On my way home, I rush into McGuire's for fish food and a new net. I love the smell of the dingy pet store and the way the floorboards creak as I walk the aisles. It's always a treat to be greeted by Flannigan, the one-legged macaw who sits in a metal cage by the entrance. I can't stay long; I don't want the gallon of Chocolate Nutty Chocolate to melt in the trunk of my Ford. But I do tell the bird he is beautiful.

"You're beautiful," repeats Flannigan. He hops on his perch, raises one green wing, opens his beak, and says it again.

I smile.

"You're beautiful," I tell Flannigan.

To which he mimics, "You're beautiful."

I swear I could keep this up all day. Flannigan is a real ego-booster.

"How is your grandmother?" asks Mr. McGuire, clad in a pair of patched overalls. His hat is emerald green and has the phrase "Thank God I'm Irish" stitched above the rim. Mr. McGuire and my grandmother are extremely proud of their Irish heritage, whereas Iva wishes she was Italian, because then she's certain she'd have dark, thick, *killer* hair. "Every man would turn to see me," she once told us with a seductive smile. "Me—dark, killer hair and red lipstick. I'd knock their socks off."

"Ducee's fine," I say to Mr. McGuire, although Iva wouldn't agree. Iva would go on and on about how Ducee is lacking zest and looking pale.

With a wide net, Mr. McGuire takes a goldfish out of a tank and slips it into a plastic bag for a woman in a pink jacket. "I don't see her much these days. Getting things ready for our family reunion?" He can call it *our reunion*, even though he's not biologically related to us. All of Mount Olive remembers that my great-grandparents loved him like a son.

"Yeah, she and Iva keep busy with all that reunion planning."

He hands the bag to the woman, who grins at the fish as though she's just won it in the lottery. I hope she enjoys her new goldfish for a long time; she seems like she'll be a good owner. If her fish does happen to die, I beg her to please not flush it down the toilet. Fish deserve a proper burial. I've had sixteen pet fish die over the course of my life, and I am honored to say that each one got not only a ground burial but a eulogy.

The woman debates about fish food while Mr. McGuire says to me, "Actually, I don't see much of any of your clan. They must not love fish. Not like you do." His smile, which covers his wrinkled face, warms my heart.

"Except you did see Monet and Grable the other day. Or maybe you heard Monet the other day."

He laughs. "Monet is an energetic lass, isn't she?"

I do love the way his accent rolls off his tongue. Some days I think I'd like to speak with an Irish accent. Ducee says everyone has a story, and I've heard the pet store owner's many times. At eighteen, Mr. McGuire came to New York City from Dublin in

search of a better life. Although the city held many of his relatives, he chose to leave and head farther south. North Carolina
beckoned him, and he was hired to work the tobacco farm of
Mount Olive's Seven Arches. This was Ducee's parents' farm,
and being Irish, they accepted Joseph wholeheartedly as one
of the family.

At the age of twenty-five, he saved enough to make a down
payment on a tiny feed shop on Main Street. Born with a fascina-
tion for fish, he added fish and aquariums to the inventory. Soon
he was selling more fish than feed. That was when he changed
the name of his store from Mount Olive Feed to McGuire's
Pet World.

I watch Mr. McGuire ring up the cost of the goldfish and
fish food on his cash register. He won't go modern; he has used
the same ancient register for decades. And I know he will never
get a computer.

The woman thanks him; the bell on the door chimes as she
walks out.

Remembering why I'm here, I pick out an orange cylinder
container of fish flakes and search for a net.

After he rings up my purchases, a solemn look encompasses
Mr. McGuire's green eyes. "Monet's father was here."

"Oh, really?"

Mr. McGuire is silent, as though contemplating whether or
not to continue talking.

I stick a thumbnail in my mouth and wait.

"Monet's father wasn't with Monet." A significant pause.
"Or with Grable. He wanted minnows. Appeared to be going
fishing early this morning. A canoe was on top of the SUV."

I wonder why Mr. McGuire's voice is getting lower. I step
nearer to the counter so I can hear better.

That's when he says, "A young thing was with him."

"With Dennis?"

Joseph McGuire holds my eyes with his gaze and nods.

I feel my mouth dry up like water evaporating under a scorching sun.

"I don't mean to be nosey, but the two were acting all cozy together." He wriggles his eyebrows. "Like they were headed to the Southern Belle Motel. A wee time out in the canoe and then some time under the covers, if you know what I mean."

I can't find my voice. I want to dismiss everything he's told me. Perhaps this is a dream and my alarm will go off soon.

At last I say, "Don't tell anyone." I repeat this line twice, just like Flannigan would. As I head out of the store, I am faced with a huge dilemma. Do I tell Grable tonight that her husband was seen with another woman? That her mother's image of him as a playboy is correct?

In my car, it hits me—Dennis had an early flight to Boston this morning. Or did he?

I don't bother turning the heat on; my car is toasty. Or maybe it's me. I am sweating with sheer disbelief.

Chapter Eight

After our dinner of pepperoni pizza and hot dogs sliced beside a pool of ketchup, Grable tucks Monet into the guest room's double bed.

As the two snuggle together and Grable reads *Pinocchio* to Monet, I wash the dishes in the sink. I have a dishwasher but sometimes choose to wash by hand because hot suds are therapeutic. They clear my mind and help me think. I am still wondering how to tell Grable what Mr. McGuire saw at his shop. Three times tonight Grable commented that Dennis was on a business trip in Boston. Each time I was tempted to let her know that he was really buying minnows with another woman. A woman "acting all cozy" with him. But even though my hands are deep in the hot, lemon-scented suds, the words to tell my cousin won't emerge. Why can't my therapy work for me tonight?

When Grable enters the kitchen, I have the oven on and am pouring the batter for double chocolate fudge brownies into an aluminum pan.

"Remember the brownies we made for the reunion last year?" Grable lets out a laugh. She has a book in her hand and sits with it at the kitchen table.

"You mean the ones Monet helped us with?" Monet managed to add a quarter of a bottle of vanilla extract to the mix while Grable and I stood at the front door of her house convincing a Jehovah's Witness solicitor we didn't need his literature. After a lengthy discussion and not at all convinced, the man left us with several pamphlets. Grable and I baked the brownies as we talked about the Bible, not realizing what had happened. It was at the reunion's Friday night dessert party when we heard our cousin Aaron comment on how "vanilla-y" the chocolate brownies tasted.

"Uh-oh," Grable said after she took a bite of one. "I thought they smelled awfully strong."

"Monet," I said with certainty.

"Did she help you cook?" asked Aaron, approval swelling in his voice. Cousin Aaron is the youth pastor at Third Presbyterian, and one of his beliefs is that children should learn early on what he calls survival skills. For Aaron, these include baking, cooking, sewing, and cleaning.

"She's two, Aaron," Grable reminded him. "She needs to work on the skill of potty training first, and then she can be creative in the kitchen." That summer was when Grable thought Monet should be out of diapers, even though the older relatives muttered she was expecting "too much from that poor child."

Now Grable opens a hardback book on koi, filled with photos of actual ponds and aquariums in Japan. Aaron gave me the book when I graduated from UNC-Greensboro. He thinks I should be proud of my birth land and has supplied me with the pagoda in my fish tank, a fan a friend brought back from a trip to Osaka, and a framed woodblock print of an Asian lady in an orange-and-silver kimono. "Roots are important," he tells me.

I've never bothered to explain to Aaron why I don't care to be reminded of Japan. Why should I attempt to get him to see things from my perspective? He knows my mother died there one winter night in a house fire and my father has never been the same. He's been told I flew back to Virginia with Father shortly after her death. That Ducee brought me to North Carolina to console herself and me, certain she could do a better job of it than Father's emotionally challenged family in Richmond. Father stayed with his parents awhile and then came to Ducee's to pick me up. He bought a one-story white house for us. Aaron and his parents even visited us there a few times.

Yet Aaron continues to find ways that I can be connected to "my roots." Ducee says to graciously accept these Japanese items from him. Pressing her wrinkled hands together, she explains that this is how Aaron shows he cares for me. "Sometimes," she whispers, "you just have to let people be who they are."

"This book is gorgeous," says Grable as she turns the glossy pages. "Look at the fish ponds. I heard some people really do have ponds like these in their backyards."

Does she want me to agree? To tell her that I do know one person in Japan with an outdoor pond? I consider sitting at the kitchen table with her, smiling and saying, "Grable, guess what? I've been writing to this man who lives in Kyoto."

What would Grable say? Probably something like, "Don't you know he could be a stalker or a mass murderer? Be careful."

I open the bag of M&Ms and pour them into a bowl. I offer the bowl to my cousin.

"Oh," she says hungrily to the chocolate, "I shouldn't."

I place the bowl by her right elbow. "You should."

Grable closes the book, takes a handful of M&Ms, and

declares, "I want to go somewhere!" She pops two pieces of chocolate into her mouth. "I signed up for this travel club where they send you brochures on trips. Costa Rica looks like a dream in the pictures. Beautiful mountains, beaches, and palm trees. I've never seen a real live palm tree." She chews a blue M&M. "I wish Dennis and I could go there."

I want to tell her she isn't going to Costa Rica with her husband because Dennis is canoeing with another woman. Now, just how would I phrase that? "Uh, Grable, Mr. McGuire saw Dennis this morning with a woman. They had a canoe on top of a SUV. Doesn't Dennis drive a BMW?"

Instead, I take the brownies out of the oven and ask if she'd like one with Chocolate Nutty Chocolate.

"I'll have to diet for weeks," she cries and then says she'll take one with a small scoop of ice cream. "Dennis used to say he wanted to travel. We would lie in bed on Saturday mornings and make plans."

I don't care to think about Dennis in bed right now, thank you. I want to push Dennis, and everything about him, far from my mind.

She sighs. "Oh, Nicole, I wish he would spend more time at home."

Me too, I think, but I just nod.

She licks ice cream off her fork as I bite into my chocolate brownie. It is warm and gooey, soothing every crevice of my mouth.

Suddenly, Grable says, "You're lucky you got to go to Japan."

"What?"

"You know, that you lived there."

"I don't remember anything. It doesn't count."

She takes a bite of her brownie with the mound of ice cream melting over it. "But you were at least there."

Okay, I won't argue with her. Apparently she is trying to make some point.

"I've been nowhere." She licks a smudge of chocolate off her top lip. "Nowhere."

"Well, you're still young. Your life isn't over."

Casting her eyes down, she softly says, "Maybe not."

Suddenly I wish I could make her laugh. Where is clowning Uncle Jarvis when you need him? He'd tell a few jokes and have us both feeling giddy, not that the jokes would be funny, but as he threw back his head and roared, we'd laugh *at* him.

I remind her about the time Uncle Jarvis sat on the picnic bench Ducee had just painted.

Grable's face shines. "He had paint all over the backside of his leisure suit."

"And no one could bear to tell him because he was so proud of that ugly suit."

"He got it at the Goodwill, didn't he?"

Together we chime, "For seventy-five cents!"

Grable laughs, and so do I until a small snort escapes through my nose.

"It was green, wasn't it?"

"The paint or the suit?"

She can't remember. "Didn't Richard end up telling him?"

I give her a sour look.

"Didn't he?" Finishing her brownie, she asks, "How is Richard these days?"

I shrug. "I don't know."

Grable looks horrified.

Okay, if she must know. "We broke up."

"Why?"

"Differences." I avoid her eyes by looking away. My kitchen ceiling fan needs cleaning. There are rows of dark dust lining each blade. One day I'll use a chair so I'll be high enough to wipe off all that unsightly dust. One day, but now I just stare at the fan, refusing to say more about Richard.

Grable respects my desire to not discuss Richard and me. Says she is sorry we broke up and then drops the subject. Moves on to this year's dessert night at the family reunion. "Think we should get Monet to help us make the brownies again?"

I laugh. It's not that funny, but I just want to be able to laugh at something.

She joins me.

I'm sure Mr. McGuire was mistaken. The man who entered his shop this morning was just a Dennis look-alike. Had to be. Dennis, who loves his daughter and wife, is in Boston this weekend.

———

I retrieve Sazae from the closet, spray her with a lavender spritzer to cover up the moldy orange aroma, and lie in bed with the lights out. There is a tap at my bedroom door. "Yes?"

Grable eases into view. She's wearing a salmon nightgown with lacy sleeves. She smells of cold cream. "Nicole, I'm sorry."

I sit up. "About what?"

"All the travel talk. I know Japan holds your sad past." The warmth from her voice spreads over me. "I'm sorry."

I swallow, pause, and murmur, "It's okay."

"If I could change it all for you, oh, I would."

"Thanks, Grable."

She yawns, turns to leave, then faces me again to add, "I wish we could do this every Friday night." Even in the darkness, I see her smile. "Well, good night."

After she closes the door, I think about Dennis and that other woman. I wish I could change things for Grable, too. Then it is as though Ducee, smelling of soft lilac, is sitting beside me, gently patting my hand and saying, "You aren't in control of everything or anybody."

A hard Southern Truth for anyone.

Chapter Nine

Of course I have wondered what Harrison really looks like. In my recent dreams, he is a remarkably large carp with a scaly orange body and face. He has a rich, deep voice. I don't think they let carp, even talking ones, teach English at universities in Japan, so I am certain Harrison Michaels is a human being.

As I watch my fish, I hear Kristine's squeaky voice asking, *"Is he cute?"* She doesn't know about Harrison, of course, but she would ask this if she did. He could be wildly handsome, traffic-stopping gorgeous, or as ugly as Uncle Jarvis's leisure suit. What if he has the features of a hunchback or a gnome? What if he looks like a serial killer? Maybe I prefer pretending he is the large and gentle fish of my dreams.

Then why did I ask that he send a picture? He knows what I look like because there are thumbnail color photos of each contributor on the Pretty Fishy Web site. My picture was taken by Ducee in her kitchen. My hair is tamed, my freckles barely noticeable, and I actually have a happy smile on my face. My bio says I teach English at Mount Olive Middle School and owned my first goldfish at age six.

Ducee says to look at the heart, not the face. She tells us God puts more value on matters of the heart than those of the face. That's fine to say, but how many people can really do that? I've known many wonderful people who never get second glances, yet they have hearts of gold. Those of us with only hearts of gold going for us have to strive a little harder to make it in this world where beauty is immediately appraised.

So when Harrison Michaels sends me an email message with an attachment, my fingers feel tingly. The message says:

Nicole,

   You asked for a picture and so here it is. If you look closely, you can see one of my Kohaku koi in the pond. He's to the left, by the lily. He's the one guilty of eating most of my plants.

Harrison

All I have to do is click on the attachment and I'll be looking at Harrison Michaels. Cute guy or gnome. Beast or cover man of *GQ*.

It's only eight-fifteen on this Saturday morning as I sit in my lumpy computer chair and stare at the little paper clip to the left of Harrison's email message. Just one click on the paper clip and the mystery will be solved. I lift my finger, then stick it in my mouth.

"Nicccc!" Monet is by my side, tousled brown curls swinging as she greets me. She climbs into my lap, breathing heavily as she moves, her stale cheese breath filling my nose. The pink Dora the Explorer pajama bottoms she's wearing slide off her hips and twist around her legs. She pulls at the flannel material and starts to whine.

I take her off my lap, adjust her pajama bottoms by straightening them on her tiny waist, and then lift her onto my lap again.

She giggles and starts to sing the theme song from the Dora show. I know she inherited the inability to sing from Ducee. Every note is off-key. Suddenly she stops singing and shouts in my ear, "Hooot doooo!"

Hot dog for breakfast, I think. Well, it sure beats having to make scrambled eggs or eggs Benedict.

"Hooot dooooo!"

"Shh," I whisper. Grable is probably still sleeping in the guest bedroom. I carry the girl into the kitchen and sit her on a chair at the table. "I'll make you a hot dog. Just wait."

When I place the plate with the sliced hot dog and mound of ketchup in front of her, she lifts her arms in the air and squirms in her chair.

"What do you need?"

Monet's lips are puckered, stretched as far out as they can go.

I step closer to her. "Do you want some juice?"

Her large blue eyes are on me. She is asking for a kiss.

I bend toward her lips, and she plants a fleshy kiss against my chin. I have never been kissed on the chin before.

Content, she laughs and dips a hot dog slice into the ketchup.

I watch her eat. Last night Grable said another appointment was scheduled for next week with a neurologist at Duke. He's new, straight from London or New Delhi. What will he find wrong with Monet this time? It's a good thing Dennis has exceptional health insurance.

The phone rings, Monet reacts by mimicking the sound, and a coughing Iva says in my ear, "Nicki, is Ducee all right?"

I pause. "Yes."

Iva sputters, "She invited me over for tea this morning, and she's not answering her door." She gasps for air.

"Did you ring her doorbell?"

"I did, Nicki. She didn't come to the door. What do you think is wrong with her? I counted to at least twenty waiting for her to answer. Remember you told me to always do that since Ducee can be slow getting to her front door?"

Well, this certainly puzzles me, because I never recall giving my great-aunt this advice.

Iva inhales. "But she didn't come to the door."

"The doorbell is broken." Doesn't she remember this about Ducee's house? Broken doorbells, phones the woman won't answer.

"What? What?" Iva sounds like a kid who has just learned that there is no Santa Claus.

"The doorbell doesn't work." I use my calm and clear teacher's voice.

"I thought she got that fixed."

"No. Knock loudly."

Slowly, Aunt Iva says, "Are you sure?"

"Sure as the sun."

"I called her on the phone after I got home. There was no answer."

"Aunt Iva, you know that Ducee never answers her phone."

"What am I going to do?"

"Ducee is fine."

Iva's coughing reminds me of my garbage disposal when a fork gets stuck in it.

After clearing her throat, Iva says, "Are you sure?"

Aunt Iva is a lot like one of my students. Clay's known for asking questions, and while the rest of the class might be bothered by them, these very questions are what endear me to Clay. "Ms. Michelin," he'll say as he raises his arm, "how do you know that Walt Whitman was a man? Huh? George Eliot was a woman. How do you know?"

I can't find fault with Clay or Iva. I'm the one with a past of uncertainties, the looming questions. It is only fair for me to allow them their barges of apprehension to motor down their streams of life.

Softly I say, "Ducee is fine. She was fine yesterday, remember?" Yesterday, Iva called wondering where Ducee was, only to find her in the backyard feeding a baked potato to Maggie, the donkey. Maggie is fond of baked potatoes, making my grandmother convinced that the beast is Irish.

"Why won't she let us have cucumber sandwiches?"

Is Iva whining now? "She's just being Ducee."

"Do you really think it's not proper etiquette?"

"I don't know."

"Cucumber sandwiches are my favorite."

"I know."

"Do you think she's okay?" Iva is lighting a cigarette; I hear the lighter click. I know it's the silver lighter she received upon retiring from the Mount Olive Pickle Company, where she worked for thirty years.

"Yes, you better hurry over there for tea."

After inhaling, Iva says, "I suppose I should. If it gets cold on account of my tardiness, she'll never let me hear the end of it."

I smile. "You know Ducee despises cold tea."

"Unless it's iced tea."

"That's right."

Monet is now jumping on one leg and laughing. The hot dog has been consumed; the ketchup is smeared on her mouth.

"Nicki? It's hard to hear. Is your TV on?"

"No."

A slight pause and then, "Nicki?"

"Yes."

"I hope there's room."

"Where?"

"What if someone takes my plot?"

Her plot! She must be talking about The Meadows, the cemetery where all of the relatives from North Carolina are buried, even Mama. "If you've paid for it, it's not going to be given to anyone else." I rest the receiver against my right shoulder and neck. I hear Monet squealing in the living room. She was just here in my sight. I hope my fish are okay. I carry the phone into the living room to find Grable cradling Monet on Aunt Lucy's chair, *Pinocchio* open in her lap.

Grable sees me and gives me a sleepy smile.

"But what about Usella?" Iva's voice cracks.

"What?" I enter the kitchen again.

Iva lets out a long cough. "In the paper this morning. Do you get the *Tribune*?"

Okay, I'm cheap. I've never subscribed to the local paper, the *Mount Olive Tribune*. If I really want to read the news, I can always find a wrinkled copy in the teachers' lounge at school.

Iva continues. "She bought a plot to be buried in, and when she died it wasn't hers anymore."

This doesn't make sense. "What do you mean?"

"They had no room to bury her. They had to take her body to Canada. And the car broke down so they had to carry it the rest of the way in a taxi and the bill came to over one thousand dollars." Iva sounds as though she's going to cry.

Before I can think of anything to say, Iva blurts, "Do you think Ducee will get there first?"

"I don't think she cares about going to Canada."

"No, no, Nicki. Do you think she'll get to The Meadows?"

"No, she has nine lives, remember?"

"I remember, Nicki." She lets out a cough, and I'm reminded of a freight train rolling into the center of Mount Olive. "I just don't think I could live without her, so it's good that everyone thinks these cigarettes will kill me before she kicks the bucket."

"I know."

"Why won't she go to the doctor?"

Here we go again. "She doesn't like them."

Iva makes a sniffling noise. "Who does? Unless you meet an eligible one." She then laughs, deep and strong. "Oh, Nicki?"

"Yes?"

"Do you reckon we could tell Ducee we need to have cucumber sandwiches at the reunion?"

"Well . . . we are in the pickle capital of the world."

"I think that might work. We have to have cucumbers because we grow them here. It would just be un–Mount Olive–like not to have them." She seems satisfied, and I have this beautiful feeling rising from my marrow that seeps into my veins and makes me want to jump on one leg. This might actually be the end to this conversation. I chance it by saying, "Good-bye."

"Good-bye, Nicki."

———

Monet and Grable leave only after Monet begs to feed my fish. I give in when the ketchup-smeared puckered lips say, "Pleeeze, Niccc," about a dozen times.

Together we stand by the fish tank, she on a dining room chair, as I show her how to sprinkle a little food from the container onto the water's surface.

After she watches the fish eat, she looks at me and asks, "Niccc maaddd?"

I'm confused. "No, Monet. I'm not mad."

"Nicccc maadddd?"

It dawns on me. Last time she overfed the fish, I was angry. I'd better give her positive reinforcement for the job well done today. Smiling, I say, "You did a good job this time, Monet."

Monet claps her hands, loses her balance, catches herself against the sharp corner of the aquarium. I grab her elbow before she does any damage. I'm still catching my breath when she frees herself from my grasp, slides off the chair, races across the hardwood, stops midway, hops on one foot, and sails into her mother's arms. "Niccc nooo maaddd!"

Grable gives her a kiss, and then I kiss the wild child, too.

Of course, moments later, after she and Grable have left my driveway for Lady Claws, the salon where Grable gets her nails done, I'm ready to raise my voice at Monet. I cannot find the most recent email message from Harrison. The attachment he sent earlier today is nowhere in my mailbox. I check, scroll here and there and wonder what happened. Then I know. Monet deleted it while I was on the phone with Iva. This is not just a theory; it is a fact. There is a ketchup stain on my keyboard. A little dollop on the right corner of the delete key.

I sit in my fuzzy desk chair and shake my head. In my mind I can see Monet's rosy cheeks with the wayward curls framing her face, hear her sing the Dora the Explorer song, and the robust shrills and shrieks of excitement. Has there been a happier child to walk the earth? The doctors in the white lab coats don't know what's wrong with her; perhaps in her defiant way she is determined not to fit into any of their array of diagnoses. What if she were somehow wiser than they, and all of her strange antics were carefully skilled methods to outsmart the lot of them?

I call Grable's cell phone. She answers on the fourth ring and tells me she's getting her nails painted a rusty red while Monet looks at fashion magazines on the salon floor. "I think it'll be a nice color. Flora Jane is painting my left hand now."

Flora Jane has been at Lady Claws since the discovery of fire. She likes to dye her hair sky blue in the summer and violet in the cooler months.

"Thanks for coming over," I say. "I'm glad you and Monet could come here."

"Really? Because I know Monet is loud and destructive and hard to—"

I cut her off. "Grable." With ease I say, "Monet is fine."

She is silent and then I hear her talking to someone else. I also hear Monet squealing and laughing. "Nicole?"

"Yeah?"

"Monet found an angelfish in one of the magazines. Some shoe advertisement with a fish swimming in a high-heeled shoe."

"She really likes fish."

Grable says she has to go because Flora's ready to paint her right hand. But before she ends the call, she tells me, "Monet really likes you, too."

I sit in the chair and just breathe in and out for a bit after hanging up the phone. Out the window I see two cardinals darting around my oak tree as the neighbor's gray cat prowls by the trunk.

Then I write to the carp owner in Japan.

Harrison,

My cousin's three-year-old daughter Monet was here and deleted your message. I know that sounds a little odd, but she is quite gifted at causing chaos. I didn't get to see the photo of you at all. Could you send it again?

Thank you.

Nicole

I hope he writes back, but if he doesn't, I tell myself it's really okay. He lives in Japan, and I am, after all, avoiding anything to do with that country.

Chapter Ten

As the finicky month of March swirls through eastern North
Carolina, Ducee tells us after Sunday dinner that we must finalize
our reunion planning. She uses her large spiral notebook with
a lopsided pineapple on the cover to jot down the menu and
other items needing attention. She is filled with questions and
poses some of them. Should she use the local florist, Flowers
by Deena, or should she ask her cousin Tweetsie in Goldsboro
to make the arrangements for the reunion events? Tweetsie
would be honored, yet can she be told—nicely, of course—that
the arrangements need to showcase more than just white roses
from her garden? Color is key here. We don't want to offend her.
We do remember that her roses received a blue ribbon at the
Goldsboro Home and Garden Show. Oh, and should the invita-
tions be printed on four-by-six cards like last year? With a larger
font. Last year's was so tiny ninety-seven-year-old Aunt Louise
in Morehead City thought she'd received a floral postcard with
mere black lines on the backside. Ducee spent a day trying to
appease the woman, telling her the lines were words, and no,
the small font was not a conspiracy to keep Aunt Louise from
the gathering.

Between Ducee and Iva, the questions and concerns mount like mashed potatoes. What about a trip to the coast in the church van? You know those Wyoming folk need to see the ocean and get some fresh salty breezes in their faces. They don't have the privilege of living close to the coast like we do, bless their hearts. Will Aaron be able to secure a van for the ride? Will the Friday evening dessert be at Third Presbyterian again this year? If so, we need more folding chairs. Is Clive up for the Sunday breakfast at his house? Back to the dessert, are the twins going to play the harmonica and flute for the entertainment that night?

Iva says she heard they were going to The Netherlands.

"What?" Ducee cries. "Who is going where?"

"The twins."

I am always amused that these grown men, Ivan and Patrick, are not known by their given names but referred to as The Twins.

"The Netherlands?" Ducee says the name of the country as though it's a disease. She removes her bifocals and rubs her eyes.

Iva sighs. "I know. How can they choose that weekend to be away? Where is their family loyalty?"

Ducee fits her glasses over the bridge of her nose. "No, Iva, the twins wouldn't do that. You probably got the dates wrong. They wouldn't miss a reunion." For Ducee, not attending a family reunion is equivalent to not getting into heaven.

Iva shrugs and moves the ashtray toward her plate, which holds half a slice of pound cake.

I've already finished my cake, enjoying each buttery bite.

"Tell us the menu for Saturday's picnic again," Iva pipes out.

Adjusting her bifocals, Ducee reads as I sip from a cup of

ginger tea. "Potato salad, chicken salad, honey-baked ham, corn on the cob, green bean casserole, egg salad sandwiches, iced tea, lemonade, and chutney. And Mrs. McCready will bring a few pies." Mrs. McCready isn't related to any of us, but like Mr. McGuire, she is considered family.

Iva puts down her cigarette. "We are missing something."

Ducee looks over her page, shakes her head, and looks up. "No, I read it all."

"You didn't say anything about cucumber sandwiches."

"Well, Iva, as I've told you before, you can't have egg salad and cucumber at the same meal."

"All right, I got that theory of yours."

I grimace. Ducee does not think her Southern Truths are mere theories. She takes offense to anyone not realizing she is the queen of etiquette. But I have learned, over the years, to stay out of these sibling spats. I try to relax and sip my tea.

"If we can't have cucumber sandwiches at the picnic on Saturday here, then we can have them at the breakfast at Clive's."

"Whoever heard of cucumber sandwiches for breakfast?" If Ducee were a rocket, she would be through the roof, halfway to Mars.

"Clive eats fried oysters for breakfast. So he'll let my sandwiches be on his breakfast menu."

"Clive will let you have sandwiches for breakfast?" Ducee sounds as if she is ready to march over to Clive's small farm and take him down.

"If we have the Sunday breakfast at his house, he will."

Ducee closes her eyes as though she is praying.

We wait.

When her eyes open, she says, "Okay, why not?"

"What?" Iva's cigarette hand is suspended in midair.

Ducee lifts the cloth napkin from her lap to wipe her mouth. "I said, why not?"

"Why not what?"

She tosses her napkin onto her left thigh. "You can have them—cucumber sandwiches."

Iva gives me a wide-eyed look and quickly cries, "Write it down! In the book."

With great effort, Ducee flips open her notebook and slowly jots down a few words.

Iva's beam is so bright, I think I need sunglasses to shade my eyes. She gives me a light kick under the table. "Did you write cucumber sandwiches, thinly sliced, no skins?"

"Yes." Ducee sighs as she puts down her pen, picks up her napkin, and carefully wipes the edges of her mouth one more time.

Later, after the dishes are cleared and washed, Iva and Ducee sing a few Irish ballads.

Ducee's eyes form tears during the last stanza of "Danny Boy," and that's when I head out the door to go home.

All day I've wanted to sit at my computer and write to Harrison. Even during the sermon this morning, based on one of Ducee's favorite passages, Matthew six, about God caring for the birds of the air, my mind was coming up with comments to make on Harrison's latest email message.

After Monet had deleted his picture before I got a chance to view it, Harrison resent the photo as an attachment with a note. His words on the screen made me smile and think, what a sweet guy.

Nicole,

Monet sounds charming. I don't blame her if she deleted my picture after looking at it. She's not the first. An ex-girlfriend of mine still throws darts at a 5 X 7 of me in her spare time.

If you look at the pond, by the lily, just behind me, you can get a glimpse of my Kohaku, my most gluttonous koi. I think he is guilty of eating the plants.

Harrison

Charming? Monet? Harrison used the same word to describe Monet as Ducee once did. In my mind I saw her ketchup-stained face, her one-legged stances, her puckered lips. I let out a light laugh but was not sure I agreed to *charming*.

Then I closed my eyes, pressed the paper clip to open the attachment, let out one single breath, opened my eyes, and was face-to-face with a man of more or less average build seated on a stone bench by a pond framed in foliage. He was wearing dark blue jeans and a long-sleeved blue shirt that brought out the blue in his deep-set eyes. His hair was brown and cut short. His eyes were alive with a smile and his lips parted to show two rows of white teeth. I searched for his shoes, but his feet were hidden by the cattails growing beside the pond.

I studied his face and then found the fish's white-and-red spotted back, barely visible in the pond. My eyes moved to Harrison's face again.

It was then that I had the urge to tell someone about Harrison. If only I had a girlfriend, I could call to say, "Guess what? Harrison sent me a picture of himself. Come over and see!"

Oh, I knew I could call Ducee. Ducee has always let me know she wants to be right in the center of my life, but telling Ducee wasn't the same. Besides, I wasn't sure I was ready to talk to Ducee about this. What would my grandmother say? "You met him online? Isn't that very dangerous? Yes, that's it, yes."

Aunt Iva would throw in that she knew someone who had met a guy online and was now at the bottom of the Neuse River as fish bait. Cousin Aaron would likewise tell me to beware of a stranger. His pastoral warning would sound something like, "Beware, Nicole. God's given us discernment for times like these." Or would he be glad that I was finally dealing with the Japan part of myself?

Carefully, I went over every aspect of the photo from the pond to the cattails to Harrison's face. I concluded that Harrison was not a movie star, but sure as the sun, neither was I. He did have a cuteness to him, though.

In the quiet of my house that night, I moved from my computer to plan my lessons for Monday's seventh- and eighth-grade classes. I opened the literature textbook. Half an hour later I'd read nothing from any of the pages. But I had written Harrison's name in bold letters on a page in my lesson planner.

Back at my computer, I clicked on the photo attachment again.

Harrison does have nice eyes, I told myself. They are blue and a little crinkled at the edges due to his smile. They seem to embody a cross between warmth and ease, and something else, something I couldn't quite place.

Grandpa Luke always said when you met someone for the first time not to neglect his eyes. His instructions were to hold the eye contact and see what your gut told you. "When I met Ducee," he told me, "I locked my eyes with hers and saw into her pretty and strong soul. Yes, I thought, by golly, this is the woman for me!"

As I fed my fish, I said to them, "His eyes are kind. They're blue like the ocean. I bet they'd gloss over when he was told a sad story."

My angelfish and clownfish just opened and closed their button mouths.

Yet I didn't say a word to Harrison about my birth in Japan or Mama. I simply replied that I was very glad to get the picture and that his outdoor fish pond looked great.

————

On Sunday afternoon after I get home I write until the sun sets. I answer Harrison's questions about teaching, why I became a teacher, and why I like living in Mount Olive. "It's tiny and quaint. Have you ever been to the South?" I tell him about the family reunion in July, the food we'll make, including pineapple chutney. "We use an ancient recipe my grandmother says comes from Ireland, although we know there are few pineapples, if any, in Ireland." I say that the green bean casserole is made with heavy cream instead of milk, which adds about five thousand extra calories to each serving, but somehow, on reunion Saturday at my grandmother Ducee's, we don't care.

Chapter Eleven

As we walk out into the fading late-March sunshine after school one Tuesday, Kristine wants to know why I look sad. When I don't reply but just push my hands into my coat pockets, she tells me I can't brood over Richard any longer. "Nicole, you have to get out there and circulate again."

Richard? I haven't given him a thought in weeks. He is probably circulating with the tattooed librarian and that is just peachy by me.

"You're cute," Kristine tells me with one of her wide smiles and a flick of her gently wind-blown hair. "I know this guy who would like to date you. He's about your height, has brown wavy hair. Since he's been out of jail he hasn't found anyone he's attracted to." Then she turns to walk toward her red Mustang. "Let me know, okay?"

As I get into my car to go home, I look at myself in the mirror and can barely see my eyes. The wind has ruffled my frizzy mane in all directions. It's hopeless. My hair will never look like Kristine's, nor will my smile or eyes or legs. I speed out of the parking lot, return Mr. Vicker's wave, and sail down the street.

What is wrong with me? Other than my wayward hair? It was a good day at school, I think. My eighth-graders wrote poetry and some of the poems, especially Clay's, were electrifying. Maybe they were paying attention last week as I taught them how to string adverbs and adjectives together. Perhaps my students will make it to Fortune 500 companies. Once they pass middle school, high school, and college, that is. And as adults, they may even look back upon their eighth-grade year and thank me. After all, Henry Adams did say that a teacher affects eternity.

But it is not teaching that has me on edge. The teaching aspect of my life has been going well for a while now. It's really quite simple. Sazae knows; my aquarium of swimming beauties know. I haven't heard from Harrison in over a week.

I reread the previous messages I've sent, analyzing each one, trying to find the line or word that may have caused him to be offended and quit corresponding. We've been writing constantly and now the inevitable has happened—one of us is tired. And it's not me.

For the whole month, I've sent messages in the afternoon and received replies the next morning. He writes at night, while I am still sleeping and on the brink of waking to a day that he is just about to complete. I learned early on that during the spring, Japan is thirteen hours ahead of America's East Coast.

I wrote on a Saturday after cleaning my fish tank. In a cheerful mood, since I'd just completed the tedious chore of scrubbing the insides and outsides of the glass tank, I made a bowl of grits and wrote about the first goldfish I ever owned. He'd recently written about his first fish, which was a minnow he caught in a stream at a local park in Kyoto.

I typed,

My cousin in Mount Olive gave me my first fish. My father and I lived in Richmond at the time and I was visiting my grandma Ducee the summer before entering first grade. Aaron came over with a glass globe container, and it held one piece of seaweed, a blue rock and a green and red pagoda. He poured the contents of a plastic bag into the container and out gushed water and a bright orange goldfish. I was attending Vacation Bible School that week and we were studying Jonah and the big fish. So, naturally, I named my fish Jonah. He lasted all summer, swimming happily in his home, which I kept on my grandmother's kitchen counter. I still have the green pagoda, and every fish tank I've had since then gets this childhood item placed on the gravel.

I looked forward to hearing his response. But the next morning before heading to church, my inbox was empty. I didn't hear from him the next day or the next. Why isn't he writing? I asked myself. Did I say something wrong? My mind spun with confusion.

I even prayed that he would write as I walked the halls at school, listened to Kristine in the teachers' lounge, and tried to ease Iva's worries about Ducee's failing health. Then I thought, what a silly prayer. He's just a guy across the ocean who likes fish. Big deal. Get over it. God must think you are awfully frivolous to ask Him for such a selfish thing.

But he writes poetry. His blue eyes are kind. And when I look at his picture and read lines from his email messages, it is as though I can see his eyes move and light up and—

I have to stop sitting in Aunt Lucy's chair. I am not only crazy, but obsessed.

It doesn't matter what I try to tell myself; I want to hear from Harrison.

As I unlock my front door, I promise myself I'll do five things around the house that need to be done before checking my new email messages. Promise.

In the kitchen there is an answering machine message from my stepmom, Bonnie. She emphasizes how wonderful it would be to hear from me. I suppose it's time I give her a call.

First, I make a cup of Earl Grey and sip it at the kitchen table. Maybe Harrison has been on vacation. He did say he was going to southern Japan, to Okinawa, to snorkel, but wasn't that in July? I finish my tea, realizing I didn't even taste it.

Then I pick up the phone.

She answers on the third ring. I'd hoped to get by with the easy method—leaving a message.

"Hi, Bonnie, how are you? How's Father?" I try to conjure a cheery voice, sort of like Kristine would sound.

"Oh, Nicole. It's you. How nice of you to call." I hear it in her voice. What she really means is, finally, you are returning my phone calls. At last you are showing some concern for me and your father. Well, girl, it is about time.

"How are you?" I repeat.

"We are doing." Which means she is busy with the women's club of Richmond while Father sits on the couch and eats sardines from a can. "How are you doing?"

I tell her school is fine and my fish are fine and then ask if she and Father will be at the family reunion.

She sighs. "When is it?"

Same as every year, I want to say, but instead tell her the first weekend in July.

"Oh," her voice sounds hollow. "No, I don't think so. The Club is having a luncheon that Friday. Saturday they are holding a canned-goods drive." Bonnie has never been one for conversation. I once tried to get her to describe her childhood house to me. Since she holds an interest in interior decorating, I figured this subject would cause her to tell in detail about each room, the furniture, the swing in the backyard. Instead, she replied in a sinister voice with, "Our house was cold. There was this dampness that crept up from the floors." Which brought chills over my skin. I didn't want to hear any more.

Now the silence makes my head itch. I attempt to break it. "So what is Father doing? Can he come to the phone?"

Quickly, she says, "Oh no. But he sends his love."

"Oh."

"Richard?"

"What?"

"How is Richard?"

Coolly, I tell her, "Fine." I'm sure he is, running off with the librarian.

"Will you come see us soon?"

"I hope to." Please, don't make me set a date.

"Can you come for your father's birthday? He'd like that."

"We'll see," I tell her. My students claim that when adults say *we'll see* it's just another way of saying *no*.

Father married Bonnie during an eclipse, I'm sure. That one moment in his life when the sun and moon lined up and he was actually sober and happy. He managed to put on some cologne to cover the smell of sardines, propose with a diamond he bought in a pawn shop, and she, enticed by his good looks, accepted. Since then there has never been another eclipse in his life. Just this large darkness like an overgrown shadow. The darkness has actually been around since Mama's death, I'm told. "Her death ripped his life apart," Ducee said once. "Just took everything from him. Yes, that's it, yes." You'd never guess my father is a medical doctor. But I heard he was once a good one, eager with enthusiasm to work at the Baptist Hospital in Kyoto, Japan. I've heard from some relatives that in his early twenties, right before he met Mama, he battled depression. Once the love of his life was dead, the illness consumed him, and not caring to seek help or medication, he lost his faith and spiraled downward. That's what they tell me.

"Well," Bonnie breathes in. "We do miss you."

"Thank you." As soon as the words leave my lips, I think, what a dumb thing for me to say. I know what I'm expected to say. "Oh, I miss you, too." But I just can't. I don't miss anything about her, not even the beef stew she makes, which is actually tasty. And Father. His depressed lifestyle has never been something I'm proud of. In fact, I used to worry that if depression is hereditary, I was doomed.

"Well," Bonnie says once more. "I'm glad we could talk."

"Take care of each other," I reply. Then I quickly whisper, "Bye," and hang up.

It's over. Going to the dentist would have been easier. But I did it. I've taken care of something before giving myself the luxury to check for new messages.

I ease into my computer chair. Yes! There is a message from Harrison. He's written back, at last. I let the relief sink in for a moment, enjoy it. All is well now. I glance up at my fish. "It's okay," I reassure them. "He wrote. Everything's okay." Smiling, I open his newest message.

It holds only one line. I am too stunned to read it aloud to my fish.

Nicole, my mother remembers the night you were born.

Chapter Twelve

In elementary school in Richmond, I wanted the teachers to catch every kid who lied. Those in the back row who claimed they weren't talking when they could be heard down the hallway. Those who said the markers belonged to them when they'd taken a set from someone else's desk. The ones with innocent eyes, telling the teacher their dog slobbered on their math homework, when really they'd left their fractions book in their desks with no intention of doing homework the night before.

Liars made my face burn with anger. Lying was surely the worst sin.

"God punishes you ten times more for lying," I once told Ducee as we lifted ladles of pineapple chutney into clear mason jars.

"Really?" she asked, wiping her fingers against her green apron with "Mount Olive" printed on the wide, square front pocket. "And how's that?"

"Lying hurts. Bad." I made a sour face like I did when she gave me turnip greens to taste.

Ducee studied the chutney in the lineup of jars on her kitchen counter. "The one doing the lying or the one lied to?"

I thought this was a trick question. So I answered, "Both."

She nodded, which made me think I had given the correct response.

I haven't lied to Harrison, though. I've just been a little . . . well, deceitful. Unfortunately, regardless of how I term it, what I've done is now biting at me. And it hurts. I am as exposed as a single goldfish in a glass bowl. Caught. Busted, as my students would say.

I've been corresponding with a stranger I've grown fonder of with each email message. He likes fish. He has a sense of humor. He has nice eyes. He writes well. In addition to his poem from last spring, he's sent three other poems.

We have several things in common—keeping fish as pets, teaching English to students, and much more than I care to let him know. We were both born in Kyoto, at the same Baptist hospital, and once lived in the same city. His parents were medical missionaries and so were mine. But did I need to tell him all that? I liked just reading his words and keeping my Japan life concealed. I have always kept my Japan side hidden.

Except for one night at my friend Josie's house when I was in second grade. We were talking about how sad it was that her pet guinea pig got loose, was run over by a garbage truck, and died. Josie had tears in her eyes and something inside must have made me think I could let my friend know about what happened to my mother. So I told her. "My mama died in a house fire in Japan," I said.

Josie said, "Ooh. That means she's a ghost of fire. Ghosts of fire are the scariest ones. Ooh." She quit sobbing and made eerie noises by smacking her lips and moaning. For added emphasis, she blew air through her nose.

I told myself Mama was not a ghost as I tried to sleep in

the twin bed in Josie's bedroom. But the shadows on the walls were exceptionally spooky that night, and the barking neighborhood dogs kept me from falling asleep. I lay in the dark as Josie snored. And I made a vow to myself. Never, ever, tell anyone about Mama again.

And now, my secret has been found out.

———

In a light jacket, I sit outside on the front step of my house. I wave to Mama in heaven and feel the pounding of my heart against my navy sweater. Harrison's mother must have known Mama. Harrison said his parents were medical missionaries. They might have lived near Mama and Father before I was born, and even after I was born. Or perhaps they just worked together at the hospital.

Nicole, my mother remembers the night you were born.

I imagine a woman with kind eyes like Harrison's, coming to the hospital to see Mama and me after I slithered into the world. She might have held me or at least watched my mother bring me to her breast. Maybe she cooed at me, "Why, you are beautiful. Look at all that hair." Perhaps this woman said to Mama, "Emma, she looks like you and Cliff. Such a nice mixture." She might have whispered, "Oh, Nicole is a pretty name."

Harrison's mother remembers the night I was born.

The only other person alive who can tell me about that night is Father. And although I've asked him about it a hundred times, all he's ever said was, "You were a keeper." Which has never brought me much comfort, because, I mean, what does it mean? Had I not been *a keeper,* would he have tossed me back into the ocean like a fisherman whose line has caught something too small to eat? "Let's throw her over the edge, boys. She's not a keeper!" I imagine a whole deck of fishermen in yellow rain gear each taking a look my way and nodding in agreement. "Oh yeah, too small to keep." And then after dumping me back into the rugged sea, heading into the cabin of the boat to share laughs and a few drinks.

An American woman, probably in her late fifties, a person I do not know, remembers. And she is not afraid, like Father is, to recall the night I arrived in the world.

I stare at the boundless sky as my eyes grow moist. The stars melt together, blurry, forming one large star.

"I will not cry," I say, blinking rapidly. "No, not tonight."

But it's too late. Tears are cruising down my cheeks.

Chapter Thirteen

Over the next two days, I compose a few messages to Harrison but send nothing. I eat toast without butter and drink water and no tea. Even God's creation of hot grits does not appeal to me. If I put on a black shawl, I could be the poster woman for mourners.

I don't own a black shawl.

Principal Vickers asks if I'm sick. He tells me he read on the Internet that orange juice mixed with fig skins is a great vitamin drink. I try to smile, nod, and thank him.

Kristine describes riding to the Blue Ridge Mountains on Salvador's Harley. She exclaims it was the trip of a lifetime. She still wants to know what to tell Eduardo. I tell her I have sworn off men for Lent. Surprising me, she says, "Yeah, I should try that sometime."

I sit in Lucy's chair after waking early one morning from a dream where Harrison, still in carp form, swims toward me, greets me, and takes me to an underwater pagoda with golden doors. My muscles ache; my eyes are puffy from tears. I rub the fabric of the chair and somehow, it calms me. I do my breathing. In, out, steady.

I think of the proverb about the person of integrity walking securely, but the one taking the crooked path being found out.

Just like me. Busted.

And that's when I decide to be honest.

Moving to the computer chair, I fluff the pillow on the seat, but when I sit down, the chair is still lopsided and uncomfortable.

It's four in the afternoon in Kyoto now. Harrison is probably on his way home from the university, riding the crowded city bus. Soon he'll enter his house, take off his shoes, put on a pair of slippers, and heat the water for a bath. He says an *ofuro*—a Japanese bath—is the best way to end a day.

Dear God, I pray, let the words come. Please give me the strength to be honest.

I click on Harrison's photo, see his smiling eyes. I listen to my breathing as I rub the scar in the middle of my forehead.

And then I begin. My fingers are stiff at first, but by the second sentence I am on a roll. I don't stop.

Harrison,

I'd like to blame my own father for my deceitfulness. He is the king of deceit. If the trait can be inherited, I've got it. However many times as a child I asked what killed Mama or how did she really die, he never once replied. He'd change the subject by asking if I had homework to do or if I'd brushed my teeth. I always thought that was peculiar. Why couldn't he tell me the truth? He didn't lie; he just kept the truth from me.

I'd like to think I haven't lied to you, Harrison. I have just chosen not to expose all there is about me. But now what else can I say? For if your mother remembers the night I was born, then she already knows more about my early life in Japan than I do.

I recall nothing about those years. Mama died when I was two. I try to recall some memory of her, but nothing is ever there. I don't talk about it much anymore, but it is always with me, gnawing at me. I have so many questions about my past. If I were to draw a picture of my mind, it would be in the shape of a question mark.

Nicole

I crawl into bed, clutch Sazae. It's now three fifty-one. I wait for sleep and am relieved when its soft tendrils caress my face.

———

I have often daydreamed that one day, out of the blue on a frosty winter afternoon, while I'm cleaning my fish tank, I will hear a tap at my front door. With net in hand, and the smell of algae in the air, I'll answer to see an elderly woman, a little stooped over. She'll be a long-lost relative, one I've never met before because she's never attended a family reunion. I will know her, though, because her name will be one that Ducee's mentioned.

When she takes off her heavy coat, there will be a faint odor of mothballs. I'll fold her coat on the sofa and ask if she'd like a cup of Earl Grey.

Seated in the living room by the window, she will start to tell me everything I've wanted to know about Mama: how the fire started, why I was rescued from the burning house and Mama wasn't, and who got me out in time. This relative will know why one of Sazae's sleeves is shorter than the other, and when Mama purchased this cotton doll for me. And my scar, set in the middle of my forehead—she will know how I got this tiny wound.

The sun will set and the tea will be consumed, and then this relative will stand to leave. She'll button her coat and open the

---

front door. And in some sort of Mary Poppins fashion, she will be carried off by the cool eastern wind.

I will then sit in Aunt Lucy's chair and cry a little, but above all I will be relieved that all my questions about my past have been answered in one simple afternoon.

Instead, my puzzle-solver, the one with the answers, is not at my doorstep but ten thousand miles away. And in order to learn about the past, I have to rely on my computer.

Oh, Mr. Vickers, it turns out you are right. Computers do enhance our lives. Sure as the sun.

Chapter Fourteen

Iva calls to tell me about a convict who escaped from a prison in Wake County. "Be sure to lock your doors, Nicki," she advises over the phone.

"I thought you said he was last seen in Birmingham. So we should be safe, right?" I am half teasing.

But Iva sees no room for jokes. "Nicki," she says through her cigarette, "he could easily turn around and come back here. He's a *convicted* killer. He's driving a blue Saab."

I wonder what Iva wants me to do besides lock my doors, which I do already anyway.

"Nicki?"

"Yes."

"Ducee's not going to live that much longer."

Here she goes again. "Iva, she's doing fine. Preparing for the reunion might make her a little tired, but she's happy."

"I wonder if I am."

"Tired or happy?"

"I know I don't need another man in my life, that's for sure."

Especially not one like Harlowe, I think. I can understand

why Iva is repulsed by pork and beans. To this day she won't look at a can of Bush's or Van Camp's when she goes down the canned vegetable aisle of the grocery store.

"Nicki?"

I look up at my ceiling fan, still covered in dust. One day I will clean it. "Yes?"

"Do you think Dennis is having an affair?"

I nearly drop the phone. Gulping, I count to ten.

"Nicki? He's never home. I just wondered."

"Iva, we don't know."

She coughs. "No, we don't, do we?" After a moment she asks, "What would you do?"

"About what?"

"If you found out that your husband was having an affair."

I haven't a clue. For one thing, I've never had a husband. My aunt knows that. I'm not even sure why she wants to know what I would do. I feel disappointed and frustrated with Dennis now. "I'd be angry," I finally say.

She clears her throat. "Harlowe was a rotten man. But he never cheated on me."

I want to go to bed. I've been tired lately. I didn't know that learning about your past could be so exhausting. "Good night, Iva."

But she has another question for me. "Why did God make Monet the way she is?"

I chew on a thumbnail and then say, "Well, if I knew the answer, I'd be God, wouldn't I?"

Iva finds this amusing and laughs. "You're so right, Nicki." Then she quickly adds, "Grable says they've got another appointment next week. The audio doctor."

"The what kind of doctor?"

"Audio is hearing, right? That kind of doctor."

I want to laugh. I'm sure this doctor didn't go to medical school to be called an *audio doctor* by an elderly woman with platinum-dyed hair.

Grable did tell me the last time she stopped by on her way to Lady Claws that she had an appointment to check Monet's hearing. But if I let Iva know that as of late I've had more contact with Grable and Monet than I've had in months, she may try to pry information out of me. I don't want to say anything I shouldn't right now. Besides, if I think Dennis is having an affair, Grable must be the first one I tell. Of course, the only evidence I have is what Mr. McGuire saw.

"Do you think," my aunt says after exhaling, "that Monet really has beauty within?"

"I think she does," I hear myself saying. "Iva, we all do."

A small pause and then, "Well, I don't know. I can't say Harlowe does."

"Some people keep it more concealed than others."

"Oh." She clears her throat. "Like having to dig for it to see it. Like remember the time we went to the coast and dug for clams?"

It was a scorcher of a day, and I got so badly sunburned that all I could do later while Ducee, Iva, and Great-Uncle Clive baked the clams was to sit in a tub of Aveeno and moan. Yeah, I remember that day like a bad dream.

"That was a pretty good day," Iva muses. "The lemonade we made was perfect."

I'd forgotten about the lemonade. Ducee had squeezed the juice of a dozen lemons into a large glass jug, added sugar, a little hot water to dissolve the sugar, cold water, and plenty of ice. That drink, served to me in a wide mason jar, had cooled my insides as my skin burned. And for a moment my mind took a break from thinking about my pain and thanked God for Ducee and her lemonade.

Iva says good night and hangs up.

I hold the receiver for a moment longer and think how quickly we forget, even those things we think we will always remember.

———

Harrison tells me, as my students would say, how it went down. In an email message that takes three pages to print, he explains how he found me out.

When his parents came to visit recently, they helped him put the underwater fence in his outdoor pond to separate the lilies from the plant-eating carp. As they worked, he told them a woman in Mount Olive named Nicole gave him the suggestion of the fence. His mother said, "Mount Olive? Emma was from Mount Olive. Remember my friend? I was thinking about her the other day. All these years gone, and I still miss her so much."

Suddenly something clicked in Harrison's mind and he had to stop working and sit down on the stone bench by the pond. "Mom," he said, "wasn't Emma's mom from Mount Olive, too?"

"Why, yes, she was."

"And what was her name?"

"Ducee," Harrison's mother said after a brief pause. "It's a name you don't forget."

"Emma made that pineapple stuff," Harrison recalled.

"Chutney."

Harrison was on to something. "Emma's daughter was Nicole, right?"

"Yes, she was just four years younger than you. A cute kid with the prettiest red hair. I remember the night she was born."

And then Harrison knew that I had to be that same Nicole, Emma's daughter. He showed his parents the color photo of me on the Pretty Fishy Web site, expecting his mother to say, "Yes, that looks like it could be her."

Instead, she said, "Michelin," as she read my last name printed under my picture. "That was Emma's last name, too."

Harrison wrote,

> I didn't know what to do then. So I just pretended I didn't know a thing, until as time went on, I couldn't keep pretending. I waited to write. I wanted to let you know that I knew. Keeping things hidden isn't real. I am sorry about your mother, Nicole. I am sorry that you remember nothing.

I carry the three sheets around with me while I do laundry and feed my fish. When I go to bed, I place them on my bedside table. These pages are the connection to my past.

And I think, so it is true, the story that Ducee has told me. "Yes," Ducee has said many times, "your mother brought pineapple chutney and God's Word to Japan."

When I was young, I thought she meant Mama had actually carried a jar of chutney with her on the ship that took her and Father to the port of Yokohama the first time they sailed to Asia. Later when I heard the story, I realized she'd just brought the recipe. She made the chutney for her missionary friends, explaining it was an old family tradition. Ducee says Mama even wore her Mount Olive apron as she stood in the kitchen, bent over a saucepan of sugar, spices, and pineapple. Apparently, the pineapples were flown in from the tropical island of Okinawa. Ducee always concluded the story with, "And so that is how my Emma brought chutney from Mount Olive to Japan. A real East meets West adventure." And then, with an air of pride and accomplishment, Ducee would nod her head, smile at all present, and fold her hands as though about to pray.

Sometimes, if I looked closely, I could see something in her eyes. They were soft and held a faraway look. Like she was almost there, in the past, with her beloved daughter, wearing her own green apron. Together they were stirring up a spicy batch of family tradition. And the kitchen's aroma was pineapple mixed with the perfect ingredient—love.

Sometimes, I had to purposely look away from Ducee's eyes. The feeling that my own heart was going to break was too heavy to carry.

Chapter Fifteen

Harrison writes to say he knew me as a child. Truth is stranger than fiction. Yes, that's it, yes.

Now, I figured that if his mother, Rita, was friends with Mama and was there the night I was born, then it would be probable that Harrison might have seen me, too. But remember me? No, I never would have guessed that.

He claims he remembers eating pineapple chutney on rice crackers with me at my house when I was two years old. It happened, he claims. He wore leather cowboy boots a relative in Texas sent him, and I wore a pink kimono with sakura blossoms. I draped a green feather boa around my neck. The tip of the boa often dangled in my plastic cup of Milo.

"What's Milo?" I wrote.

"A chocolate-flavored powder that comes in a can and mixed with milk makes pretty good chocolate milk" was the response.

I write to him that my mind is on overload, that reading the words on my computer screen is becoming harder and harder. And because I do not want him to think that he can quit writing to me or that I will stop corresponding with him, I type, "I'll continue in the morning."

His response, just three hours later, is, "Want to talk by phone?"

———

When asked what I do for exercise, I can't say I jog or play tennis. But I once read an article in a magazine in the teachers' lounge that said cleaning is physical exercise. Now my reply to those who ask what I do for exercise is, "I clean." They usually look at me as if I am the sinking *Titanic*, in need of more help than they can give. But like washing dishes by hand, doing chores around the house is good therapy. Cheap, too.

Tonight, dressed in my oldest and most comfortable pair of Wrangler's and a UNC-Greensboro T-shirt, I start with my ceiling fan in the kitchen. Standing on a chair, I reach the long blades and, using a wet paper towel, slowly remove the dust. As I wipe, some of the dust sticks to the towel, but most of it drifts onto the floor. I wonder if dust looks the same all over the world. Is Japanese dust identical to American dust?

When I step down off the chair to get another paper towel, there's a knock on the front door.

There, in the brisk April night, stands Richard. He has one long-stemmed red rose in his hand. He smells of cologne. Yes, I recognize it—Brut.

"I don't have your Michael Bolton CD."

He laughs. "Oh, Nicole, I'm not here for my CD."

Goodness, what are you here for, then? I run a damp and dusty hand over the hem of my T-shirt.

"How have you been?" he asks.

Do I detect sincerity in his tenor voice? I hope my eyes don't look as if I've been crying. "Fine." I let politeness step up to my side and ask, "And how are you?"

"Great!" His eyes hold mine. He smiles as I think how broad his shoulders look in the moonlight. I didn't recall them being so wide. "Would you like to go with me to the Pickle Festival?"

If my heart were a bullet, it would be shooting out of my chest now. Clear to New Bern. "What?!"

He rests a hand, the one not holding the rose, against my shoulder. "In three weeks."

I know when the festival is; it's always the last weekend of April.

He wants to come in. I block the door. "Richard, what are you doing?"

His eyes twinkle, bright and full. Why did God waste such long eyelashes on a guy? "Nicole, I thought we could just spend some time together."

"Why?" I feel like my students, like Clay asking why Shakespeare used such weird language in his plays.

"Oh, Nicole." He displays his handsomest smile. "I've missed you." Softly, "Us."

I remember falling snow and hot chocolate and the coziness of sharing an afternoon with him. I remember how he grew bored with me. How he wanted to rush me into marriage. How he crushed my heart by breaking up. I shake my head.

"Nicole, we did have a lot of fun."

"No. No." I take a few steps back. Far enough back that his warm hand can no longer rest against me.

His brow wrinkles, a sign he is growing aggravated with me.

"Richard, we said it was over. You told me I don't know what I want." I breathe in. I have always liked the smell of Brut. And Brut and the spring air, they seem to go together, like the ocean and sand.

"We could try. . . ." He is using his gentle voice, the one he uses when an irate customer at his shoe store wants to know why he can't return a pair of shoes purchased months ago, clearly worn many times.

I wonder if he is here because the librarian has rejected him.

"We could hang out and talk. Watch movies."

I look at him. He's wearing a forest green Izod shirt. He always did look good in green. He asked me months ago if I knew what I wanted in life. I didn't then, but now I think I do. Slowly, I tell him, "I don't think so."

His eyes turn dark. He extends the rose to me anyway.

I take it and watch as he walks toward his car, gets in, and backs out of my driveway.

I am almost sorry for him. He is gorgeous, but I could never love him.

As I continue with my kitchen fan cleaning, I can't believe he was just here.

Truth is stranger than fiction.

———

At the aquarium, my fish beckon me to watch them dance. Besides a clean place to live and food, that's all they really want. Watch us, see us swim. We are tranquil and beautiful. Enjoy us just because God made us. Observe the way our fins swish past the seaweed, causing the green plants to sway. State-of-the-art perfection. We know how to bask in the salty, cool water because that's what we were created to do.

I tilt my head to the left and quickly jerk it to the right to see if Monet's method of viewing my marine creatures works. Not for me. I just feel dizzy.

Chapter Sixteen

I don't wait until morning to send a few lines to Harrison. Before climbing into bed, I write, "I prefer not to talk by phone. Let's continue with email. Thanks, though. Thank you so much." He does get the idea I am appreciative of him, doesn't he? That because of him, I have a new lease on my life? I hope my words hold enough gratitude to carry over the cyberspace miles.

No, I'm not able to talk on the phone. My voice could break up or I could cry as we talk, become hoarse, or lack any words to fill the pauses—these fears, however, I don't share with him. Email is so safe—my time, my choice of words, and always the ability to delete a line or two. Spoken thoughts are so final.

Four hours later I sit up in bed, clutching Sazae. My dream was so vivid, it had to be real. I click on my bedside lamp, see Mama's smiling face in the frame, and wait for my mind to convince me that I have been only dreaming.

I swam alone in a dark, cold ocean. Water raged around me, and each time I lifted my head to breathe air, a wave slammed against my face. The pain was strong as my struggle continued. I tried to swim out of the ocean, but instead, my foot became lodged under a large rock. I screamed for help as loudly as I could, but no sound came out from my lungs. I tried again. No one came. I was desperately alone, although I kept sensing that Harrison was somewhere.

Then I heard a voice above me say, "You have to be in the same ocean for Harrison to hear you."

I looked up to see Monet, of all people. It was not peculiar to me that she was speaking clearly and in a full sentence. All I knew was, this girl—wild child—made sense.

Suddenly I was able to twist my foot from under the rock, freeing it from its bondage, and swim.

I swam for miles, knowing that I was going to find my way. At last the sun broke through the clouds and I reached warm, bright waters, the ocean of my past dreams. Inside a golden pagoda was Harrison. He greeted me in his deep voice. "Nicole," he said, "I'm glad you made it."

My foot was bruised, but I didn't mind. I had made it. I had found my way. And he was there.

————

My plans are few for this week of Easter break. Kristine and Salvador are on a motorcycle trip to Myrtle Beach. Kristine says she'll send me a postcard. She can't wait to go to this restaurant Salvador mentioned, one where you're served peanuts and allowed to throw the shells on the floor. From a large tank, guests select their own catfish for the cooks to fry up. While waiting for your meal, you drink iced tea from a conch shell and listen to a band play the blues.

Ducee is attending all of the special church services, but when I drop by for tea Thursday afternoon, I tell her I will join her and Iva only for Easter Sunday. My grandmother asks if I need to tell her something. I say there is nothing to tell. She adjusts her bifocals, wipes her mouth with a pink cloth napkin, and examines my face. "Nicole," she says after too much silence, "you know, I may be old—I suppose some would think I am—but I am here."

Quickly, I tell her that I am glad she's here and that I'd like another cup of ginger tea.

I don't really care for more tea, but I can't let her continue talking. My gut senses that she is going to add, "I am here, but one day I will be gone." No, no, I can't hear her vocalize those fears of mine.

———

While writing an article for the Pretty Fishy site on Saturday evening, I hear from Harrison. It is Easter morning in Kyoto, and he is getting ready for church. He writes that he just got off the phone with his mother, who now is in Texas. "She says Watanabe-san lives in a nursing home in Katsura. I plan to visit Watanabe-san this afternoon. I'll let you know what I find out."

Well, I think that is just dandy, but what has Watanabe-san got to do with any of this?

First off, who is Watanabe-san? I check past messages from Harrison to make sure I haven't missed anything. No, in all of the messages he's sent, there is no recording of anyone by that name.

So I write back, "Okay, I'm clueless. Tell me who she/he is."

———

I love Easter Sunday, although I wonder if God thinks it is the epitome of human deceit. On one Sunday of the year, folks show up at church. Not just the regular church attendees, but people who haven't been in, well, since last Easter. There they are in all their finery. Women in pretty, delicate, pastel-colored dresses and men sporting cotton suits with silk ties. The church looks full of life—although today as Reverend Donald preaches, I wonder if anyone is really listening. I wonder how many are pondering on the miracle of the resurrection of Jesus and how many are thinking about ham or chicken, or whether Aunt Martha will serve her delicious deviled eggs at lunch this year.

I may let my mind slip a bit here and there, especially as my own stomach rumbles with hunger. But during much of the service I thank God over and over for bringing Harrison into my life. You know, I tell God, Harrison is a much better choice for bringing light on my past than that heavy-coated mothball-smelling old relative of my imagination.

Our Easter lunch is at Great-Uncle Clive's farm. Iva excitedly tells him to make sure his cucumber crop is productive this summer because we are going to need a dozen of his vegetables for the reunion.

Clive is six-foot-four and, like Joseph McGuire, has one outfit he wears daily—faded overalls and a T-shirt with the Pepsi-Cola logo. I wonder where he finds overalls long enough. I know where he gets the Pepsi shirts. There's a small shop in New Bern, the town where Pepsi was first created, that sells T-shirts and all kinds of Pepsi paraphernalia. He bends close to his sister Iva and says, "Why do you need cucumbers?"

"For the reunion." Proudly, she announces, "We are going to have cucumber sandwiches."

Clive chews on the end of a toothpick he is holding. His hand is broad, and the wobbly toothpick looks as if it could snap at any moment. "I thought it was against southern etiquette to have both cucumber and egg salad sandwiches at the same meal."

It is the first time I've ever heard him speak such a long sentence. He usually prefers one or two words.

Iva's grin stretches across her face. "Not anymore is it against all that etiquette baloney," she tells her younger brother. "Ducee is making an exception." Iva draws on her cigarette, watches the smoke evaporate, and grins some more.

I don't think she would be any happier if she'd just gone to Virginia and won the lottery.

———

The rose Richard brought over is in a narrow glass vase on my kitchen table. The flower is elegant, regal. So much so that it doesn't look real. It only has two tiny thorns on its green stem. I wonder if that adds to its unnatural look. I finger the velvet petals as I wait. I'm ready to hear from Harrison.

By midnight, when my inbox is still empty, I decide he must be busy. Who was this person he was going to see? A connection to my past? What if she or he is a bad person? What if Harrison got in a fight because this Watanabe-san refused to disclose any information? What if Harrison's life is in danger?

A cup of hot Earl Grey doesn't soothe my worries. In fact, after only two sips, I abandon the mug and go to the computer to check once more for an email message. But the inbox produces nothing new.

As I get ready for bed, I pour the cold tea down the sink. What is wrong with me? Here I am throwing out my favorite Earl Grey.

I lie in bed stroking Sazae's shorter kimono sleeve and pray that Harrison is safe. But when the digital clock on my bedside table shows 2:00, I sigh and get out of bed. Then I do what I often do when I can't sleep—a load of laundry. As the water rushes into the machine, my mind wanders. What will happen if Harrison stops writing? Surely, he knows he holds the answers to my many questions from the past. Certainly, he wouldn't abandon me after all this. "Would he?" I ask aloud to the washing machine.

I close my eyes to try to recall something about this childhood friend, but nothing is there. No sharing drinks of Milo. No feather boa around my neck. No Watanabe-san.

The washing machine rapidly ushers in the next cycle.

Chapter Seventeen

Sometimes I think the passage in the Bible that commands us not to worry is one of the most profound pieces of advice around. "Therefore I tell you," Jesus says to the crowds following Him, "do not worry about your life, what you will eat or drink; or about your body, what you will wear. Is not life more important than food, and the body more important than clothes?" And then, of course, comes Ducee's favorite passage: "Look at the birds of the air; they do not sow or reap or store away in barns, and yet your heavenly Father feeds them. Are you not much more valuable than they? Who of you by worrying can add a single hour to his life?"

Of course, Harrison writes again—in spite of my worrying that he may have encountered something awful or decided to give up on our correspondence. Watanabe-san, I find out, is a woman in her late sixties. When Mama, Father, and I lived in Kyoto, she lived with us, in a small *tatami* room in our two-story house. She was our live-in maid.

She now resides in a nursing home outside of Kyoto, in Katsura. Harrison's mother, Rita, did some searching and found out from their former maid that Watanabe-san had been living in the home for six months.

> She's in a wheelchair. She suffers from dementia, and there are days she won't talk at all. But the nurses say that on good days, she converses. Luckily, when I told her who I was, she responded with a smile. She remembered that I used to come over to your house with my mom. Your mom and mine would sit, drink tea, and eat pineapple chutney on crackers. You and I, Nicole, would drink Milo. And you'd gobble up your serving of chutney, but apparently, I hated the stuff. (I have never been fond of pineapple and blame it on the time I was three and we went on furlough to Texas. My parents were speaking at a church in Fort Worth, and I was with my aunt and uncle in Houston when a hurricane came through. I was afraid I'd never see my folks again, and my aunt tried to console me with chunks of pineapple.) When I asked Watanabe-san about the fire, her eyes filled with tears. She kept crying, "Is she okay? Did she live?" I told her that your mother died and she nodded her head, yes, she did remember that tragedy. But what she wanted to know was if you survived, Nicole.

Here, I stop reading and walk over to my aquarium. The fluorescent light that is always on shines on the water and makes each fish sparkle. I find the eel, sunk in the gravel by the pagoda. If I were to name him, he'd be Sinker or Slinky. But the truth is, I quit naming my fish in college.

One of my professors, my favorite, Raymond Kelly, pointed out that naming something was a human characteristic and that in the animal kingdom there were no names. Lions didn't walk around referring to their cohabitants as Fuzzy or Curly. He and I actually had debates on this topic, me saying that to name a pet was to accept it and make it part of your life. He disagreed. We found arguments to support our views and, for a semester, discussed this in mutual appreciation. Sometimes I just think he liked to argue for the sake of being different. What can I say? I enjoyed it, too.

When we returned to campus after spring break my junior year, we heard the news. Professor Kelly would not be with us any longer. One day during the two-week vacation he'd gone to an amusement park with his wife. He'd ridden the roller coaster. His wife refused to ride, petrified of the motion and noise. She went to get a Sno Cone. When she returned, her husband was dead. A part of the roller coaster, the very car he was in, broke and he was flung from the car to an instant death.

I hate roller coasters. Motorcycles and airplanes, too.

And in honor of Raymond Kelly, I don't name my fish anymore. I just let them live with me as one big family. Beautiful, but nameless.

I watch my fish for a few more silent moments and then return to the computer.

The screen still holds the message from Harrison. I suppose I should read about the house fire. Isn't this the mystery I have wanted revealed for as long as I can remember?

Chewing my thumbnail for a moment calms me. I rub my scar.

When the phone rings, I run to get it.

Iva wants to know if I want to go to New Bern with her and Clive. "We're leaving in about an hour and can swing by your house to get you. Clive's driving his Pepsi truck."

I love the coastal town. And riding in Great-Uncle Clive's truck with a bottle of the drink painted on each side and a few other decals of bottles on the rear window is an experience like no other. Inside the truck, the cooler is always filled with icy cans of Pepsi, and a small, plastic, scantily clad woman sits on the dashboard, embracing a bottle of the drink.

"We'll eat at that barbecue restaurant on the way," my aunt says.

I say I'm busy, sorry.

She tells me she is sorry, too. "Maybe next time."

"Yes, maybe so."

"Oh, Nicki?"

"Yes?" Is this going to take long? I'll have to find a chair to sit on if my aunt is going to dive into her list of questions.

Iva surprises me. "Isn't it just grand that we're having cucumber sandwiches at the reunion?" I can feel her smile across the telephone line.

"Yes, Iva, it is."

That's it. She's finished. She hangs up with a quick click.

Slowly, I place the receiver back in its cradle and head back to my computer. A sensation overcomes me, one I cannot shake. My heart pounds, my ears feel as if cotton is wedged inside, and my fingers are numb. I close my eyes, breathe in and out. Steady.

Maybe I should go to New Bern instead. I do like The Cozy Barbeque, the tiny restaurant outside of Kinston on Highway 70. The iced tea served there in mason jars is so sweet it could give you cavities just looking at it. The barbeque sauce is every bit as good as Smithfield's.

What am I afraid of? What could be worse than all the years I've spent not knowing what really happened the night of the fire? Goodness, I remind myself, you've been crying out to God, just as King David did in Psalm Six: "My soul is in anguish. How long, O LORD, how long?" Well, now the answers are here. Just go ahead and read them.

In my mind I see my grandmother's face, nodding for me to, yes, yes, read.

The pep talk works.

I open my eyes. With the afternoon sun casting streaks of light across my computer, I enter my inbox. And as the expression goes, I am ready to face the music.

Watanabe-san says she rescued you from the fire. Your father wasn't at home that night. He'd gone to Tokyo to a church conference. The fire started downstairs in your parents' bedroom. Watanabe-san had an upstairs bedroom and suddenly woke to the smell of smoke.

When she got to your mother, your mother was facedown on her bedroom floor. Watanabe-san rushed over to her, and then heard your voice down the hallway. You were standing in your crib with heavy smoke all over and you were singing. Watanabe-san couldn't see because of the smoke and her eyes were burning, but she heard your voice singing a song you and she often sang together. She says your singing helped her know where you were and she was able to reach you and get you out of the house. She has always felt if she'd been quicker and younger, she could have saved your mother as well.

The fire did burn her hands. They are scarred. She thinks they were burned when she opened your bedroom door. The knob was like an iron and it took a few tries using both hands to get it opened. She says it doesn't matter.

By the time a neighbor called the fire department and the truck got to the house, the wooden house was demolished. Your father was immediately called and flew back from Tokyo. A few items were not harmed and neighbors boxed them up and gave them to your father.

Watanabe-san regrets that you and your father left Japan. She has often wondered how you were. She never heard from your dad even though she found his new address in Virginia by contacting the mission board and wrote a few letters. There are days, the nurses tell me, when her mind isn't fluid, that she is in a panic, wondering if you survived.

Nicole, I remember hearing my parents talk about the fire. I woke up the next morning and heard my mother crying. I've never heard her cry like that since.

This has got to be hard for you to handle. I would prefer to tell you over the phone but respect your wishes.

I plan to visit Watanabe-san again later this week and will ask whatever else you want me to ask.

Also, Nicole, if you want me to tell you about your scar, I can. Whenever you are ready to hear, let me know. I was there.

Only an email away.

Fondly,

Harrison

I admit, I like his fondness.

Chapter Eighteen

I have never known my face without the polka-dot scar in the middle of my forehead. In the picture of Mama and me, there is no scar, but it doesn't always show up in photographs, so I don't know if the scar arrived before or after that day when Mama and I, dressed in kimonos, smiled into the camera. I'm used to the scar; it's a part of me. Except for rubbing it, I usually don't give it any attention. What's bothered me over the years is that, like so much of my life, it's a mystery.

Once I concluded I was born with it. Just one of those things that happens. Like my apple birthmark on my lower back. Of course it clearly looks different than my birthmark; a nursing student at UNC-Greensboro told me that tidbit of medical information for free. She said she could tell that the skin had been opened, like a wound, and then healed, leaving the tiny scar.

Still, she could be wrong. She was, after all, still a student.

My cousins in Wyoming had another twist on it. One summer when they spent a week with Ducee and me in Mount Olive, they informed me it was a magic symbol, given to me at birth by the Princess of Susunanastan. I was nine before I realized, thanks to my geography teacher, that the country of Susunanastan doesn't exist.

Ducee said it was most likely a mark left by Mama's lips, where she used to kiss me every day.

And now, with the newest message from Harrison, my scar's origin has been revealed. The mystery is solved. All the years of wondering have ended with this day.

Move over birthmark, Mama's daily kiss, and even Princess of Susunanastan.

One afternoon, after school, while Rita and Mama drank tea at our house in Kyoto, Watanabe-san took Harrison and me to the park. I'd just turned two. Harrison was six.

Having no siblings of his own at the time, he treated me like a baby sister. That day, he pushed me on a swing for a bit, not very high, because he knew I was just a small girl. Then a dog, a stray mutt probably, came racing through the playground and I, terrified of animals, screamed. I either jumped or fell— Harrison's not certain—off the swing and hit my head on a scrap of wood that someone had abandoned. The wood on the ground near the swing had a nail sticking out of it.

Harrison ran to pick me up off the ground. He and our maid took turns holding me as the blood gushed from the cut on my head. Watanabe-san carried me home as Harrison walked beside me, grateful for my sobs because that meant I was still alive.

"I remember thinking dead people don't cry, so she must still be living," Harrison wrote.

At our house, Mama examined me. She, along with Harrison's mother, both nurses, decided the cut didn't need stitches. I had just received a tetanus shot the month before, so they figured I was covered. They taped a white bandage to my head, a large one made from an old sheet. It circled my whole head.

Harrison said he let me have all his chocolate milk that afternoon and even gave me one of his favorite Matchbox trucks, sent all the way from the U.S.A.

I stand in front of the bathroom mirror and touch my scar. It feels different to my fingers now. A scar with a clear story behind it is more satisfying than a magic symbol given at birth by the Princess of Susunanastan.

I thank Harrison for helping me. I still have more questions to ask him, hopeful he'll either know the answers or find out from Watanabe-san. What about my doll's shortened sleeve? Where did Mama get the doll? What was the song I was singing in my crib the night of the fire?

I tell him to please hug Watanabe-san the next time he sees her. "Hug her for me," I write. "She saved my life. Tell her how grateful I am."

How I wish she could have saved Mama, too.

I go out and sit on my front step. I don't need a coat; a light sweater keeps the spring breezes from cooling my skin. In the distance, the crickets and bullfrogs serenade each other. It's like an orchestra performing just for me.

I find the brightest star. Now when I wave to Mama, I feel I know her so much better.

———

When I look out the window, the daffodils in Hilda's front garden seem to be at the height of their beauty. I click on a message from Harrison in my inbox. He has visited our former maid once more. In the long email I see the words, "She wants you to come to Japan."

In a hurry because it is time to leave for school, I print the letter and stuff it in my tote bag. I'll read it during lunch.

On the drive to school, I feel my stomach buckle. *Come to Japan.* That's absolutely absurd. Placing a hand against my stomach, I pat it, soothe it. *Really, you don't need to worry,* I tell it, *we are not going to Japan. You won't have to deal with the turmoil of motion sickness because I won't get on an airplane. To go anywhere.*

I don't ride airplanes, motorcycles, or roller coasters.

Come to Japan.

As my students would say, No way!

Chapter Nineteen

After the last bell rings, I head out the main door with dozens of chattering students, all busting with the energy that displays itself with the approaching end of the school year. You can hear it in their steps; only seven more weeks until we are free from this institution. Seven more weeks and then, no homework, no waking up early to catch the bus, and best of all—no English class with Ms. Michelin!

The long, lazy days of summer wait just around the corner.

In my car, I take a few breaths and roll down the window. Relief hits me, too. It's Friday. No more students for a whole weekend. One thing that students don't realize—adults enjoy some time off from them, too.

Once out of the parking lot, I just drive. Pretty soon I've left Mount Olive. I have no idea where I'm headed, but I'm headed somewhere. *I don't know where I'm headed, but I am headed somewhere.* It sounds like good bumper-sticker material.

My grandfather Luke swore by leisurely drives to nowhere. He said there was nothing like an unexpected ride down a familiar road, a wonderful recipe for thinking and unwinding. Some Sunday afternoons he would let Ducee and me come along in his delivery truck, as long as we didn't insist on stopping to bargain shop or make a number of restroom breaks.

Grandpa Luke's love of driving must have sunk into my genes; already I can tell this ride is helping ease the tension in my muscles.

The warm sun soaks into my arms and legs as I sail down Route 117. Along the road, purple wisteria—bountiful and aimless—sweeps around the high limbs of trees. In front lawns, yellow daffodils stand straight and proud.

I pass Warsaw, and then Rose Hill, home to the largest vineyard and winery in North Carolina. When the Welcome to Wallace road sign greets me, I smile because now I know where I'm headed. It won't be much farther. Wow, this little road trip is just what I needed. After the email message from Harrison, I need a place to be free, like the wisteria, to spread out and absorb.

Come to Japan.

No.

I am delighted that Watanabe-san wants to see me after all these years, but perhaps if her interest in being with me is so strong, she could jump on a Japan Airlines flight and fly to North Carolina.

The clock on my dashboard reads three-fifteen. This means it's early Saturday morning in Kyoto. Harrison is sleeping. Soon he'll wake to his alarm, which is set to a classical music station out of Osaka. He'll get out of his futon, shave, and put on a cologne for men by Shiseido. For breakfast he'll eat raisin toast and oatmeal. Grits? Never. Earl Grey? He had it once, he thinks. Must not have liked it, because he's never had it since. Hot coffee, extra strong, is what he makes to start the day.

After glancing at the headlines of the *Japan Times*, he'll brush his teeth. At eight-thirty he'll catch the bus to a special school for handicapped kids. Every Saturday he volunteers at the school with a group from his church. He writes that working with these kids is the highlight of his week. "I like being the professor and teaching English at the college, but my time with these special-needs children is when I learn more than I could ever teach. The mornings are valuable lessons, molding me more into the person Christ has hope I will become one day."

———

When I cross over a bridge, I'm in the coastal city of Wilmington. At a traffic light, I roll down my window until it won't go down any farther and breathe in the salty air. Ah, this is life, I think, because that is what my grandfather used to say whenever his lungs filled with the aroma of the ocean or the Blue Ridge Mountains.

I park on a side road by a gigantic beach house painted a salmon color, complete with a wrap-around white porch. In the summer months this side street would be filled with cars and I'd have to venture to another, but today, in early spring, my car's the only one.

I stop along the sandy public beach access path to take off my shoes and socks and roll up my cotton pant legs. The sun is settling in the western sky, yet it feels hot on my arms.

As I approach the ocean and hear the crashing waves, I know this trip to Wrightsville Beach is one of the best decisions I've made in a long time.

Not quite as good as deciding to continue writing to Harrison months ago, even though I suspected he lived in Japan.

Then there it is before me. Sun-enriched brilliant blue sky and deep, dark blue sea. Right in front of me to enjoy as though I am the only one alive. The grand waves dissolve into foam as they crash against the shore.

A sigh rises from my lungs and out into the inviting air.

The ocean calms me as much as it floods me with awe. Beside it, I am one little creature. My problems seem microscopic.

Digging a plastic clip out of my purse, I pull my hair into a ponytail. I walk toward the moist sand by the shore. I love the way the sand oozes through the spaces between my toes.

A woman with a broad-rimmed straw hat and a little girl with a green bucket walk past and smile. The girl looks about three years old and has hair the color of Monet's and just as much energy as she dashes ahead of her mother. She yells, "I can run faster than you, Mommy!"

For a second I wonder what Monet is doing today. I think she was scheduled to see a neurologist in Chapel Hill. I hope Dennis isn't with that woman who drives an SUV. But then I push away thoughts of Dennis. I came here to the coast to spend time thinking. I will deal with the likes of you another time, Dennis.

Following the woman and child is an elderly woman, dressed in shorts. Her rich, even tan makes me feel as if we've already had months of summer. I wonder if she's just back from the beaches of Puerto Rico.

I remove my sunglasses, rest them on top of my head, and closing my eyes, lift my chin upward so that the sun can warm my eyelids. The heat of the coastal sun is a balm for my eyes, eyes that have felt many tears.

Since I didn't prepare for this spur-of-the-moment trip, I have no towel to sit on, but nevertheless, I find a spot on the damp sand. A timid hermit crab making its way over a large shell scurries away from me.

I did a science project on crabs once. There is the blue crab, the king crab, and the—

I make myself stop. I came to the beach to ponder my life, not to recite animal life.

Slipping on my sunglasses, I take crumpled pieces of paper from my purse. They rattle with the ocean wind, and I clutch them tightly. One gust of wind could send them into the water.

These pages are from Harrison, his words to me earlier today. At lunchtime, I read his whole email message inside the janitor's closet. It was the only place I could find free of noise.

He'd been to the nursing home again to see Watanabe-san. This time the older woman had a photo she grasped in her scarred hands. She said it was of Michelin-san and the little daughter, Nicole. In the black-and-white picture, both are wearing kimonos and smiling into the camera. The little girl holds a doll against her shoulder.

Watanabe-san said she gave you that doll. She went to Kobe one weekend and found the doll at a shop on Centagai. Centagai is a covered street that stretches for almost a kilometer with stores and restaurants along each side. Watanabe-san kept saying how you loved that doll. You cried for it the night of the fire and she picked it off the floor as she pulled you from your crib. One of the sleeves of the doll's kimono was singed by the fire and she later cut off the damaged part.

Sink. Sink in.

With my free hand I uncover a tiny scallop, its half shell the color of a Magenta Queen tulip. I trace my finger along its rim. How nice to be a shell and just be, no thinking, no pondering, no endless questions with answers you never expected.

Mama did not give Sazae to me.

In the bleach-smelling janitor's closet when I read Harrison's message the first time today, I wanted to scream. All that came out was a little "Oh no" as my heart raced like the cars on the Charlotte Speedway.

Now I let my mind come up with whatever it wants to. I had to keep it in check as I taught today. I made myself play the teacher role, writing on the whiteboard, assigning homework, and grading quizzes on Emerson.

First, I think of Sazae and wonder if our relationship will change, since I know she is not a gift from Mama. She is from our family maid. Which means that now nothing I own is from Mama.

The waves collide into each other and all I can come up with is: She gave you life.

That is my gift from my mysterious mother. That, and my eyes. My unruly hair and freckles come from Father. My nail-biting and scar-rubbing traits are probably no one's fault but my own.

I close my eyes to see a woman lying on a floor, flames consuming her. A Japanese maid fighting to save the life of a child as fire burns her hands. A child singing in the fire so that the maid can find her amid the smoke. And a doll, a cloth kimono doll, with a singed sleeve.

This is my past.

And this is my present.

The pain inside immobilizes me. I am like the half shell, lifeless.

I breathe in and out, taking my time. There is no hurry. Time at the beach is meant to pass slowly.

Chapter Twenty

Sitting on the beach, I grasp the sheets of computer paper and read some more.

> Watanabe-san tells me the two of you used to sing together. You would wear your kimono and sometimes a green feather boa, and stand on your tiptoes, waiting. From your side she would call out, as though making an announcement, "And now, we have the Kimono Lady. Nicole is our Kimono Lady. She is going to sing!"
>
> As your mother played the piano, you would smile and start to sing the song Watanabe-san taught you. It's called *Ame Ame* and is about how a mother comes in the rain to pick up her child. She carries a large old Japanese umbrella made of wood. It's called a *janome*. The child is so happy to see her mother.

Oh, my. "Oh, my!" I cry right there on the beach. I sang in Japanese. I had no idea I could once speak Japanese. "I'm bilingual." The laughter collects in my throat, and I let it out.

A young couple, walking hand in hand, smile at me.

Yeah, don't mind me. I'm just having a little information overload.

They linger, bodies close, an embrace, a passionate kiss. Then they amble farther down the shore.

I wonder if they're dating, in love, married, or cheating on their spouses. Grable's husband is threading his way into my thoughts yet again. Dennis, no good from the get-go.

My eyes scan back to the beginning, and I read the first lines of Harrison's letter.

Nicole,

I visited Watanabe-san again today. She is so relieved to know you are alive. I guess sometimes she is confused about whether or not you were rescued. The nurses say she has her good days, and then the days when she wants only to sit in her wheelchair and drink tea.

Today was a good day. She talked constantly. She wants you to come to Japan. She says you can sit beside her and ask all the questions you have. She will do her best to answer them.

Think about it, Nicole. I would like it if you came to Japan. I think it would be a good experience for you.

I laugh again. Neither of them understands that I can't go to Japan. Nicole doesn't fly.

Three sea gulls soar on the surface of the waves; one catches a small fish in its beak and, with great force, flies from the others. Squawking, the others chase after him in the air.

I watch the ocean for a while as my thoughts tumble all over each other until they are a tangled mess.

As the sun sets, the sky is filled with little puffy orange clouds that look like the bellies of goldfish.

I wonder what a sunset looks like in Kyoto, Japan.

She wants you to come to Japan.

First off, even if I could transport myself across the ocean without having to succumb to the confines of an airplane, what would I do? Go where in Kyoto? Walk up to a hotel and check in? What if I hate the food, especially the *unagi*, the broiled eel, that Harrison claims doesn't taste like fish and is delicious? I could get sick. Kristine says that an ex-boyfriend of hers went to the Philippines and ate some uncooked vegetable or something like that and got an amoeba. The parasite was living in his intestines and he had to drink some horrible-tasting medicine to get rid of it. What if an amoeba makes me so sick I have to spend days in bed? What if I can't speak the language, unable to mutter even a proper *konnichiwa*?

And Harrison. What if I'm so nervous around him that all I do is bite my fingernails?

He's wonderful in his email messages. But there are those who can write well and can't mutter an intelligent word when face-to-face with another human. What if Harrison stutters or mumbles? What if I do?

And what if I can't find my way on the trains and get lost in the subway stations? What if the crowds of people that Harrison describes are *everywhere* smother me and I get claustrophobic, can't breathe, and pass out? And what if the hospital they take me to is a skyscraper and my room is on the fiftieth floor? How will I ever look out a window that high up?

True, I was born overseas, but I am really a small town southern girl.

———

On the way home, with the smell of the beach sand and air filtering through my car, I have a craving for shrimp. I stop at Shady Palm, a little seafood restaurant outside of Wilmington. The place looks as if it hasn't been dusted in centuries, but it has some of the best seafood on the Atlantic coast.

When I enter through a front door that jingles, I see a large group seated at a booth enjoying a meal. They have ordered salmon, fried shrimp, and scallops in butter, with sides of mashed potatoes. Shady Palm seasons its potatoes with a smoky barbecue sauce. If you can get past the reddish color, they are unbelievably tasty.

I walk up to a counter that's in the shape of a palm leaf and order a pound of fresh jumbo shrimp to go.

"Anything else?" asks a cashier with chestnut hair and fingers donned with silver rings. Her nails are painted black. She looks at me expectantly.

Anything else? Well, yes, I have a question. Do you believe that God grants wisdom to those who ask for it? And also, how does one know the wisdom is from God, God-ordained, so to speak, and not a human product? To put it simply, do you think that in light of the recent happenings in my life, they have all occurred for a reason? And that if I have to make a decision, that God will help me do the right thing for me and for all involved? I know I'm not deserving of Him to whisper in my ear or put His hand on my shoulder, but the Bible does mention a lot about His mercy and grace. What do you think?

The cashier is bored; I can tell by her incessant yawning. Her painted nails keep reaching up to cover her mouth. I am weary of watching her.

She is bored, and I haven't even begun to tell her my woes.

I give a small smile and say, "No, thank you, that will be all today."

She yawns again, tells me what I owe, and passes my order written on a scrap of green paper to the kitchen crew.

Within minutes, I am handed a Styrofoam container of jumbo shrimp. My hands are happy just to hold it.

As I leave, a mother strolls a little girl out of the restaurant door ahead of me.

The mother asks the child, "Got your soda?"

The daughter nods, her little chubby hands clasped around a plastic cup with a lid and straw.

"Are you thirsty?" The mom emphasizes each word, and I wonder if she is an educator. We tend to do that.

"Yes." The child takes a sip from her drink.

"Are you big thirsty or little thirsty?" Her animated voice has a distinct rhythm to it.

The girl drinks again. "Big!" she shouts and nearly drops her cup.

I watch the mother push the stroller to a parked van. "Yes, you are a big girl!" The woman claps her hands and then reaches toward her child, lifting her daughter—a toddler with rust-colored hair—out of the stroller. The two embrace, spin around once, and giggle. "Then are you ready to see the big wide world?"

I place the Styrofoam box of shrimp in the trunk of my car. And as I do, that same question looms at the center of my mind. *Are you ready to see the big wide world?*

I can answer that. *No. No, I'm not.*

On the way back to Mount Olive, I make another spur-of-the-moment decision. An hour later, I stand in Ducee's driveway, my car parked beside her lilac bushes.

Maggie McCormick wedges her nose between the slats of the wooden fence and sniffs at the box of shrimp. I pet the donkey as the moon glistens like the belly of a white koi.

Harrison told me that instead of the man in the moon, the Japanese see a rabbit pounding rice. He wrote, "Leave it up to the Japanese to see something more dramatic than a simple face."

Chapter Twenty-One

Ducee doesn't lock her front door until she goes to bed, so I know with a shove, it will open. It swings, causing the ivy wreath on it to rattle. Ducee believes an undecorated front door in any season is cause for dismay. Bare doors look empty, uninviting. One should hang some sort of greenery, artificial or real, on one's front door at all times. This is a Southern Truth.

Inside the hallway, I hear the TV blaring, and sure enough, as I enter the living room, Ducee's asleep in her recliner. It's after eight when these catnaps usually begin. Sometimes she sleeps, wakes to watch more TV, and sleeps again before calling it a day, locking her front door and retiring to her bedroom.

On a small TV tray, her bifocals rest on top of her maroon Bible. A cloudy orange bottle of her heart medication leans against the remote control.

Her feet, encased in white tennis shoes with lime green laces, are propped up on the ottoman. I bought the tennis shoes for her from Richard's shoe store in Goldsboro. He gave me a discounted price and even found a box in the storage room that was one of Ducee's favorite colors—lavender. Together we placed the shoes inside. Ducee was thrilled to open the box and try on her new sneakers when I brought them home to her. I don't think she's taken them off since.

On TV, Columbo, dressed in his tan trench coat, scratches his head and maintains a puzzled look. "So if you were asleep in bed last night, then why is your lipstick on this wine glass?" he asks a jittery woman in a short scarlet dress.

I leave Columbo for a moment to straighten the family portrait. This oil painting by Aunt Lucy hangs to the right of the TV on the wood-paneled wall. As I give the frame a little push to adjust it, I think how often I've come into this room and done this very thing.

"What would you do without me to straighten the picture?" I ask Ducee every now and then.

"You are the only one who straightens it," she replies. "If it weren't for you, the picture would always be tilted."

It is a portrait of Ducee, Grandpa Luke, Betty, and my mother Emma, done in heavy oil by Lucy. I know Ducee loved her baby sister, but does the love have to be shown in such an overtly visible way? The portrait would never be accepted by any artist I know. Ducee's eyes are crooked, and my mother, a girl of about ten when it was painted, looks as if she just saw a ghost. Her eyes have a wild, frightened look, and her eyebrows are arched into her scalp.

"Well, well," Ducee said once, "it was just so kind of Lucy to paint our picture."

Kind, yes. And looking at the picture must give Ducee some satisfaction, for the walnut-framed picture has been on the wall for as long as I can remember. Grandpa Luke is holding a pipe in one hand, and Betty has two double chins. I have heard that my aunt was on the chubby side as a girl, but two double chins? Perhaps this distortion was not Lucy's inability to draw faces well, but her deliberate stance against the way society had treated her. An attempt to fight back at life for making her give up her infant immediately after its birth. Or maybe she was going for the late Picasso effect—plain ol' wackiness. All the bourbon she consumed might have kept her from seeing clearly. I don't know; I never met Aunt Lucy.

Once Iva looked at the picture, blew out consecutive rings of smoke, and asked, "Why?"

It was one of Iva's most profound moments.

All of us ask that question when we view the painting.

If it has to hang, at least make it hang straight, is my plea. I will be keeping that piece straight until my last living day.

After a commercial break, Columbo is back and eager to solve the case.

Ducee jolts, opens her eyes, and smiles at me. "Hello, dear. What's in the Styrofoam?"

"Shrimp. From the beach."

"And how was the water?"

"It's too cold to go in."

"Want to cook them now?" Ducee stretches her tiny arms over her head and yawns. "I'm well rested and ready to cook. Butter and garlic?" She knows that's the way I like my shrimp seasoned.

She points at Columbo and says, "It's that woman who killed her husband, the one in the red dress. He took out a two-million-dollar life insurance policy on her. But she took a three-million one out on him." Then she presses a button on the remote and Columbo and his famous trench coat vanish.

After she puts on her glasses, we peel shrimp together in the kitchen. Ducee asks if we should buy new picnic tables before the reunion. "Both of mine are rotting around the legs."

I tell her we could try the flea market in Raleigh.

She wonders if someone will donate two. That's Ducee, always hopeful for a bargain or a freebie. Sometimes she jokes about herself. "Me and my frugal Irish ways," she'll say. Deep down I think she prides herself on being frugal, just as she prides herself on being Irish.

As the garlic sautés in butter, Ducee hums a few lines from "Molly Malone." Next she sings—off-key, of course—"My Wild Irish Rose." Hearing her sing takes me back to when I was little, all those times of standing in her kitchen helping her prepare jars of chutney. No matter where I am when I hear "My Wild Irish Rose" or "Molly Malone" or especially "Danny Boy," in my mind I am back in my grandmother's bright kitchen as a little girl.

She doesn't ask how I am. I know she'll wait until we are seated at her table. Then she'll dish out the questions, one after the other. It's a good thing I'm eager to talk to her.

I watch as she spreads a yellow-and-white daisy tablecloth over the pine kitchen table and sets two plates. She removes a vase of orange day lilies from the counter and places it in the center of her table.

I pour iced tea into two crystal glasses as the cooking shrimp fills the house with its savory aroma.

After bowing her head and thanking God for the food, she fills my plate with shrimp. Picking up a spice container, she sprinkles a little fresh oregano on top. Then she places a few shrimp on her plate. "I ate too much this afternoon," she confesses. "Mrs. McCready brought over an apple-cinnamon pie, and I had a big piece. Too big, I'm afraid."

Suddenly I feel very hungry. I haven't eaten since breakfast when I wolfed down a bowl of grits before opening Harrison's email. I spent lunch in the janitor's closet reading Harrison's message. I bite into a fat shrimp. Ah, this is a taste of heaven.

"So, any reason you went on an outing to the coast?" Ducee asks.

I swallow. Twice. I've been over in my mind what I plan to tell her. But how should I start?

"Something bothering you, dear?"

Where are the words I rehearsed on the ride back to Mount Olive? Did I leave them on Route 117? "Do you think . . ." I begin and then give in to hesitation.

"Take your time," Ducee says. "I know you must be hungry."

I follow her advice and eat a few more shrimp. Then I try again. "Do you think that people can care about each other deeply before ever meeting?" My eyes bulge, and I sit there in shock. That was not at all what I planned to say.

Without missing a beat, Ducee says, "It's been done many times."

"When? How?"

Ducee pats my hand. That gesture has always comforted me over the years.

She closes her eyes, as if in thought, then opens them and wipes her mouth. All my life I have watched my grandmother wipe her thin lips on linen napkins. No paper ones for her. Southern etiquette has a rule about this, I'm sure.

"Let me tell you," she says. After a sip of tea, she begins. "We go back to Ireland. Our motherland." There is no doubt that pride flows in Ducee's voice. "There was Lizzy McCoy. She was a beauty. Yes, yes." Ducee's eyes close. When they open she says, "She looked like you, in fact."

I want to say that she couldn't have been a beauty, then, but it's my grandmother's turn to talk.

Ducee's small hands clasp under her chin. Her eyes hold that looking-into-the-past stare. After a moment of silence, she places her hands on the table. "Yes, yes. Lizzy was an Irish rose. And she was in love with her brother's best friend, who happened to be in England. Now we Irish weren't too fond of the English, as your history books will tell you. Edgar McCormick was living in London at the time." She whispers, "As a spy."

I wonder why, when I came to talk about me, my grandmother is diving off into her storyland. Patience, patience. I should have talked when I had my chance. I finish my shrimp.

Ducee continues, "Lizzy first heard courageous stories about this Edgar from her brother. He would come home from battle and talk about this young man. Edgar was a warrior. Strong, big, bold."

Like sitting on the beach, Ducee's storytelling is an art not to be rushed. I stretch my legs and chew on a nail.

"Edgar," says Ducee, "would be Ireland's salvation. Lizzy listened to the stories, and as she listened, her heart grew quite attached to this hero. She'd never laid eyes on him. But the stories, if they were true—and her brother was an honest man—then, this Edgar McCormick was most certainly a man she respected and admired. She asked her brother to please tell Edgar about her, just to see if perhaps this lad might be interested. Many battles were fought after that. Lizzy wondered if her brother had forgotten her request."

The grandfather clock lets out nine chimes.

Ducee waits for the last one and then says, "And then . . ." With her eyes toward the ceiling as though she is reading the ancient words of this story there, she whispers, "Yes, yes. One night, at midnight, a peasant knocked on Lizzy's door and told her a boat was waiting for her at the shore. The arrangements had been made; she was to set sail for England immediately. It was all done very carefully and secretly. She rode with soldiers, Irish soldiers, all sworn to secrecy. For many nights she was on that boat. Oh, she got seasick and a storm nearly killed them all. But she made it to England to see this man she had never met."

A rumbling occurs in my stomach as I think of Lizzy out on a stormy sea. What in the world would make anyone do what she did? I drink some tea.

Ducee, as though reading my mind, says, "That is the power of love."

The room is silent.

"So? Did she make it?"

"Ah." It's as though Ducee has left her kitchen, transported to her beloved Ireland. I wonder if she sees rolling green hills dotted with wooly white sheep. She moves her head a bit to the left and smiles. "Let this be the clue. McCormick."

When I don't respond to her smile she repeats, "McCormick."

"Oh." Sometimes with Ducee you have to act like you follow what she's trying to convey.

"McCormick." My grandmother says the name with a pride and a strength I have heard many times over the years. "Yes, that was Edgar's surname." Then she folds her hands together as though that ends the story.

But I know better.

"Yes, yes. Lizzy married Edgar McCormick and worked with him as a spy. I understand they were quite a team. He became my great-grandfather. She became my great-grandmother."

Well, I have never heard this story before from any of my Mount Olive relatives of Irish descent. Which makes me wonder, is it true?

"And so." Ducee pats the table. "We sit here. Generations later. Here because Lizzy took a risk and went to England to meet the man she loved, the very man she'd never laid eyes on before."

Chapter Twenty-Two

Before Ducee starts another tale, I'd better tell her what I came here to say. Jump right in, I urge myself. It's now or never. But the words seem stuck in my mouth, trapped back behind my molars.

Ducee provides a questioning look.

Okay, now or never. "You know how I want answers to what happened in Japan."

Ducee gives a gentle nod.

"Well, I've found some things out."

Ducee's look reassures me that it is safe to continue. "The maid we had was the one who carried me from the fire."

"Oh, I used to know her name. What is it?"

"Watanabe-san." I have no idea how to pronounce the name, but hey, neither does my grandmother. "The fire started down-stairs. That's what Watanabe-san said."

Ducee's eyes grow wide. "You heard from Watanabe-san?"

"Yes. No. Well, Harrison has talked with her."

"Harrison?"

"He lives in Kyoto. He was born there. He's an English

professor at a university. His mom and Mama were friends."
I pause between each sentence, hoping something will make
Ducee say, "Ah! I recall. I remember."

"I see." Ducee only nods.

Mama wrote letters to Ducee; didn't she mention Harrison?
"Harrison's mom is named Rita."

Ducee has either forgotten or Mama never wrote about
these two.

"He grew up in Kyoto. His parents were missionaries like
Mama and Father."

It doesn't seem like any buttons of recollection have been
triggered for Ducee. She says, "I don't remember hearing about
a Rita."

"Well, she and her son, Harrison, were often invited over
for chutney. Mama served it on rice crackers."

Ducee laughed. "Really? That Emma, she knew how to connect the East and West, didn't she?" I smile as Ducee squeezes
my hand. "So you have found some answers."

Her eyes, framed by her bifocals, look exceptionally happy
tonight.

I nod. "Oh, and even my scar."

Ducee looks at me with a hopeful expectation.

"I fell off a swing. Harrison was pushing me at a park and
a stray dog scared me. I either jumped or fell off the swing and
hit a board with a nail in it."

"Oh, my." Ducee shakes her head. "No magic blessing from
the Princess of Susunanastan."

We laugh.

She reaches over to kiss my forehead, and her lips rest against
my scar. "I have always thought that scar beautiful. I can't imagine your face without it. It has given it character." With hands

in her lap, she speaks just above a whisper, "God gives us faces when we are born. They are innocent and pure, young and without a crease. As we grow, as we live life, we develop them, these faces. Yes, that's it, yes. They develop us. Your scar is part of you and now you know its story."

And I can't forget Sazae. "She wasn't from Mama," I tell Ducee. "The maid gave her to me."

Ducee searches my eyes. "I'm sorry." She seems disappointed, just as I was, to learn this. "I assumed your mother bought you that doll."

After a moment, Ducee pats my arm and whispers, "I bet you're tired."

I hadn't thought about it, but now that it's been mentioned, yes, I am.

"It sounds like you learned a lot lately. Learning can be exhausting."

Suddenly it is as though all the twists and turns of the day have caught up with me. It seems as if weeks have passed since I printed out Harrison's newest message and carried it into the janitor's closet to read. My muscles ache just thinking about the whole day.

Ducee has a question for me. "How did you find Harrison?"

"He read one of my columns at Pretty Fishy. He has carp in a pond in his garden and asked me a question about them."

"The Internet," says Ducee with a small nod. "I heard it does connect the world."

As I carry our dishes to the sink, she stands and cries, "Leave them. I can do them in the morning." Then her arms circle my waist. "Oh, Nicole, isn't it wonderful?" She lifts her face to kiss my cheek. "I thank God you have met someone from the past." Her next question makes me jump. "When are you going?"

"Where?"

"To Japan."

"What do you mean?"

Ducee winks. "What do you think I mean?"

"I can't go there!"

"Why not?"

Why not? I hate flying. The last and only time I've flown, I threw up on the airplane. My roots are here; I can't leave Mount Olive. I ask, "Who will take care of my fish?"

"With half of Mount Olive being related to us, we can surely get someone willing and capable." She tilts her head. "Monet would be my first choice."

Monet! I envision my whole aquarium murky and lifeless as three-year-old Monet laughs and hops on one foot. "Oh, Ducee, I hate to fly."

"Lots of people don't like to fly. One out of eight."

I ask, "One out of eight what?"

"Americans. One out of eight of us is petrified to fly. Even Loretta Lynn."

"The country singer?"

"That's right," says Ducee. "I heard it on this program on TV." And according to Ducee and Iva, if it's on TV, well, then, it's pretty close to truth.

Even Loretta Lynn hates to fly. Imagine that. For the first time, I don't feel so alone with my fear.

"Okay. Okay. Don't go, then." Ducee's voice suddenly is firm, and a stern look shifts into her eyes.

"What?" My mind is still on Loretta Lynn.

"See?" Ducee's face breaks into a smile. "Hard to think of giving it up, isn't it?"

Ducee sure has some strange psychology.

"Risk!" she tells me as I make my way to the front door.

"What?"

"Lizzy risked her life. Young girls didn't just leave their homelands and take off to meet strangers every day, you know. Eventually she and Edgar risked their lives to come to this great land of opportunity. They believed in a dream that this land could provide them with brighter futures than the lot they had been given in England or Ireland. So they came here. Risked it all. Yes, yes."

"I don't know. . . ." Lizzy was courageous. I have yet to find a brave bone in my body.

"Be like the duck that jumps into the pond."

In my mind I picture a yellow duckling diving headfirst into a pond. Her webbed feet vanish into the water, the last visible sight of her. The older ducks surround her place of entry, watch the ripple from the splash, and wonder. "How does the duck know if she can swim?"

Without hesitation, my grandmother says, "She doesn't." With a wink she adds, "But there's a good chance she can."

I kiss the top of Ducee's head, breathe in lilac, and whisper, "Good night."

"Nicole, I think it will do you good to go" are her last words to me.

In the driveway by the fence, I touch Maggie's wet nose. Maggie sniffs, possibly wondering where all the shrimp I had earlier went.

The moon is still a beautiful glowing ball. And yes, if I squint, I can see a pair of eyes and an imprint that could serve as a mouth. I have always seen the man in the moon. If I cross the Pacific and go to Japan, will I be able to see the rabbit within?

———

At home, my first stop is to see Sazae. In my bedroom, I take her from her spot on the pillow and cradle her. "You were not from Mama," I tell her. Of course she has no reaction. Did I expect her to stand up, plant her hands on her hips, and demand, "And why not?"

Seated on the edge of the bed, I trace her kimono sleeves with my finger. Back and forth, my finger travels across the sleeve singed in the fire and later trimmed by Watanabe-san. "She gave you to me," I say. "She saved you, too, and altered your burned sleeve." I clutch her, press her head to my nose, and smell that moldy orange aroma. "She risked her life to save us, Sazae."

Her expression doesn't change. Same black eyes and fading thin lips.

Perhaps knowing Sazae wasn't a gift from Mama will make it easier to give my childhood doll to Monet. I smile at Sazae, examine her *geta*, and feel her cotton body against the bend in my arm. She feels like she did when I was six and nine and twenty-nine.

This doll has been with me for as long as I can remember. Her presence has comforted me all these years.

Oh, Monet, she is still my, my, my.

Chapter Twenty-Three

I explain to Harrison about Sazae and ask if he could possibly find the shop in Kobe and purchase a doll like Sazae. "I'd like to give her to Monet."

Harrison writes that he will certainly try. "Of course," he says, "you could come to Japan and I'll take you to Kobe. We can look for the shop together. And while we're at it, we can have lunch at this hole-in-the-wall restaurant that serves the best *unagi*. It melts in your mouth."

In my next message I write that I don't fly. "Some people don't eat meat. (And while we're on the subject, I am not sure I could eat eel.) Some think it's a sin to read your horoscope. I don't travel by plane."

He writes to me about Dramamine, and I reply that no medicine could possibly be potent enough to take away my fear of flying.

"Well, then," he writes, "you may have to be like our parents and the early missionaries and take a ship to Japan." In the same message, he says he's going on a weekend trip with Jurgen to Shikoku. I'm glad he told me, because otherwise I would have worried when I didn't hear from him for two whole days.

Sitting in Aunt Lucy's chair, I have a view out the window of two bluebirds sailing around the oak tree, now full with new spring leaves. The birds dart under and over each other. They take turns perching on a limb. They are stunning against the green. Then suddenly they've disappeared. Flown off to some-one else's yard. As though they were bored with mine.

I feel panic spread across my skin. What if Harrison decides to leave? How can I be sure he will continue writing? Do I really expect to still be corresponding with him, say, five years from now?

Oh, I hate thinking about those five-year plans. Teachers think it is a topic students should contemplate. "Where do you see yourself five years from now?"

And the answers fly out: Happy, wealthy, living the life of ease.

Isn't that what each of us really wants?

And no one gets?

Instead of that smooth path filled with greenery and frolick-ing birds, it's a winding, uphill climb in the desert, with scorpions and rattlesnakes at every bend.

The five-year plan doesn't know that the spouse will get sick and die, or that the boss will lay you off one morning when you come to work all ready to go, cup of steaming coffee in hand.

"Life is a series of unhappy and happy events," Ducee told me once. "But it's in those moments that we grow. Most of life is made up of single happy moments. And sometimes a few moments are all you get."

———

My grandmother was given many happy moments with her daughters, Betty and Emma. Ducee took the girls each Saturday to the five and dime, and sometimes to the movies, where they bought popcorn when there was money to spare. While her little girls played dress-up with old hats and shoes from the attic, she sat in front of her sewing machine with patterns and pins, creating school clothes for them to wear.

She had many proud moments—graduations from high school, nursing school, and weddings. Births of grandchildren.

Then one winter afternoon, twenty-nine years ago, she received a telegram that let her know there would be no more moments with her oldest. Emma was dead.

Every year on Mama's birthday, Iva, Ducee, and I make our annual pilgrimage to The Meadows, the cemetery where Mama is buried. Ducee wears a black fisherman's hat and a solemn expression. Iva is usually late.

Once we're all gathered, Iva and I help Ducee take three purple helium balloons, tied with long white strings, from the cab of her red truck. We each hold one, protecting it, guarding it from flying away too soon. Then we stand in a circle, talk about Mama, and wait for Ducee's cue—"We love you, Emma!"—to release the balloons and watch as they dance into the April sky.

This year I am early. Against the wind, I walk carefully on freshly mowed grass over to Mama's gravestone—still white, even after twenty-nine years.

When I was small, I'd lean my whole body on the stone, resting my head against the inscription. *Emma McCormick Dubois Michelin. April 30, 1938—January 30, 1970. Our Loss, Heaven's Gain.* With my eyes closed, I would say, "Mama?" A pause. "It's me. It's Nicole. It's me." Another pause. A small hand touching my mother's name. "Mama?" Rubbing her name, hoping, somehow, the action would bring her to life again.

One summer afternoon when the ground and air were sticky with heat, I swore I heard a rustling sound followed by a gentle female voice. "Oh, Nicole," the voice whispered, "of course, I know it's you. I love you."

It was a day I'll never forget, one of those fleeting happy moments Ducee refers to.

When Grandpa Luke was alive, Ducee, Luke, and I would come to The Meadows with a picnic and spread a red-checkered cloth on the ground by Mama's grave. We'd eat ham biscuits, homemade pineapple chutney, chips and coleslaw, and pour chilled lemonade from a thermos into Dixie cups.

Ducee would say, "Emma loved lemonade," and I would think that I should love it too, then.

It was after one of those lunches that I heard the tender voice speak to me. Quickly, I opened my eyes, certain that I'd see an illuminated, parted sky, and angels descending with harps and halos of purest gold. Surely this was a miracle, the kind recorded in the Bible.

Instead, the sky held only the same thick clouds it had earlier. Grandpa Luke and Ducee were leaning against the tall pine tree on the hill to the left of Mama's grave and talking calmly as though nothing spectacular had happened. Perhaps Mama had only spoken to me—Nicole Delores Michelin. Perhaps this could be our secret, like our special family pineapple chutney recipe.

Today, I listen as intently as my ears let me.

I wait.

Even as we grow older, our childhood hopes don't leave us. I would give almost anything to hear that voice of summers ago whisper in my ear.

But I hear only the wind.

And then there is a rumble. Ducee has arrived in her truck. I see the purple balloons bouncing inside the cab.

Fifteen minutes later, Iva walks across the grass toward us, muttering something about the police blocking part of the road a mile from here. She's sure they are trying to catch an escaped convict.

Ducee hands us each a balloon and kisses hers. With her free hand, she pulls the black fisherman's hat down over her ears.

The wind whips across the silent graves.

"We remember this day," Ducee says. She lets the tips of her tennis shoes touch Mama's tombstone. "This is a day to celebrate. Without this day, Emma wouldn't have been born. This is the day she entered the world and made it a sparklin' place." Then Ducee calls out, "Memories." It's a cue for any of us to share a memory of Mama.

I hold no memories, so my tradition has been to say, "I love you, Mama."

Iva clears her throat and says, "I remember the time you ate the soap in the bathtub."

I wonder if I'm allowed to laugh.

Quickly, my aunt adds with a flourish of passion, "We miss you, Emma."

Ducee closes her eyes, and except for the wind, there is silence. Once, Ducee stayed silent for a full eleven minutes. I checked the time on Iva's wristwatch. It was the April I was thirteen and the minutes seemed long and stretched, like my patience.

This afternoon, within seconds, Ducee raises her head, shouts, "We love you, Emma!" and we know it is time to let the strings to the purple balloons go.

I release mine reluctantly, as though I am letting Mama go.
Which is silly to think of because she left a long time ago.

With energy, the purple globes fly into the sky.

We watch in silence as we do every year. Sometimes the
balloons head east, sometimes north, but always, they disappear
too quickly for me. And I wait with Ducee till all we can see is
a speck against the crystal-blue spring sky.

"They go to heaven," Ducee once told me.

"Really? Does Mama get them, then?"

"Yes," breathed Ducee. "Yes."

All these years that is what I want to continue to hear. The
balloons make it to heaven, against all of nature's laws of grav-
ity, against birds that might pop them with their beaks, against
all forces. Those very balloons grace Mama on her birthday in
heaven.

We head over to Ducee's for a dinner of hot biscuits, cold
beets, pineapple chutney, meatloaf, and mashed potatoes. This
meal is prepared every April thirtieth; it was Mama's favorite.

I've grown to love the meatloaf Ducee makes. She flavors
it with tomato sauce, a little brown sugar, and a host of spices.
However, the beets I can't seem to acquire a taste for. I still keep
them well away from the mashed potatoes on my plate so that
they won't make the white, fluffy potatoes red.

After the meal we have the customary angel food cake Ducee
buys from a bakery near the pickle company. Iva and Ducee
usually sing a song or two from their collection of favorites.
This year they croon "When Irish Eyes Are Smiling."

After the second verse, I excuse myself from the living room
and wash dishes.

This is our tradition. Tradition keeps us strong, Ducee tells us every year. As long as she doesn't break out into the song "Tradition" from *Fiddler on the Roof*, we'll be okay.

———

"Did my mom really like meatloaf and beets?" I ask Harrison after returning from Ducee's. It is a little strange to be asking someone I have no memory of about another person I hold no memory of.

As Harrison told me earlier, he will be gone from his computer this weekend, taking a trip with Jurgen to visit fishermen friends in Shikoku. This is also the week of Emperor Hirohito's birthday, which means lots of traveling and time off during this week, known for some reason as Golden Week. So I'll have to wait to find out about Mama and the beets.

A weekend stretches before me, offering what? All I want to do is hear from Harrison. I look at his picture on my computer. Then, since there are no new messages, I read old ones from him. The words "Come to Japan" pop out at me.

In his most recent message, Harrison tells me I can freely ask Watanabe-san as many questions as my heart desires if I just come to Japan. "I visited her today and she was in her brooding mood. She only shared tea with me, no memories," Harrison wrote. "I'll visit her again when I get back from Shikoku."

———

Just for fun, I search at Google and before I know it, I am at the government's official passport Web site. In order to get a passport—not that I ever would—I'd need to apply as a new applicant. Since my old passport was issued when I was under sixteen, it can't be renewed.

I need to fill out a form and take it, along with two two-by-two-inch recent photos and a picture I.D., to a government building. There are a number of government buildings in the state of North Carolina that provide passport service.

I search some more, fascinated by the assortment of information on international travel. I can't wait to tell Principal Vickers. We might even be able to chat about the Internet's wealth of information in the hallway on Monday.

With a few more clicks, I am at the U.S. Department of State's Web site. I type my zip code into a little search box to see where the closest passport location would be. Up pop six locations, the Clerk of Court building on East Walnut Street in Goldsboro being the closest at only fourteen miles away. I jot down the address and phone number.

Am I going to apply for a passport and fly to Japan? Hop on a plane and let it take me over the sea? Thirteen hours of motion while cooped up with strangers? When I throw up, who will hold my hand and give me a sip of water to drink?

I exit the U.S. Department of State's Web site.

I'll swim to Japan before getting on a plane.

———

Harrison writes that his trip to Shikoku was enjoyable and that he and Jurgen have made plans to spend the last two weeks of July and most of August working at a fishing village on that island's southern coast.

"So," he says, "why don't you come here the first of July and spend two weeks?"

Without a moment's hesitation, I shoot back a message. "I can't travel then. The weekend of July Fourth is our family reunion."

Miss that event? Never. Those of us with any McCormick

in our blood take attending the annual family reunion very seri-ously. Why, if you don't show up for the reunion, awful things can be said about you. If you are dead, then and only then are you excused from a McCormick reunion. As for the bad things being said, that will happen if you are not present—dead or alive.

Chapter Twenty-Four

The sunshine streams through my bedroom curtains and I see, to my shock, that I've slept until noon. When was the last time I did this? In college on a Saturday, perhaps. I turn onto my side to save Sazae from toppling off the mattress. I set her on the spare pillow and smooth out her kimono.

Resting against my pillow, I imagine a Japanese woman staggering through a smoky room to hear the voice of a little girl singing. I see her carrying that child, along with the child's doll, outside to safety.

The mother is dead inside.

The father is out of town.

This woman's hands are burned.

The girl is fine.

Except for her heart, which will always have a hole because the night she lost her mother, she lost her father, too.

Her father will never be the same. It will be stated, over the years, that he is now just a shell of the man he used to be. Like a shell abandoned on Wrightsville Beach.

After eating a bowl of grits drenched with butter, I call my father to wish him a happy birthday. It is May fifteenth, and he is sixty-four.

Bonnie claims he can't come to the phone.

"Is he sick?"

"No." Her voice is filled with hesitation. What is the woman hiding from me?

"Is he sleeping?"

Quickly, "No."

"Is he there? Has he left?" I feel anger start in the pit of my stomach and rise like a wave in my chest.

"He's just a little . . . under the weather."

"On his birthday?!" I shout, as though one isn't allowed to be sick on his birthday.

"Yes." And that is all she's going to tell me, the person of few words that she is.

"Tell him I hope he has a happy birthday." I spit out the words.

"I will." Silence. "Anything else?"

You mean like I love you? "Yes."

She waits and when I say nothing, prods with, "Okay . . ."

I close my eyes and count to five. "Tell him . . ."

"Yes?"

"Tell him I'm going to Japan." Then I hang up. Just like that.

———

I sit in Aunt Lucy's chair for most of the day, thinking. It is amazing how our minds can think so much, loaded with a multitude of ideas and plans. I'd like to turn my mind off some days, but I haven't figured out how to do that yet.

At four, I head out to a little shop I've seen on First Street that has a neon sign with "Passport Photos Taken Here" in the window. I circle the location three times before parking in front of it.

A red-and-black sign on the door invites me inside: Open. There is even a dusty green plastic wreath under the sign. I should feel most welcomed, since according to my grandmother, this is an inviting place, but my sweaty palm can barely turn the doorknob.

This is a camera shop and the walls are covered in glossy pictures of mountains and ski resorts. Cameras—Nikon, Sony, Olympus, and Panasonic—rest under a clear glass counter. I study a Nikon silver digital camera so tiny that it fits in a human's palm. If I owned something this small, I'd be sure to drop it or lose it, I think, and carefully move away from the cameras.

In a drawl as sweet as honey poured over a hot biscuit, the young girl behind the counter asks, "May I help you?"

Taking my eyes off one of the posters—the jagged Swiss Alps—I look at her. Her nails are painted green. I wonder if Flora Jane at Lady Claws painted them. "How much are passport photos?"

"Let me see."

She's probably a high school student, or college, it's hard to tell; kids are looking younger to me these days. She glances at a card taped to the cash register. "Two photos for eleven dollars." She eyes me a minute and then says, "Our guy who takes photos is out right now." Reacting to my frown she tells me, "If you want, I could try to take them for you."

I swallow. "Sure. If you don't mind."

The girl is so nervous; I wonder if this is a good idea. Then I smile because we are the perfect match—I am nervous, too.

"I'm not very good," she warns as she asks me to sit on a

stool in front of a white cloth draped from a horizontal rope. "But I have done it before." She picks up the Polaroid camera. "Once."

How hard can it be? After I view the first set of photos where my head is cut off at my scar and the next set where my chin is sliced away, I see it must not be too easy. "Take your time," I tell her. "I'm in no hurry." I sit up, smile, and let her snap again.

The third time is a charm. Two glossy pictures of me with my full head and chin captured. I thank her, pay, and carry the pictures to my car.

I don't know what I'm doing, but I'm doing something. Bumper-sticker material.

Harrison would say I know what I should be doing: take a dose or two of Dramamine, get on the plane, and come see Japan for yourself. In a recent message he wrote, "It is your birth land. It'd be like coming home. Watanabe-san wants to see you. And, besides, I haven't had anyone to eat pineapple chutney with in thirty years."

I smiled at the last line and replied with, "You don't even like chutney. And I don't like eel."

He responded, "You love eel. As a child in Kyoto, you ate it every Saturday. Your mother would take you to a restaurant in Karasuma and you licked your bowl clean. Watanabe-san told me this."

Me and *unagi*? I gulp. Surely, she is mistaken.

Driving home, I wonder what I have done. Then I realize the Polaroid pictures of me don't have to be for a passport. I could send them to a friend or keep them in a scrapbook.

I listen to the voices in my head.

Now, who would you send a Polaroid photo to?

And why would you want two identical poses of you in a scrapbook?

You don't even have a scrapbook.

———

The phone is ringing when I enter the house from my passport photo outing, and the voice on the other end is soft.

"Hello?" I speak loudly, hopeful the person will do the same.

"Nicole."

It's amazing how we humans can distinguish voices even upon hearing only our names spoken. I'd know this voice anywhere. "Happy birthday," I tell Father.

"Bonnie said you are going to Japan."

"Well, yeah. I've been—"

He interrupts. "Don't."

"Why not?"

"It isn't a good idea."

"Why not?"

"Don't go."

Why can't he expand on his reasoning behind his insistence? "I think it's a good idea," I tell him with mock enthusiasm because I am not fully convinced it is the right thing to do.

"Don't go to Japan."

Something starts to burn in my gut and expands through my veins. It feels like fire. "I am going!"

"Don't."

"Father." I try to calm my voice, try to shove my emotions aside. "I would like to go."

"Don't." Is that all he can say?

Perhaps if I explain that there will be people on the other

side to assist me, maybe that will ease his fears. "Our former maid and Rita's son want me to come."

The silence on the other end scares me.

"Rita? You have been in contact with Rita?" His tone is muffled, as if he's a million miles away, not just in the next state.

"I've been emailing Rita's son, Harrison."

"No." It comes out as a moan.

"Father, I've been making my own decisions for some time now."

In a tone that makes my skin and everything beneath it crawl, he tells me, "Nicole, you can't go. Japan is a land of terrible remorse."

All my life I have been avoiding this Asian country, one of the reasons being because my own father is so consumed by what happened there. We have been in bondage, chained, unable to move freely, due to our fear.

"I need to go there, Father." Sometimes I wish I could call him Daddy. "I hope you have a good birthday." For the second time that day, I hang up the phone.

Instead of tears of frustration, I feel a new strength fill me. As I look at the passport pictures now on my kitchen counter, I wonder who that photographed woman is. Red hair, blue eyes, freckles. Her tentative smile makes me wonder if she will be able to carry through with this unbelievable plan.

I hear my father's repeated plea for me not to go to Japan. He is fearful of something, I think. My solemn father has a closet of ghosts, and one of them is trying to make its way out.

Chapter Twenty-Five

On a typical muggy and wet June afternoon, Grable and Monet stop by to drop off linen napkins. Ducee has asked all of us North Carolina relatives to supply her with napkins for the reunion. We think paper is the way to go, but she informed us about southern etiquette.

Grable swung by Ducee's, but my grandmother isn't home. She and Iva are at the Piggly Wiggly buying pineapple for our next chutney-making event. Fresh pineapples are on sale this whole week.

Grable pulls up in the driveway and pops open the trunk as I slip on a pair of sandals and walk out to meet her.

As I stand by the car, Monet, strapped in a car seat, pounds on the back window screaming, "Niccc! Niccc fissssz! Pleeeeez!"

"Can I let her out?" I ask Grable.

Grable, looking worn and sullen, shrugs.

Free from the constraints of the vehicle, Monet scampers up the brick steps, and just as Grable warns, "Be careful, Monet," slips on the wet pavement.

I have never heard such a holler come from any one human.

Grable places her fingers against her temples. I think she just might cry. Which mystifies me—I have yet to see her tears on any occasion.

Sure, Monet's wild, but Grable's always known how to handle her daughter. I saw firsthand at the hospital how the maternal instinct to care for a child different from the rest kicked in. Only Grable knew the trick to soothe the fussy and hyper infant to sleep. I also remember the way she gained control when Monet was in my bedroom wanting Sazae.

Maybe Grable wants to cry about Dennis. I'm still wrestling with whether or not I should tell my cousin what Mr. McGuire saw at his store.

There is no time to ponder on Dennis's extracurricular activities. I walk over to Monet still flung upon the top step. "Are you okay?" I check her knees, elbows, and legs as she continues her noise.

She's not crying, for her face is clear of tears. She is all volume.

"Careful, okay, Monet?"

She lifts her head, bounces up like a jack-in-the-box. She tries to open the front door.

"Wait!" Grable commands. She is taking out a large box of linen napkins.

"Wow," I say. I didn't know a person could own so much cloth.

"Tell Ducee she can keep these. I don't need them. We haven't had dinner guests in ages." Grable's eyes glaze over.

"Are you . . . all right?"

Monet is yelling for her mother to help open the door so she can get inside my house and watch my fish.

"Monet, stop!" Grable's voice makes me shudder. "Stop it now!"

Monet stops fighting with the door and throws herself onto the stoop, wailing.

Grable sighs, making no attempt to help Monet.

I walk over to the child and sit beside her. Placing a hand on her back, I say, "Monet, it's all right. When you stop crying, we can see the fish. Okay?"

"Nicccc maadd?" she sobs, her face buried in her hands. This time there are tears glistening across her face.

"No." I slowly rub her back. She is wearing a pink Dora the Explorer T-shirt and a pair of green-speckled cotton pants. Grable has told me Monet dresses herself.

"Maaaaam maadd?" Her tearstained face peers into mine.

I look at Grable, standing there holding a box filled with cloth napkins she will never use to entertain guests at her home because her husband never comes home for dinner anymore. "No," I gently reassure the child, "Mommy is not mad." Tired, frustrated, weary, overburdened, but she loves you, Monet. Oh yes, she clearly sees there is beauty within.

Monet moves toward me, wiggles into my lap, and wipes her eyes with the palms of her hands.

Oh, Monet, I am so sorry. I wish our daddies had time for us. I wish we could all go to the park together and swing and slide.

Grable gives me a look of appreciation. There is a faint flicker of light in her eyes.

The doorknob opens with ease once I show Monet how to maneuver it, and we all go inside. Under cautious supervision, Monet feeds the fish. She opens her mouth like they do, her lips forming a tiny circle. After she hops on one foot and then switches to the other, I tell her to sit in Aunt Lucy's chair because I have a surprise for her.

Monet races to the chair, squealing as she goes.

From my bedroom, I carry out a cardboard box wrapped in brown paper, stuck with postage stamps of cherry blossoms, bamboo, and carp. I hand the box to the child.

She embraces it, smiles, claps her hands, and almost falls off the chair. She lets her mother lift out a cotton kimono doll, just like Sazae, only without fading lips and with both sleeves the same length.

As Monet hugs the doll, she asks if it is hers.

"Yes," I say. "All yours. You can take it home."

"My, my, my!" the child squeals.

Grable wants to know how I got a doll for Monet almost identical to mine.

"One day I'll explain," I say. We'll eat M&Ms after Monet is asleep, and I'll tell you everything. When I'm ready.

"My, my, my!" Monet shouts.

I wish Harrison could see how happy he has made this child.

We watch Monet plant kisses all over the doll's face.

"What will you name it?" asks Grable.

Monet gives us a large smile. "Nicccc!"

Wait until I tell Harrison that the doll he sent for Monet is named Nicccc!

———

That evening after Iva calls to tell me that we are scheduled to look for new picnic tables next Saturday, the phone rings again.

"Nicole."

"Hello."

My father's voice sounds strained. "Did she tell you about the baby?"

Baby? What baby?

"Did she?"

I have no idea what he's talking about. "What baby?"

He's crying, I think.

"Will you tell me about the baby?"

"It died." He barely has enough strength to get the words out.

"It died?"

"Your mama was pregnant, so the baby died, too." Now he is sobbing. My father is crying on the phone.

"Father?"

The sobs are out of control, heavy, and gasping in my ear. I can't stand it; I want to put the phone down.

Suddenly the sounds are gone, disappeared. He must have stepped away from the phone. No one stops crying that quickly.

"Father?"

I hear some noise on the other end.

I wait a few seconds before asking, "Father? Where's Bonnie?"

He's blowing his nose. "At the club for dinner."

"Are you going to be okay?"

He tells me he's going to hang up.

When he does, I am like a robotic being, an alien even, out of space, out of time, just standing alone in my kitchen. Uncertain what to do next. What is the southern etiquette for learning that a baby died? My sibling-to-be?

I stand and listen to my own rapid breaths, like bullets being fired. Rain starts to splash against the kitchen window, the pellets hitting the pane as fast as the questions that shoot into my mind. Soon I am a heap in Aunt Lucy's chair. This is too much, this finding out about my past. What other surprises are around the corner?

Minutes later, I email Harrison. "Did Watanabe-san say anything about my mother being pregnant?" I don't use spell check or hesitate for one second before letting this message speed over to Harrison's computer.

Did Ducee know Mama was pregnant? Had Mama told her in a letter? How far along was she in her pregnancy?

It's a pathetic feeling knowing that a child, forming in a womb, a human with eyes and hair and a personality, was snuffed out just like that. And not just any child. My brother or sister. Had Mama lived, I would have had a mother, a father, and a brother or sister. I know we would have been happy. People would see the love and happiness oozing over us like barbecue sauce on chicken. "Do you know the Michelins?" people would say. "Oh yes, such a happy family."

The story changes.

The mother is dead inside.

The father is out of town.

The maid's hands are burned.

The girl is fine.

And now, the baby inside the mother is dead.

I sit in the wingback chair, trying to imagine what a sister or brother of mine would look like. Would he or she have red hair, too, and freckles? A brother might be the opposite of me—laid-back, one of those easygoing types, able to help me out with my fears. Fun-loving and surrounded by friends, able to get me dates with the most interesting men.

I'll never know. It is one of those chapters in the book that ends without satisfying the reader at all.

My father's sobs fill my ears. I can't remember ever having heard or seen his tears before.

Chapter Twenty-Six

Night surrounds me. The fish tank's fluorescent beam is the only light on.

I sit close to my fish in the darkened dining room and watch the clownfish glide through the water. They are so safe in their contained paradise where all of their needs are met. They never harm each other. Never speak words that can be misunderstood. There are no secrets between them.

If only humans were this simple.

Heaviness sets in my heart, making walking to the computer painful. The computer's screen lights my face and the keyboard, but the rest of the living room is shrouded in darkness. The clock on the bottom right-hand side of the screen says it's midnight. One in the afternoon of the next day in Japan. Harrison is teaching an English class right about now.

I am not Lizzy, the brave soul from the past who ventured to meet the man of her dreams. I am a wimp. I am my father who won't get help with his neuroses. I have red hair and freckles like him; we are two peas in a pod. My mother was the adventurous one—it was she who convinced my father to make the plunge and apply with the mission board to become medical missionaries in Japan. Her determination, zest, and faith were enough for both of them.

So I've been told.

I step outside and sit on the brick step in front of my house, viewing the sky. The heavens host clear, glittery stars tonight. I find the brightest but am too sad to wave to Mama.

I imagine Mama, her hair pulled back and a smile on her face as she and Father take off from California on that large ship to Yokohama, Japan.

Dreams, the night sky seems to say. *What are yours?*

And all those teachers from the past, their voices crowd around my ears, "Where do you see yourself five years from now?"

Where do I see myself? In Mount Olive? Safe and secure? Plagued with questions? Unable to face the part of my past that lies on the other side of the ocean?

Ducee's word rings out over my lawn. "Risk."

I see Harrison, smiling in the picture. Kind, warm, blue eyes that go along with his comforting words sent in email messages. Can I trust him?

Can I trust that God has put him in my path to help me?

A breeze blows, rustling the nearby leaves. It makes me think of the lines in the old hymn, "In the rustling grass, I hear Him pass. He speaks to me everywhere." Ducee says that was one of Mama's favorite hymns and that she often quoted from it.

I smile and wave to Mama.

Back inside, I sit on the fuzzy, uncomfortable desk chair. As my aquarium hums, I slowly hit the letters on the keyboard to form my words.

"I am coming to Japan."

I read this sentence aloud to my fish seven times before pressing the send button.

Once I've sent the message to Harrison, my shoulders relax, free from the weight that burdened them.

I'm too excited to sleep; I take out the Windex and paper towels and buff all my mirrors until they shine like every star in the Big Dipper.

Chapter Twenty-Seven

I remember a sermon Pastor Donald preached years ago on the theme of what trust looks like. It was a while ago, and I can't recall all his points or Scripture references, but I did get one thing out of it: It's scary to trust a God whose face we have not seen. That's why we need faith, faith to travel the unseen. And when we think we have no faith, we can ask for it. Even the gift of faith is supplied by God.

It all made sense to me as I sat listening to him that Sunday morning. It was winter, the heat was on, and my toes were toasty. I knew a lunch of barbecue was coming up at Ducee's.

Living his sermon when the days are damp and the heat doesn't work and food is bland because I'm sick with a cold is another story. Why, even God's chosen, the Israelites, had trouble with faith. Except for those mentioned in the book of Hebrews.

I've often wondered if I'd lived back in Old Testament times, if my name would have been recorded thousands of years later in the book of Hebrews. Would my name be in that New Testament book, recorded right next to Abraham and Moses? Even the prostitute Rahab got her name in this worthy portion of the Bible.

Then I laugh.

You are a gutless one, Nicole. You have never watered your gift of faith. It is so small; it's still a seed in the ground.

———

Summer vacation has hit and the plans for the reunion are in full force. I am still on the planning committee, so to speak, even though I don't plan on being present at the festivities.

Ducee tells me this can be our secret. Giggling like a little girl, she says she'll drive me to the airport in her truck for my scheduled flight. Then she tells me she'll make a good excuse for why I won't be at the reunion. "Leave it up to me," she adds with a broad smile. "Remember Lizzy. It is going to be just peachy. Yes, yes."

Sometimes I think Ducee confuses my trip across the ocean with a walk in the local park.

———

Iva calls to talk about the reunion. She is still pleased that Ducee has agreed to cucumber sandwiches. "We did it, Nicki." She laughs and coughs at the same time. "We did it."

Then, without missing a beat, she says she thinks we all are going to die at the beginning of the next year.

"Why?" I ask. I chew a nail and wonder if I could just for once in my life let my nails grow so that they can be tapered and painted for my trip. That way, when I throw up on the plane, at least my nails will look nice holding the air sickness bag.

"Two thousand," says Iva.

"Two thousand what?" Certainly not linen napkins. We are only expecting two hundred tops at our reunion.

"The year." She chokes, clears her throat, and adds, "I read in the *Tribune* that our country isn't prepared for the next century."

"We aren't?"

"No, the computers will cause us all to blow up."

"Really?"

"Nicki?"

My aunt sounds sad, so I answer with gentleness. "Yes, Iva?"

"I really did want to see the year two thousand."

"Me, too."

"Ducee says it will be fascinating to write two-oh-oh-oh on a check."

Except that all my checks have the numbers nineteen followed by a line already printed in the right-hand corner where the date is written. What will we do in the year two thousand when we don't need the ones and nines? Use White Out? Will the bank accept that?

"Nicki, you have a computer, don't you?"

"Yeah . . ."

"I'd get rid of it. Before it has a chance to blow up and kill you."

Well, if we aren't going to live but another half a year, I might as well just go for it. Get on that plane, flash those painted nails, hold that air sickness bag, and fly across the ocean. It would certainly be better to leave the earth this way than being blown up by my computer.

———

I have no idea what kind of flowers Mama liked, so I have brought her a calla lily from Flowers by Deena. True, Ducee says she liked purple lilacs, but I never heard Mama say from her lips what her favorite flower is. And what can I believe? For years I thought Sazae was a present from Mama, and look where that led.

At The Meadows, I wait for the cemetery's maintenance man to move his riding lawnmower away from this side of the land. Then in my clearest and strongest voice, I say to Mama's name on her gravestone, "I'm going, Mama." I step closer. "Oh, I may hate it there. But I'm going."

I listen, hopeful for something that will let me know she hears me. It is a still day, and the only noise comes from the lawnmower over by the pine tree.

I continue, "Mama, I am really heading to Japan. Father doesn't want me to go." My knees feel weak. Why did I bring Father into this? I try again. "I have to go. For me. Remember Harrison? He must have been a nice kid. I must admit I've grown quite fond of him. I think that if there is any chemistry between us, I could fall in love with him." I pause to comprehend the words I've just told her. "Scary, huh?"

I brush away a pinecone and sit beside the grave. Who cares if the freshly mowed grass stains my shorts? I have to start letting some things go. "Am I crazy? Crazy like Aunt Lucy?" I ask.

Mama knew Aunt Lucy. She stood there as her aunt painted her distorted eyebrows in the family portrait. She knew what Aunt Lucy's soft skin felt like and if the mints she chewed covered the heavy odor of liquor on her breath. All I have of this relative are stories. What if the stories aren't true? Perhaps Great-Aunt Lucy was the sanest of the bunch and it's the others who are crazy.

I steady my voice and say words that come from the deepest part of me. "Mama, there is just so much more to learn. I can't do it here. I have to get in the same ocean as Harrison in order to find out. I want to walk along the streets of Japan and see what you saw."

I touch the stem of the lily and take a breath. "I'm going, Mama. And if the plane crashes or I die in it from claustrophobia after inhaling the same stale air for thirteen whole hours, well, then . . ." I lift my eyes toward heaven. "I'll see you soon." I rest both hands against her engraved name. It is warm from the sun. I stretch my fingers as though I am pushing my fingerprints into the stone.

Sighing, I take a thin, light blue ribbon and a pink ribbon from my pocket. Deena at Flowers by Deena cut the strips for me without asking why I needed them, which was considerate of her. Explaining about a dead sibling would have been difficult for me to do.

Slowly, I tie both delicate ribbons to the flower's stem. These are for the baby—blue for boy and pink for girl—my unborn brother or sister.

Harrison told me Watanabe-san had been asking about the baby and he, at first, thought she was referring to me. After my question to him in my email message, he asked the older woman during a visit to the nursing home, "What about a baby?" She broke down in tears and said Michelin-san was pregnant, just three months along, and what a shame the baby died with her. Watanabe-san's outburst brought in a few nurses. Then she was wheeled away to calm down with a cup of *ocha*.

I hate to think this woman was so distraught all because of me and my need to know the past, but Harrison told me not to worry. "She may cry, but she also smiles often when she recalls her years of being your family's maid. She said those years were some of the best. Until that terrible night. She's never gotten over that night your mother died."

———

It's never easy leaving the cemetery, but the maintenance man makes it a little easier today as he cranks his lawnmower up a notch. Perhaps that's just as well. There are things to do during this summer vacation.

My passport may arrive in the mail today, as well as the plane ticket Harrison found for me at a discounted price. First I am to fly from Raleigh-Durham to Atlanta, where I'll have a three-hour layover, and then on to Detroit. At this airport, which is so huge it can make you crazy, or so I am told, I'll wait for two more hours. At last, with a belly filled with Dramamine, I am to hop on a plane for Osaka. And fly for thirteen hours.

Nonstop.

Just like that.

The whole plan makes me queasy, but in all reality, I can't think of anything else I'd rather do than spend two weeks in Japan with Harrison and Watanabe-san.

Of course, I still hope for that instant *Star Trek* beaming-me-to-Japan method. Maybe someone will discover how to implement this way of travel before I step onto a plane. It is almost the year 2000, after all.

I still am not sure I can actually go through with this, but the truth is, I've gone too far now to go back. It's as if I was once happily swimming in one stream, but a warm current suddenly caused me to turn and change my direction. I was a fighting fish at first, not wanting to be transported to anything different and unusual. Now I'm enjoying this new current, even though

I know that down the stream, I may be faced with some disap-
pointing waters. I know because this is life, life with its fleeting
moments of happiness.

As I whisper good-bye to Mama, words ring in my mind as
they have so many times before at this place. Words that will
forever live inside my heart.

I miss what we could have had together.

Chapter Twenty-Eight

Harrison made reservations for me to stay at a *ryokan*, a traditional Japanese inn with futons laid out to sleep on the *tatami* floor. "Breakfast at these is usually steamed rice and fish with a bowl of *miso*. I'll make sure the fish is deheaded before your tray is served. And if it gets too bad for you, you can bring out the granola bars. They do still have those in the U.S., don't they?"

He said that he'd like to take me to Nagano to see the mountains and to Hiroshima to see the peace museum. He asked where else I'd be interested in going.

I hate to sound naïve, but I have no clue. I suppose seeing Mount Fuji is important, and Harrison agrees we could take the *shinkansen*—what we Americans call the bullet train. I ask him if this train is like riding on the Charlotte Speedway. He has no comment.

"Actually," he writes, "I may be biased, but the city where you and I were born is the best Japan has to offer. It's a great combination of the traditional Japan and the modern. I'll get us tickets to see a local Kabuki play. Or would you rather see Noh?"

I reply with, "It's all Greek to me. You choose."

After that reply, I think I'd better educate myself. I take Mr. Vickers's advice and tour the Internet. Just by typing in "Japan" and "Kyoto" at Google, I am led to beautiful color pictures of temples, shrines, ponds, gardens, and mountains. The cherry blossoms look exceptionally delicate, like cotton candy floating on tree limbs.

One site shows rows and rows of decorated folding fans and another pictures of flags in the shape of carp, strung on bamboo poles. The caption under the photo of the billowing carp flags reads, "Koinobori." These carp are flown on May fifth, which is Children's Day in Japan.

May fifth is also my birthday. I've lived all these years not knowing I was born on Children's Day, the day carp fly in the air.

With eagerness to learn, I read until my eyes itch from the light of the computer screen. I amaze myself. I am not the girl of yesterday, avoiding all things Japanese.

_____

As I enter the house from a short outing to Friendly Mart, the phone is ringing with fervor.

"Nicole?" The voice of my stepmom is never cause for celebration.

"Hi, Bonnie." I muster a cheery tone, or at least try to.

"How are you?" Her tone is dull, like a knife that is useless in the drawer.

"Pretty good. How are you?"

"Your father says you are going to Japan."

I'm tempted to put down the phone or pretend I can't talk now. "I am."

"Well." A significant pause. "Well."

Is this it? Is this all she called to say?

"Be safe." It is a command.

"I will."

"He doesn't think you should go."

I know, I know.

"However, if you must, please be safe." She sounds like a recording.

And why wouldn't I be safe, I almost say to her. Isn't basic safety high on everyone's list? Do we wake in the morning vowing that today we won't be safe? That instead we'll purposely drive recklessly or jump into the middle of oncoming traffic? "Of course," I tell her.

"Japan was hard for him."

I rub my scar as I cradle the receiver between my ear and my shoulder. I don't want to talk about this anymore. Speaking of safe, Father and Japan are not safe topics.

"Just be careful. He wants you to be careful."

"Okay," I say. The word sounds empty all alone, so I enhance it by adding, "Tell him that I said thanks." I don't ask if he can come to the phone, because I don't want to hear any excuses of why he can't talk to me, his only living child.

"Bye," I quickly toss out and am ready to hang up.

She tells me to have a good night, and then once more with urgency, "Be careful. Be sure to be careful."

I stand staring at the phone, wondering what possesses her to act so strangely. It has to be from living with Father. She chose this life; she continues it.

Some days I think she'll snap, ending up at the mental institution in Butner. Other days I imagine her squeaking out of the house in Richmond just before her sanity completely disappears. I wouldn't be shocked to get a postcard from her, written in her loopy style of penmanship—the kind that puts circles instead of dots over the letter i. "Hi Nicole, I'm in Tahiti. I've left your father."

It wouldn't surprise me. How can she put up with a man who eats sardines from a can and watches TV all day long?

———

Now that Harrison doesn't have to continue to convince me to take the plunge and fly to Japan, and now that I have many questions about my past answered, I tell him it's his turn.

"My turn?" he writes. "Am I going to like this?"

I say most people do. The average person likes the limelight, enjoys getting to talk about a subject of vast importance—him or herself. "I hope it's not too nosey to ask," I write one evening as my fish swim and I sprinkle salt on grits, "but are you happy that you grew up in Japan? Was it worth it?"

He is intrigued by my last question and replies with a long message.

> Was it worth it? I assume you mean being away from my peers in America and missing out on Hershey bars, apple pie, and Chevrolets. Was getting the experiences of *unagi* at the hole-in-the-wall restaurant, being submerged into another language, and taking an *ofuro* every other night worth the trade-off? Good question.
>
> Japan held my childhood. I don't know what growing up in America would have been like.
>
> At eighteen, after a childhood in Japan, I came to the U.S. for college. Then I went to graduate school and got my Ph.D. in English. After that, I returned to Japan to live. Why? There are many reasons, but I think the biggest one was because life in America, my own country of citizenship, was too strange to handle. I am clearly a foreigner here, often the only Caucasian in the room or train station. I know my place here—considered an alien because I am not from Japanese parents, yet so familiar with this country

because of having lived here for twenty-six years total. I choose to be the foreigner here instead of the foreigner in America. Many don't get it, but since I have lived for so few years in the U.S.A., I feel that country is alien to me. I am more familiar with Japan and its customs. It is home.

I don't know if this makes sense to you.

My younger sister lives in New York City now and has immense cultural shock. Her husband works near Times Square and she fears taking the subway to meet him for lunch.

Used to crowds in Osaka and Tokyo, she says New York crowds aren't familiar.

She was always the "celebrity child" in Japan. With her blond hair and blue eyes, the Japanese asked her to pose for English language school posters and brochures. In America, especially in New York City, she is a dime a dozen. No one stops her on the street to ask if she'll teach English or tell her she's beautiful or comment on how long her legs are. She is another face in the crowd, and she is having a hard time adjusting to this. As an American in Japan, it's like the horns blow and the red carpet is rolled out wherever you go. The only people who ask her for attention in the city of New York are the beggars on the street corners. In time, she may get used to it all.

We like to act like we had the life of ease and fun. Deep down, there are so many insecurities and worries. I wouldn't trade my upbringing in Japan for anything. It is who I am. But that doesn't mean it was without difficulties.

I've written a lot. You may want to be careful when you think about asking me a question like that next time. I may never stop. Thanks, by the way, for asking.

I read his response many times. Then I print it on sheets of copy paper. Even though I don't fully understand where he is coming from, I am honored that he took the time to share his thoughts with me. Perhaps when I actually get to Japan, I'll comprehend better how he feels.

I can't wait to meet him. Again.

———

Being female, I don't know what to wear. I've never understood other women who complained about their lack of nice clothes or clothes that fit. Just put on a pair of jeans and sweatshirt and go wherever you need to go. That *was* my attitude. Who needs loads of clothes?

How things can change. I've spent the last hour trying on all my sundresses—all two of them—and three pairs of faded jeans, one khaki skirt, T-shirts, and a skirt with a ruffle that was probably passed down from Aunt Lucy. I feel like a frumpy old schoolteacher. That is not the image I want to give Harrison when he greets me at the Osaka airport.

My savings account tells me I have one hundred sixty-two dollars to spend on clothes. I check out a flyer from Julianne's on Main Street. How convenient, it's having a sale this week.

The sky is a shiny blue without a cloud in sight, and the summer sun beats down on me with all the heat it can muster. It is summer in the South.

Thank you, God, for a working air-conditioner in my car.

Inside the cool car, before backing out of my driveway, I step on the brake and laugh. Throw my head back and let a laugh start in my stomach and work its way out of my mouth, just like Uncle Jarvis does. Then I laugh at the sound of my own laughter.

It is the sound and feel of sunshine and waterfalls mixed together on a beautiful southern day.

The Good Lord willing and the creek don't rise, I am going to the land of the rising sun.

———

I don't shop much. The few times I have gone to the mall, after about an hour, I'm bone-tired. Forget standing over racks of seasonal clothes, I just want to be home on my comfortable sofa in a pair of worn jeans and my tattered Mount Olive T-shirt with a mug of tea. It seems like trying on clothes and looking in the store's dressing room mirror should be fun. Aunt Iva considers it a treat. Perhaps because she has long legs, so clothes look good on her. Sometimes I am able to admire the way a dress or pants fit and feel like a model, albeit a short one. Those are the few-and-far-between times. Usually, I'm mortified that the mirror could do such an injustice and make me look so awful. Once I do make the tedious decision to buy the particular dress, I wonder if I'll wear it five years from now (another way the five-year plan haunts my life) and basically get my money's worth out of it. All this wondering makes me sit even longer in the dressing room and debate.

While in the dressing room at Julianne's, I listen to other shoppers trying on clothes.

"Oh, Susie," one says in the stall next to me, "do you think these shorts make my butt look big?"

"Well . . ." I hear Susie suck in air. "Well . . ."

I figure if there is a slight hesitation and no immediate, "Oh, of course not! Your butt isn't big at all. I wish my butt was as small as yours," then really, it is time to forget those shorts.

Susie continues with, "I like the color. Everyone needs a pair of pink shorts."

"Really?" A pause. She is probably studying herself in the

full-length mirror. A turn to the left, a glance over her shoulder at her reflection, and then a slight twist to the right. "Okay, I'll get them."

Her mistake. She will not get her money's worth out of those shorts, regardless that they are the color pink and everyone needs a pink pair of shorts. Because, sure as the sun, she'll get home and realize too late—"Wow, I knew my butt was big, but not this big!" And the shorts will either go in the Goodwill section of her dresser or she'll return them to the store two days from now. If she's remembered to hold on to the receipt.

I know I won't buy shorts today. Harrison says that only children wear shorts in public in Japan. Showing too much skin is taboo.

After Susie and her friend leave the dressing room, I stand. The dress I have selected to try on has vertical green and black stripes. As I slip it over my head and look in the mirror, I smile. The colors glow a little against my pale skin. Twirling around, I feel thinner than I have in years. Then I scrape my heel against the door and muffle a moan. Rubbing my heel, I peer once more into the mirror and manage another smile.

"Hello, Harrison," I say to my own reflection, practicing for when I see him at the airport.

I imagine him smiling back, eyes filled with light and warmth, and maybe he's even thinking, "Wow, she looks good in that dress!"

My heart feels as if it will pop out of my chest. I decide then to purchase the dress.

———

As I pull into my driveway, I'm ready for some lunch and a

glass of iced tea. Shopping not only makes you tired, it makes you hungry.

I make a glass of instant iced tea. As I add three ice cubes, I'm glad Ducee can't see me now. She'd be shocked if she knew I used iced tea mix. She always makes fresh tea from distilled water and tea bags. She instructs that the key to dissolving the sugar is to add it while the tea is still hot, right after the tea bags have been removed. Then to stir the mixture *emphatically*. I like watching her, at barely five feet tall, *emphatically* spinning a silver spoon around a glass pitcher. Sometimes the pitcher looks bigger than she does.

She plans to make ten gallons of iced tea for the reunion's Saturday picnic.

It is going to be hard to miss the reunion. I wish I could be in two places at one time. I have never missed a reunion, except for my short years in Japan.

As I drink my iced tea, I note that right now in Japan, it's four in the early morning. Harrison is sleeping in his futon on the straw floor. Much of the time when I think of him, he's asleep.

The ringing phone breaks into my thoughts.

"Hello?"

"Nicki? Oh, Nicki." Iva is out of breath.

"Hi, Iva," I say calmly, expecting to hear my aunt clear her throat and then tell me something about either a runaway prisoner or details of our upcoming reunion. The last time Iva called she said Great-Uncle Clive's cucumber crop was producing many lovely green cucumbers. "I can taste those cucumber sandwiches, Nicki. They are going to be the best," she said.

"She's had a heart attack."

I am confused. "What?"

"Oh, Nicki."

"You're at the hospital?"

"Yes."

With my aunt you can never be sure, so I ask, "Ducee?"

"Yes, yes!"

"I'm on my way."

———

Ducee is in the intensive care unit at Wayne Memorial. Pumps, tubes, and machines that make gurgling noises surround her as she lies motionless in a sterile bed of white. She is breathing softly and on her own. Her eyes are shut, the veins in them the color of her blue crocheted throw rug.

I approach a nurse and ask what happened. The nurse asks another nurse. Suddenly out of what seems like nowhere, a doctor with a white mustache stands at my side. I don't remember his name, but his worn face and bushy white eyebrows are familiar. I'm certain he was Ducee's doctor the last time she was brought here in an ambulance, the time Mrs. McCready found her slumped in her recliner.

"She had trouble breathing," the doctor tells me as his eyebrows wiggle. "Pain in her chest. I heard that the donkey's braying alarmed the neighbor. When the neighbor came to your grandmother's yard, she found her on the ground by the donkey."

Good ol' faithful Maggie McCormick.

Then the doctor makes the Hippocratic Leap—at least, that's what I call it. The huge leap into using medical jargon. I want to scream, "Just give me the layman facts, good doctor. Just the layman facts!"

But he's already taken off, using those five-hundred-dollar

medical terms, terms that make my head spin. Greek would be easier. Of course, the doctor has to use them. Learning them cost him a pretty expensive tuition.

I stand by Ducee's bed, watching her and all the machines. My eyes dart back and forth—her, machines, her, machines—until my knees grow weak and I leave the room, while I can still walk.

In the waiting room I am greeted by familiar faces. Almost a dozen of them. Iva, her daughter Clarisa Jo, Mrs. McCready, who is frantically reciting the Lord's Prayer, Cousin Jerome from Elizabeth City, Tweetsie from Goldsboro, Great-Uncle Clive, and his daughters Chloe and Jackie Sue. Then in comes Cousin Aaron and his wife, who likes to be called, believe it or not, Puddin'. They take turns hugging me. I smell their cologne, lotion, hairspray, and perfume.

Not one of them smells of that familiar scent I have grown to love—Ducee's lilac.

Chapter Twenty-Nine

The waiting room is tiny, with straight-back chairs and one lumpy fluorescent green sofa. Aside from the scents we've brought to it, it has its perpetual aroma of lemon furniture polish and chlorine. After all the hugging, no one knows what to say.

Mrs. McCready keeps scratching her silver hair. "I'm not going to use that conditioner anymore," she tells the assembled group. "It said it would make my hair soft and shiny and . . ." Sitting up in the chair, she reprimands herself, "Oh, how can I be talking about my hair at a time like this?" Silently, she adjusts her glasses, places her hands in her lap so that they form a small mound, and then scratches her head once more.

"I know all about bad conditioner," Clarisa Jo tells us. She raises her short arms to her own head of dyed-blond hair. Neither she nor Grable inherited Iva's long-limbed-and-tall genes. "Believe me, I used some awful product last year and was miserable, just plain ol' miserable." She looks at her mother. "Wasn't I, Mama?"

Iva's mind is yards away, in the intensive care unit with her sister. I know because mine is still there, too. Iva manages to produce a nod.

"I don't use conditioner," Chloe tells us. Her southern accent allows her to replace every word ending in an "er" with an "ah" sound. "Makes my hair too soft. Such a bother to do anything with it."

Her sister Jackie Sue agrees. "My hair just flies away when I use that Herbal Essence stuff."

"Although it does smell nice," says Chloe.

"It does, but I like Pantene. That's what I use now," says Jackie Sue. "Only every other day, though."

There is a page over the PA system for a Dr. Williams.

Iva's face loses its color as she grabs my hand. "That's Ducee's doctor," she tells us.

The one whose name I'd forgotten, the one with the bushy eyebrows.

Suddenly, hair conditioner doesn't matter anymore. We're back in reality. In this moment of crisis, we are knit together unlike any previous reunion. I look at each anxious face in the waiting room. We are truly family.

———

Later, Iva takes note of the No Smoking sign as she's about to light up. "I guess I'll have to go outside," she says, but doesn't budge.

I know she won't chance leaving this floor where her sister lies motionless, even for a coveted Virginia Slims.

I pick up a copy of a dog-eared *Time* magazine. The sound of my flipping through the pages is loud in this tiny, anxious room. I try reading an article on Taiwan's economy, but it is no easier than listening to the doctor tell me what is wrong with Ducee.

Iva leans over and whispers close to my ear, "Nicki?"

"Yeah?"

She lets out a moan. "I was supposed to die first."

"Iva."

"I'm the one who smokes and is difficult to get along with."

I pat her hand the way my grandmother pats mine. "You're not difficult."

An hour later Monet bursts into the room with Grable. Grable looks exhausted, bags billowing under her eyes.

Monet rushes over to me and buries her face in my chest. She's brought her Sazae doll, the one she named Niccc. After dangling her in front of my face, the little girl embraces the cotton doll at the waist with both hands.

Just the other day Grable said Monet takes her new doll with her no matter where she goes. She even took it to her last MRI and screamed that the doll had to be scanned too.

As evening approaches and we have all taken turns seeing Ducee in the room where none of us chose to stay very long, Grable's mom and Iva's daughter, Clarisa Jo, calls Howie, a distant cousin of mine, twice removed, who runs a sandwich shop. Howie delivers a large hoagie filled with turkey, ham, cheeses, pickles, tomatoes, olives, and lettuce.

"That must be nine feet long!" Iva says as she eyes the sandwich and watches her daughter set it on the table in a small kitchen connected to the waiting room. Clarisa Jo unwraps the clear plastic and paper surrounding the hoagie. Grable opens a few random drawers, finds a knife, and cuts the sandwich in pieces. Everyone enters the kitchen and stands around the table like a vulture, ready to eat. We wait. We're used to Ducee giving the blessing. Finally Clarisa Jo mutters, "We thank you, God."

Monet mumbles, yet for some reason we all understand each word loud and clear tonight. "Duceeeee get weellll soooo."

"Yes," says Clarisa Jo to her granddaughter, "we do ask God to make Ducee well really soon."

It is eight o'clock at night in Mount Olive, and we are famished.

Ducee would enjoy this, I think as I bite into the bread filled with turkey, ham, and cheese. It's fresh and full of flavor. Oh, she might think it needs a little salt, but because of her blood pressure, she'd use a salt substitute instead. I chew the sandwich and feel a vast improvement. Then I realize why I'm more hungry than usual; I skipped lunch.

Iva says the food is wonderful and I agree.

Is it wrong to feel good about eating when someone in the next room is unable to eat?

Monet tugs at Grable's pants and asks for a hot dog. A low groan springs from Grable's throat.

Quickly, I tear off a piece of ham and pretend to feed it to Monet's doll. "Yum, yum, the doll likes this. Do you want to try some, Monet?"

Monet frowns, starts to cry, and then as I continue acting like Monet's doll is enjoying the ham, the wild one screams, "Me! Me! ME!"

Monet patiently stands in front of my hand as I feed her a bite of ham.

From across the room, Grable smiles.

Monet asks for more. Then she grabs my arm and starts talking about my fish. "Fee! Fee at my hommmm. Fee! Fisssz swwi, swi mmmm." She sticks a finger in my stomach to let me know she now wants to know about my aquarium of fish.

"Yes," I reply. "My fish are at home swimming, too." It's

surprising to me that I can actually understand this creature when I used to think it impossible. Ducee says sometimes ears have to be trained in order to hear what they need to hear.

I'm grateful when Clive inquires about her new doll and Monet leaves my side. We all watch as Monet is swooped up into Clive's large lap along with her Sazae look-alike.

Monet fingers Clive's eyebrows, squeals a few phrases, and then settles down. Her doll faces me, and for the hundredth time, I wonder what my own Sazae felt like brand-new when Watanabe-san first gave her as a gift almost thirty years ago.

I look around the room and suddenly recall why we are all here. Ducee is stuck in intensive care, and we have no idea if she'll pull through. It is much too much to comprehend. I chew on a pickle as the conversations in the room become a dull din. A tinge of panic overcomes me as I am bombarded with questions. What were my last words to Ducee? What were her last words to me? Did I let her know how much I love her? That she makes the best barbecue in the world? That she is the only mother I can remember having?

I almost choke on the pickle. Tears well in my eyes, and conscious of the others in the room, I sniff a few times. I will not cry, not tonight.

Luckily, Pastor Donald steps into the room then, rescuing my mind from the endless worry, as well as any more tears. He has just been in to see Ducee. He says he'd like to pray with the family before leaving.

I close my eyes and attempt to concentrate on his words, asking for Ducee's speedy recovery and telling God how much Ducee means to all of us. I suppose God knows how much she means to each of us in this room, but I also suppose appreciation for His creation is something He never tires of hearing.

At the end of the prayer, my heart no longer feels as if it's on the racetrack.

Iva blows her nose in a crumpled tissue she takes from a corner of her overstuffed purse.

When Pastor Donald says he must go, I hate to see him leave. He shakes hands with Great-Uncle Clive and Aaron, and pats the women's hands, saying he'll be back tomorrow and to be sure to call him if anything changes.

Monet clutches her doll, rushes into his arms, and plants a kiss on his left cheek. "Thannn youuu," she says, her tone booming to the ceiling of the small kitchen. "Thannn youuu praaaa." She smiles into the pastor's eyes.

He takes her hand and smiles back.

Suddenly everyone else is smiling too, grateful for Monet, the little wild thing, somehow able to express at this time how each one of us feels.

Chapter Thirty

The next morning, after a troubled night of sleep where Iva kept shouting in my dreams that Ducee was dead, I toss on a pair of jeans and a UNC-Greensboro T-shirt and check my answering machine. Seeing that no one has left a message, I feel Ducee must still be alive. If anything happened, Iva would have let me know.

Quickly, before heading to the hospital, I open my email. I ignore all the messages—mostly spam—except the one from Harrison.

Nicole,

   Do you remember the day we went to the park and two Japanese girls made a crown out of clover for you to wear? There was a patch of clover and you were in the middle, the other girls surrounding you, creating this crown for your head. They were mesmerized by your red hair. I visited Watanabe-san today and she regrets that the picture she took of you wearing the clover crown didn't survive the fire. She has lots of pictures on her bulletin board that she was able to save. She wonders if your father has that clover photo in the boxes of items packed up for him. I said I'd ask you.

Harrison

Clover crown, I muse. I do wonder what that looked like. As for the boxes neighbors apparently packed for Father after the fire, I have yet to see the contents of those. They were shipped to his parents' house and stored in their attic.

I went up there once. That was the day I broke my ankle and was told never to enter the attic again.

"There is nothing up there for you," my father's mother sternly told me. "Nothing."

———

Two days later, Ducee is moved to a private room. The nurses cart all the flowers, balloons, and cards she's received to her new room, a room with yellow walls, the color of her own kitchen.

Alone with her in the room, I gradually make my way to my grandmother's side and remove strands of her gray hair from her pale face. Gently, I run fingers across her cool forehead, cheeks, and eyes.

Ducee doesn't make a sound.

Sitting on the stool by her bed, I remember how Ducee cared for me one summer when Father drove me down for a four-week visit. I'd been in Ducee and Grandpa Luke's home only three days when I came down with the flu.

"Why do my eyes hurt? Why am I so hot?" My questions had been constant, even back then.

Ducee smoothed my hair back from my flushed face.

"Why does my foot feel funny?"

"Just rest, dear. It'll be okay."

I started to cry.

"Oh, honey," Ducee whispered. "Shhh. Shhhh." She brushed

her fingers over my aching arms. "There, it's okay. Don't you know you are my chutney girl?"

At the time I thought, "I am Ducee's chutney girl. I guess I am going to be okay."

Now Ducee twitches just a tiny bit, which makes me think I should phone every relative.

I wait and watch as she opens her eyes. I feel I am viewing a child's first steps. I want to hurry the process, yet I know I need to be patient.

Ducee swallows, and then mumbles.

I lean in, place a hand on Ducee's shoulder, and touch my fingers to her left cheek.

Ducee's lips are colorless as she moves them.

"Just rest," I manage to say. "It will be okay." And, oh, how I want to believe this.

I tuck the white sheet against Ducee's shoulders as her eyes shut.

Later she asks for a sip of water and gets frustrated when some of the liquid dribbles onto her checkered hospital nightgown.

"Shh," I tell her. "Shhhh. Don't you know you are my chutney girl?"

I hope that is a smile I see on my grandmother's lips. She looks peaceful. On second thought, it could be her dying face. A face I have yet to see. How do I know that it isn't?

This could be the day her heart, which was under the surgical knife years ago, decides it can take no more, and stops.

"Emma." Like a blessing, I hear my mother's name float from Ducee's lips. "Emma."

"Ducee?" I edge closer to her.

Ducee's eyes flutter open, catch mine in their gaze, and she smiles. I know it is a smile. She is not going to die. Not now. Ducee slowly whispers, "Did anyone ever tell you . . ."

"What?" I strain to hear.

"That you . . ."

"Yes?"

" . . . have hands . . . like your mother?"

———

The attic belonging to Father's parents was dank and musty. Somehow I knew that there were boxes up there, boxes that had been sent from Japan, filled with items that survived the house fire. I suppose Ducee had told me. Curious, one afternoon while the adults were downstairs watching a game on TV, I snuck upstairs and pulled down the attic steps. The dark hole leading up to the attic gave me goose bumps, but I told myself that the wonderful reward would be opening those boxes and finding pictures of Mama in Japan. Perhaps there was even some of her jewelry that had been rescued from the fire, like the turquoise bracelet she received after graduating from nursing school. I had heard about that bracelet from Ducee and imagined how it would feel against my skin, on my wrist. The thought of having something to wear of Mama's produced a happy sensation within my twelve-year-old heart. With determination, I embarked on the steps, slowly making my way up. Downstairs, a door opened and slammed; I felt my heart freeze in my chest. Fearful of getting caught in the act, I quickly bounded up the last steps. In the darkness I could smell the coolness and ancient odors of the attic. One more step and I'd be inside, but instead, I lost my balance and fell six feet to the floor. Pain seared my whole body as I lay in a lump on the rug in the hallway, certain that blood was pouring from every crevice. I couldn't move. I was sure I was dead.

"Nicole?" I heard my grandmother Michelin approaching me. "Nicole? Where are you? What have you gone and done?"

I had to wear a cast on my ankle for six weeks. No bracelet of Mama's to dangle on my wrist, or photos of her and me to gaze at—just an uncomfortable piece of plaster to add to my clumsiness.

———

Ducee's room is silent after the doctors make their rounds. I sit, stand, look out the window, think about Harrison, and sit again. I guess I could write to tell Harrison about the failed search for my mother's belongings. For all I know, the boxes could contain a picture of a little American girl in a clover crown woven for her by two Japanese girls. But someone else will have to venture to the attic to sort through boxes to find it.

In the early afternoon as a thunderstorm brews, Grable visits. From the minute she enters the room, I feel anxious.

Seated beside me on a stool, she's unsure what to do with her long nails. They are painted a rosy red, the color of Monet's cheeks when she's flustered. She runs the back of a finger over a thumbnail, studies another nail, and then folds her hands so that her nails cover her knuckles. "The doll has been wonderful. Thank you." Her smile is fleeting, just a quick gesture.

I think that perhaps I'll now tell Grable about Harrison. It would pass the time as we sit beside Ducee. I could tell her how we met online and build up to my plane ticket to Japan. She can keep a secret.

As I am about to begin, clearing my throat and wishing for a glass of water, a nurse opens the door. Systematically, she marches over to check on Ducee. We watch as Ducee has her pulse and blood pressure taken. The nurse refers to Ducee as "Mrs. Dubois." I forget sometimes that my grandmother has another name besides Ducee.

Ducee remains quiet, breathing slowly. How can she sleep so much?

When the nurse leaves the room, Grable says in a voice that hangs heavy in the air, "Dennis is in love with someone else."

I want to tell her that isn't true, that Mr. McGuire isn't sure it was Dennis and another woman at his store that morning months ago. I want to tell her that Dennis loves her, that their wedding ceremony is something Ducee still mentions, that Dennis is going to take Monet to the park this afternoon and embrace her when she sails down the slide.

"He's tired of us. Tired of Monet and nobody knowing what's wrong with her. He's tired of me. Of me being tired." Grable's sigh expands to fill each corner of the room.

"He says he loves Monet." She pauses to take a breath, a breath that seems to swallow her. "But he wants to move out. Away from us. Away. For good."

I fight the desire to chew a nail, a short and broken nail, one that will never be tapered and glamorous, frosty, and red. I fold my hands instead. Rain pelts the windowpane by Ducee's bed, angry and fierce. "Grable," I say over the noise, "I'm sorry."

"We used to have it all. He used to love me, and I was enchanted with him." She looks at her shiny wedding diamond. "But it crumbled."

I hate not knowing what to say.

"I hope the divorce doesn't harm Monet. Sometimes at night she just presses her nose to the window in hopes she will see him coming home."

"I'm so sorry, Grable." It is such a lame thing to say. A time like this needs a symphony of mellow and heart-wrenching violins playing. Not little ol' me, unsure of what to say and so aware of my bitten nails.

Looking out the window, Grable muses, "Why do we need to find out what is wrong with Monet?"

I hope she doesn't expect me to have the answer to that.

"There is no cure, anyway. All these doctors poking and prodding and trying to come up with some sort of neurological or behavioral reasoning for why she's unique." She inhales and lets the air out slowly, deliberately. "She is who she is." Her words seem as though they're coming from a well-scripted play, one of optimism and strength, yet her eyes are shadowed by a forlorn look on her face. "She might be autistic or have some condition no one has ever been diagnosed with before." Shrugging, she folds her hands in her lap and stares at them.

Time ticks away; I'm aware of the clock on the wall.

Thunder crackles in the distance as the rain picks up speed.

My cousin continues to watch her hands, as though if she were to take her eyes away from them, they might disappear.

I think about reaching over to hug her or saying that she can bring Monet over anytime to feed my fish. But before words form in my mouth, Grable rises from her seat.

She is gone as quickly as she entered.

The room is consumed with pain. I feel its heavy weight pushing against every sterile crevice, each tile on the floor. The sound is booming in my ears, louder than any thunder. I want to comfort, yet I need to be comforted.

I touch Ducee's cheek. "You can't leave me now, Ducee. Please, not today."

And as the room grows dark, I wonder at how we humans are born to pain, experience it constantly, and yet never learn the techniques of dodging it. We just learn to cope, to live. And some of us, if we are lucky enough, to thrive, in spite of it all.

Chapter Thirty-One

The news I hear at the coffee-scented nurses' station when I arrive at the hospital this rainy June morning is that Ducee asked for pineapple chutney. The nurses on duty are clearly amused.

"Pineapple chutney!" A short nurse in a pink smock laughs and takes a sip from her Starbuck's cup. "Sounds very tropical."

Tropical, I think. I've never heard that said about our family's pineapple chutney. If the tradition of making the sweet condiment really started in Ireland, and Mama took the recipe to Japan, there is nothing tropical about it at all. Except for the pineapples, which grow in balmy regions.

I walk into Ducee's room and swallow hard. She is still here, still in the white bed, living, being tended to now by a nurse named Violet.

Just as Violet begins explaining her concern over Ducee's blood pressure, the door swings open and Iva bounces into the room with a jar. It's pineapple chutney; she went home to get a pint for her sister.

"The chutney is here. The party has begun," Iva says with delight.

I know Ducee would like tea with chutney and crackers,

and Violet is kind enough to provide us with both crackers and tea.

We help Ducee sit up in her bed, two pillows propped at her back.

I get the task of opening the glass jar. It takes me only two tries—not bad—and the lid is off.

With a knife, Iva spreads dark yellow mounds of sweetness on the tops of a few crackers. She hands a cracker to her sister.

Ducee takes three meticulous bites, leans back on the pillows that seem bigger than she is, and says, "Ah, did that hit the spot."

Violet asks what it is that she's eaten.

"The finest food this side of heaven," replies Ducee.

"Fried chicken or pizza?" asks Violet with a smile.

Ducee says with all the enthusiasm in her tiny body, "Pineapple chutney."

Violet looks as if she might be sick.

"It's tradition food," explains the older woman. "It's what keeps us strong and united."

Violet says, "United?"

"Yes, yes. Like family. Do you know what the difference between united and untied is?"

Iva and I shoot each other looks of, where is she going with this?

Ducee smiles. "The letter *i*," she says. "It just depends on where it sits, doesn't it? Yes, that's it, yes. Where one sits determines how she hears and views the world around her. In unity or untied." She shifts her body slightly under the sheet and repeats, "Untied."

Violet is used to all types of patients, I'm sure, and in her medicine chest of replies, finds a response to my grandmother. "You are quite wise, Mrs. Dubois," and then she takes her blood pressure and heads out the door.

Iva fidgets, moving from Ducee's bedside to the window and back to her bed, like a caged animal.

Finally, Ducee cries, "Oh, Iva, go have a smoke!"

Iva stops in her tracks, and I see relief spread across her face. "Really? I won't be long."

"I'll be here. It's okay," I reassure my aunt. I know she would never want her sister to be alone, especially during the day in this hospital room.

We watch Iva slide out of the room, dodging a potted Begonia sent from The Twins, her long legs gliding over the linoleum.

When we are alone, Ducee turns to me and gives a warm smile. "How are you, my dear?"

"Me?" I snort. "How are you?"

She smiles again, and I see flecks of life in her bluish-green eyes, eyes that were sallow just days ago. "My heart just fluttered," she says.

"It wasn't just a flutter this time. You had a heart attack."

"Did I?"

"Yes."

Ducee grins. "Well, well."

She asks for a sip of tea, and I apologize that it's not ginger.

"I don't know what happened to me. It was a glorious morning. Brilliant."

It was. I'd been shopping. Shopping as if all was well while just miles down the road my own grandmother was having a heart attack.

"Did you see the sky?" Ducee closes her eyes. "As blue as a Staffa Aster. Yes, yes."

I couldn't pick an Aster out of a lineup, much less a Staffa kind.

"Maggie McCormick and I did enjoy a few sugar cubes, and she ate a whole baked potato as I gave her a good brushing. And then, quick as a flash, here I am." She smiles broadly, her thin lips barely visible.

"Your heart must have hurt. You had a heart attack." I wish the woman would realize that she's not at a picnic in the park.

"Aren't those nice?" she says referring to a lime green vase filled with pink and white roses, yellow daisies, and purple horns of plenty.

There are so many vases and baskets of flowers on every flat surface of this room. Relatives, neighbors, and church friends have come out of the woodwork to send flowers and cards to my grandmother. The fourth-grade Sunday school class even delivered a stuffed brown bear with an attached red balloon that reads, "We can't bear to be without you." The get-well card from a grandniece in Elizabeth City with the pink-tongued poodle on the front is ironic, since Ducee is far from fond of the breed. Lou Anne, the relative who is a Realtor and sold my house to me, sent a tin in the shape of a house. The tin is filled with peppermints.

Ducee looks at me as I admire the newest addition from Cousin Aaron and Puddin'. It is a stone sculpture of two opened hands, palms cupped, and on the index finger of one of the hands sits a tiny sparrow. The line from a song Ducee often hums, "His eye is on the sparrow and I know He watches me," is printed in silver letters across the other palm.

Birds of the air. Lilies of the field. Here today and gone tomorrow. God cares for them and oh, how much more He cares for you and me. This is one of Ducee's Southern Truths she's paraphrased from the book of Matthew.

Suddenly she says, "Don't miss your flight."

I look at her, my little grandmother in a bed surrounded by tangible love—all these gifts from others.

"You haven't missed it now, have you?"

I shake my head. I am about to protest.

"I wish she'd written more." She yawns. "Nowadays we have video cameras. I so wish she had one back in the sixties so that she could have filmed it all. Then I could have watched, and you could see what it was really like then. But no, all we had were letters. And I'm afraid your mama didn't write enough of those."

So Mama didn't send enough letters back home to her parents in Mount Olive? Mama wasn't perfect.

Ducee seems to be in a talkative mood. Perhaps her heart attack has triggered her memory. Maybe she will say that she knew Mama was pregnant when she died.

"Ducee, what else do you remember?"

But Ducee is asleep, her head against the pillows, her mouth in the shape of a tiny O.

I make my way to the stool by her bed and just watch.

She's told me that she used to hover over my bed as I slept during the first nights at her house after Father and I came back from Japan. She says she would cry because she missed her Emma so much and that to watch me without my mother tore her heart to pieces. She knew her lap would never be large enough to hold me and give me what I needed from a mama.

But she made a promise that she would certainly try to be the best grandmother she could be.

And although a part of her wanted to die and join her beloved Emma because she didn't think there could be life without her daughter, she knew her work on earth was not complete. "My, my," she has told me over the years as she caresses my arm, "I thought what a huge task God has given to me in my old age—to care for this tiny one. But you know what? The task was not a chore at all. No, no. Every moment with you has been a gift."

At this point, I always feel honored, special, and immensely worthy—like a beautiful quilt has been swept over me, engulfed me, and warmed me with sunlight even brighter than the sun beaming over the Carolina coast.

Ducee's mouth is fully opened now, and she is snoring. Many times as a child the husky sound of her snoring annoyed me. Now I welcome it; it means she is alive.

I lift the sheet that has slipped around her stomach, tucking it over her chest and around her shoulders and neck. When I pat her shoulder, it feels fragile to me. Like a Japanese porcelain doll I once saw displayed in a glass case at an Asian store in Goldsboro. I was so afraid it would topple off the shelf, shatter, and break. I worried that if my footsteps were too hard or loud, the doll would come crashing down. I didn't want to see damage come to that delicate porcelain face.

Ducee murmurs something I can't understand, and a slight smile forms across her mouth. Then the door to her room is flung open and a frazzled Iva announces, "Clive is here. He was in a fight."

Chapter Thirty-Two

In the emergency room of the same hospital, seated on a crisp bed, is Great-Uncle Clive. His head is wrapped in a white bandage and a scarlet-and-blue bruise lines one side of his jaw. His right arm rests against his side in a bulky cast. There are streaks of blood around the neck to his white "Drink Pepsi" T-shirt. His denim overalls are torn at the knees.

"He hit first" is all he says.

Iva, who cajoled her brother into telling, relayed the incident to me as we headed down to the ER in the elevator. Clive heard Dennis had come back to see Grable and collect his things. Furious, Clive asked where Dennis was staying. Grable told him he was at a friend's apartment in Goldsboro. Clive found the telephone number mounted to Grable's refrigerator with the forest green Mount Olive magnet and tracked Dennis down, entering the apartment this morning. Dennis yelled at him to get out, and the fight began. Clive left town right when Dennis threatened to ram an axe into one of the truck's doors—the one heavily adorned with the Pepsi logo. It wasn't until Clive's daughter Chloe saw him hours later, in his broken condition, that he agreed to take her advice and head to the ER.

Of course, Iva didn't know that Dennis had left Grable and Monet. Her brother's fight with Dennis was the first she'd heard that Dennis had not been living at home in ages.

"I just don't know why Grable didn't tell me or Clarisa Jo," Iva says with shock.

I am surprised that our clan has kept a secret. Grable didn't want her mom, Clarisa Jo, or her grandmother Iva to know that Dennis was gone more than he was home and that she knew of his affair. She confided in Clive, and a little in me.

"He had it coming to him," Clive tells me through clinched teeth and eyebrows that rise in fury.

"What does he look like?" I ask tentatively. "What did you do to Dennis?"

"He's a selfish good-for-nothing."

Clive, even as a child, I'm told, was a person of few words. He has nothing else to say. He waits for the doctor to release him to go home so that he can tend to his cucumber crop, sit on his newest John Deere and mow the grass, and work on a playhouse he is building on his property for Monet. I heard he painted a bottle of Pepsi on one side.

I touch his arm, the one without the cast. "I'm sorry, Uncle Clive."

"She needs her daddy." His eyes hold flames.

I nod, knowing he is referring to Monet. "She needs so much." I let the sentence hang in the air and then am tempted to add to it, but what is there to say? Monet is suffering without her daddy. And Grable is clearly at her wits' end.

"How's Ducee?" Clive asks after moments of silence pass between us.

"Better . . . I think."

He stares at his cast. "She can't leave us."

My sentiments exactly.

When a nurse enters with what Clive calls his exit papers, I leave the room.

Among the relatives, it has always been said of Great-Uncle Clive, "He has a temper. You think he's all silent and strong, but when his temper boils, it boils."

It boiled today.

I'm sorry I missed all the drama. I would have liked to have seen what really happened. I have a hard time believing that Dennis, who can act so refined in his pressed lawyer's suit, threatened my great-uncle's Pepsi truck with an axe.

No wonder he reminds many family members of Aunt Iva's ex, Harlowe.

———

Ducee sleeps when I visit the next day. It seems the flowers in the room have multiplied overnight. I read the new cards and notes attached to the vases of day lilies, roses, and one delicate purple orchid. Against one of the vases is a thick piece of paper with a picture painted on it. In the picture, the sun is shining through a set of dark clouds. Below the clouds is a square fish tank with a little angelfish inside. Around the tank are strands of purple, green, and blue. The picture, obviously drawn by an elementary school student, makes me smile. I wonder who painted this artwork for Ducee. The artist used acrylic paints and did quite a good job.

Violet enters Ducee's room and greets my sleeping grandmother by touching her cheek with one hand and exclaiming, "How are we today, Mrs. Dubois?" Then Violet sees me studying the picture. "Nice, isn't it? That little girl does love your grandmother."

"Which little girl?" I ask.

"The one with the Chinese kimono doll and the Dora the Explorer T-shirt."

My eyes grow wide. "Not Monet!"

Violet nods and laughs. "She's a noisy thing, but when I gave her paper and some paints I found in a drawer, she went right to work."

"She was here?"

Violet manages to convince a sleepy Ducee to open her mouth for the thermometer. "Last night after you left," the nurse says as she sits on the stool by Ducee's bed. "I squeezed paint from a few tubes onto a paper plate and filled a small tray with water. She did all the rest."

I shake my head and want to laugh. All these years we've been giving Monet the wrong artistic medium to use for her drawings. We've supplied her with crayons and markers when the child needed—who would have guessed—acrylics!

The colors in Monet's painting are like a rainbow, a promise of hope. I imagine her holding the brush in one hand and dipping it into the pools of paint the way she dips her hot dog slices into ketchup. She's even given the fish eyes and fins.

If the original Claude Monet were here, what would he title little Monet's masterpiece? I'd like to think he'd agree with me and name it Beauty Within.

———

Harrison wonders why I haven't written. "I guess you're busy preparing for your trip," his message says. "I do miss hearing from you. I'll see you soon. I can't believe how much I'm looking forward to your visit."

His words stir within me an excitement—a feeling of magic—like a child experiences on Christmas morning.

I haven't written to him since Ducee has been hospitalized. I guess I don't know what to say. I do not know if I will go to Japan after all this. My longing is for my grandmother to be back on her tennis-shoes-encased feet.

Chapter Thirty-Three

Mrs. McCready is a dear woman in spite of the recent trouble she has had with hair conditioner. Forever this woman will be esteemed by all of the clan because twice now she's found Ducee, called 911, and overseen Ducee being lifted into the ambulance and taken to the hospital. There is no way we can repay her for being a neighbor that is like a sister to my grandmother. But as kind as this elderly woman is, she's not going to look after a donkey. That much is clear.

It is up to me to feed Maggie McCormick while Ducee's in the hospital—only because, perhaps, I am the only one dumb enough to volunteer.

I brush the animal and give her clean water. I let her eat a baked potato, taken from Ducee's hospital tray at dinner, and a carrot, out of my hand. Before leaving, I guide her out into the field by Ducee's house. The rustic barn door is ajar; Maggie can go inside if she needs to. But the weather's so warm that Maggie will be just fine in the grassy land enclosed by the fence.

"Maggie, you are more than a beast. You are a lifesaver," I tell her as I hand her the apple, the gift Mr. McGuire gave me yesterday for her. I stopped by his store for fish food. Eagerly, he told me he knew that Clive had been in the ER. Nothing stays secret in this town.

"I hope," Mr. McGuire said, "that Dennis ended up in the ER, as well."

I told him that, according to Iva, Dennis threatened to take out a gun but punched Clive in the jaw instead. Clive fell backward and landed on his arm. Clive knocked Dennis in the teeth and possibly, although no one knows for sure, a few of them broke.

Maggie McCormick chews the apple, shows her large teeth, and gives a slight bray. She must know she is special to have alerted Mrs. McCready about Ducee.

I check Ducee's doors to make sure they're locked. Everything seems secure and tranquil, right down to the two dormer windows protruding out from under the black roof. Even the wreath is hanging squarely on the lavender front door this June evening, but the door doesn't look inviting now, perhaps because no one is home.

The gardenia bush on the side of the house fills the air with its sweetness. Now, that is a fragrance that can calm any uneasy nerve. If Ducee dies, I'll take the gardenia and plant it in my yard. Each day as I walk past it, I'll be filled with an aroma that will soothe me almost as well as watching my fish swim.

When I back out of the driveway, I take one last look at Ducee's house. Part of me fears that Ducee will never return to it again. Perhaps the nine lives we've kidded her about having have come to an abrupt end.

I feel badly that I even considered taking the gardenia bush if Ducee dies.

I drive home unaware of my surroundings, making the familiar left and right turns. When I pull into my driveway,

Hilda waves from her open garage. She's standing over a stack of cardboard boxes while a burly man I've never seen before washes her van. He soaps up the body, his large muscles flexing. I bet lots of people are willing to wash Hilda's van. They may even think that cleaning the vehicle of a saint secures a place for them in heaven.

Before I take the keys out of my car's ignition, the dashboard's Check Engine light ignites. Oh no. I wait for the light to disappear as though if I stare at it long enough it'll fade. Cars are fine, I always say, unless they refuse to run smoothly and need servicing.

Luckily, I can call Great-Uncle Clive. He's still in pain and doesn't sleep well since the fight with Dennis, but maybe he can come by and take a look under the hood.

———

Inside my house, I settle in my fuzzy chair to check for email messages. There's a pink-and-purple-colored message from Kristine asking how my summer is going. She adds that her car is in the shop because she backed into a telephone pole after her salsa lesson last night. She hopes the repair won't be costly. I can relate. She and Salvador just returned from three days at Emerald Isle and they'd like to bring over a gift for me. "We might just stop by and surprise you one of these days," she writes before ending her message.

I hope their visit isn't too much of a surprise. I would hate to have just stepped out of the shower when they arrive, or burned something on the stove.

The phone rings.

Aunt Betty heard from Iva about Ducee and wants to know how her mother is doing. "Should we come now?" She poses this question a few times, using a variety of intonations. "We could come earlier than planned for the reunion. I can fly out tomorrow. How is she? What do you think? Should we come now?" Her questions spill into each other, and I don't know which one to answer first.

One thing I do know is that my grandmother would prefer that people not make such a fuss over her, even if one of those people is her own daughter.

"She's going to be fine." Who am I trying to convince? "Just fine."

"How is her heart?"

"The doctors are going to change her medication."

"Oh, should we come now?" I hear the worry over the phone lines.

I firmly tell her to wait. "I'll call you tomorrow. Meanwhile, don't worry." I hope I sound as calm as anyone, even though I've twirled my index finger around a strand of hair so tightly that my finger, for a few seconds, is stuck.

Uncle Jarvis gets on the phone and, true to character, tells a joke about two men who went fishing with an elephant. The joke is wasted on me because I don't think it's funny. But when my uncle roars with laughter, I can't help letting out a little laugh. His next joke is about a bottle of Tabasco and a moose; it must be only for those in Wyoming to understand. I pretend it's a good one. As he delves into a joke about a buffalo in hiding, I realize my mind is a thousand miles away—somewhere over the Pacific Ocean.

Aunt Betty yells in the background, "That's enough, Jarvis! You need to mow the grass."

Uncle Jarvis chuckles, says he'll see me at the reunion soon.

He wonders if he should bring some buffalo steaks for the grill. "They might taste good with that chutney Ducee makes."

I take a thumbnail from my mouth and say, "Sure."

When we tell each other good night, I wonder what kind of shape Ducee will be in for the reunion. Although we've already made the chutney for the event, she's not going to be able to make the casseroles, the gallons of iced tea, the egg salad sandwiches. She might still be in a hospital bed. The weekend is just around the corner and how can she possibly get things ready when she sleeps half the day?

It's ten-fifteen at night eastern time, eleven-fifteen in the morning Japan time.

I wonder how Harrison's church picnic at Minoo Park is going today. He wrote that this particular mountain park has monkeys that roam freely. They often grab food from visitors. He said once a tiny monkey crept up to his picnic table, snuck under his elbow, and ran off with a whole bag of potato chips.

Smiling at the thought of a monkey stealing chips, I wonder if Harrison thinks of me as much as I think of him.

I can't believe how much I'm looking forward to your visit.

I would never admit that sentiment to him in a message across cyberspace. I would hold it tightly, secretively, in my heart. As I already do.

Chapter Thirty-Four

In two days, on Thursday, July first, I have a flight to Japan. And except for Ducee and me, no one in Mount Olive knows. This must be the best-kept secret of the whole McCormick-Dubois-Michelin clan. It will go down throughout the generations as the story of Nicole Michelin's trip to Japan. Families will crowd around the tables eating chutney, drinking ginger tea, wiping their mouths on linen napkins, saying, "She and her grandmother Ducee didn't tell a soul. Nicole applied for her passport and purchased an air ticket and planned her trip just like that. No one knew. Isn't that amazing? The whole time everyone thought she was going to be at the family reunion, bringing that Mount Olive centerpiece. You know, the one with the olives on a large fresh pineapple? But no, she was on her way to Japan. And that is the story of how Nicole missed the reunion and went to Japan."

The downside of a well-kept secret is that there is no one to talk this over with.

Do granddaughters leave their grandmothers in hospitals and sail across the skies, away from them? If I could ask Grable, or even Iva, what they think of me leaving at a time like this, that might help me know what to do.

Maybe the tale of how Nicole skipped the reunion and flew to Japan will never be told.

My new clothes are still in the striped pink-and-blue bags with Julianne's written in gold on them. The drugstore bag holding lipstick, perfume, and nail polishes sits next to them on the kitchen floor where I dropped them when the phone call from Iva about Ducee being in the hospital arrived. They are crouched together, expectant, waiting to hear. What is the verdict? Will the items remain in the bags forever, or do they get let out and have their price tags clipped off? Will they get placed in the large gray Samsonite suitcase?

I stare blankly at the bags. What was I thinking? What possessed me to buy nail polish? Why would I paint my nails and draw attention to their short, stubby characteristics?

After buying clothes at Julianne's, I guess I went crazy. Stopped at Franklin's Drug and came out with three bottles of nail polish. And a tube of coral lipstick. And Elizabeth Arden's Green Tea perfume. When was the last time I purchased any of these products? I've prided myself on not needing any of them. These frou-frou products of society are for other girls, not me. Not Nicole Michelin, the simple English teacher.

The bags bulge and beg with wanting to know if they will forever hold their contents.

So what is the verdict?

Bits and pieces of Harrison's previous email messages start to pop up in my mind, the way the letters pop over when Vanna turns them on *Wheel of Fortune*.

We can take the train from Kyoto to Tokyo. For lunch we can eat the *obento* they sell at the stations. Rice, pickles, fish, and seaweed, I tell you, it is a traveler's delight. There is nothing that can be compared with riding on the *shinkansen*, looking out the large glass window, watching rice fields and bamboo groves, little towns and children on bicycles, as you eat an *obento*.

I want you to meet my koi. I know as an expert in fish care, you will be able to convince them not to eat the plants. They'll listen to you.

Nicole, it will be so good for you and Watanabe-san to reconnect and talk together. Of course, I won't mind translating. Watanabe-san appears a bit confused at times, but seeing you will make her so happy.

I think I'd like to buy another Tashio Sanke koi. It has a white body with a red pattern and black accent marks. The last one I picked out was sick and didn't live long. I bet you could help me get a good one this time. Then you can meet the fish store guy. He has a saltwater aquarium that takes up half of his apartment and is always telling me he needs advice.

When the bullfrogs and crickets sing in my garden and my koi swim in the pond and then raise their heads to eat out of my hand, and the sky is filled with stars, I think I live in a corner of heaven. And you, Nicole, just might agree.

I go to the computer and view a picture he sent of Watanabe-san seated in a wheelchair at the nursing home. She's in a white *yukata* with a dotted blue pattern; her hands that look like flower buds are folded in her lap. Her gray hair is pulled back from her forehead into a bun. What catches my attention most is her smiling wrinkled face—like she can't wait to see me.

―――――

At midnight I could use some Uncle Jarvis. Instead, I turn on the television and dig into a pint of Two Times Nutty Crunch. A balding comedian in a plaid shirt starts to tell mother-in-law jokes and the audience finds him hilarious.

Watanabe-san and Mama, Mount Fuji and the *shinkansen*, they are all on my mind. I think of questions to ask Watanabe-san. There are several concerning my doll. First, why did the doll get named Sazae? What does that mean? Assuming it is a Japanese name, do I pronounce it correctly? Throughout the years, I've wondered if I've been mispronouncing the name of my cherished companion.

I have a recollection of deciding that Sazae was too strange a name and so I started calling my doll Belinda Sue. I was seven and, to me, Belinda Sue was the most gorgeous name. Oh, why, oh, why hadn't my parents named me this?

For one full day while we played house where she sat in the doll high chair and drank from a plastic tea set, she was Belinda Sue.

But the next morning when I looked into her coal eyes and stroked her black hair, I knew. She was not Belinda Sue. She was Sazae, and changing her name would be denying who she was and where she came from. A gift from Mama, a gift given to me in that country I wanted nothing to do with—Japan.

I finish the container of ice cream and throw it in the kitchen trash can. I could use another pint, but my freezer holds no more of the creamy treat.

There are other questions I want to ask Watanabe-san, questions regarding Mama and Father. How was their Japanese? Did Mama go to the market to buy fish and pickles made of radishes? How often did she make pineapple chutney? How did she and Father get along? Did they hold hands as they strolled in the Imperial Palace grounds?

And then there are the questions about my relationship with Mama. How had Mama mothered her only child? Was she laid-back or overly protective? Did she insist I wear shoes, or did she let me run around in the spring and summer grass barefoot? Did she kiss the top of my head as I've seen mothers often do? Was she the type of mom who would twirl her daughter around in a parking lot and ask if she was ready to see the big wide world?

I sit in the wing chair as these questions take turns coming to sit beside me. One by one, they pose themselves, wanting answers.

Then they leave me alone. And when my mind is clear of them, thoughts of Harrison arrive. Harrison—dear carp owner with the soft blue eyes. Harrison—poet, email buddy, mystery solver, and childhood friend. Of course I wonder if when I greet him at the airport there will be that spark, that deep sense of knowing that I could love him.

Oh, really, is this the time to be such a romantic?

In my bedroom, I pull the blinds shut and then take out my passport from the dresser drawer. It's in pristine condition with its navy blue cover and crisp, unmarked pages. United States of America—how much more official can you get? The photo of me looks almost as pale as the page it's glued to, but that's okay; it's a known fact that passport pictures, like driver's license photos, are not supposed to be glamour shots. Nicole Delores Michelin—I signed it using my most flamboyant signature.

I see Ducee in the hospital bed, still weak, her heart damaged. Again. A worried doctor from the other day. Why was he worried? She has to live to see the year 2000, don't you see?

My passport will remain starched and clean. It's not going to know the mark of the immigration stamp. It will stay here in my dresser drawer, along with the framed picture of Richard.

The TV audience laughs as a profound sadness fills every silent laugh line on my face.

Chapter Thirty-Five

The word at the nurses' station is that my grandmother, Mrs. Dubois, was not a happy camper last night. She complained of being uncomfortable and told a nurse that it was time for her to go home to her soft and familiar bed. She talked nonstop about Maggie and baked potatoes. The nurse on call did not know that Maggie is a donkey with a white hoof. Apparently, Ducee tried to convince this nurse that not only was she needed at home, but that her family was flying in from Wyoming and from all over North Carolina, actually, yes, yes, that was right, and she needed to go home to take care of everything. Right now.

"And so," my grandmother said sometime around three in the morning, "if you will just sign me out of the hospital, I'm sure I can get someone to come pick me up and drive me home."

To which the nurse promptly stated, "Mrs. Dubois, we will get you home. But first take this pill."

Ducee took the pill, and the pill put her out. Just like that.

This morning Violet warns me, "Your grandmother may be a bit groggy and sleepy today. But don't worry."

She is asleep as I slip into her room, her room still packed with flowers.

The stool beside her hospital bed is probably as uncomfortable as the bed, I think. I take a towel from the adjoining bathroom, cover the top of the stool, and sit. Much better, just like a bit of padding helps make my computer chair at home tolerable.

Ducee's heart rate is still being monitored, but the IV bag has been removed. Surely, that's a good sign. Unless you're dead.

Every part of me aches, even my bitten fingernails. I will never know what Japan looks like in the summer. I will never know if Kyoto feels as humid and hot as Mount Olive can in July. But the truth is, I used to know. I just don't *remember* what it was like.

Ducee stirs. When she opens her eyes, she seems alarmed.

"Ducee," I say in my reassuring voice, "you're in the hospital."

"Oh," she breathes. "I dreamed I was in heaven." She reaches up to touch my face. "Child," she says, her eyes focused on mine, "please don't miss your flight. You have the adventure of a lifetime before you. Be ready to go. Don't let anything get in the way."

"I love you." Sometimes saying these words can make your eyes fill with tears. Using the back of my hand, I wipe a tear from my cheek. She is my mother and grandmother, all wrapped in one. I can't lose her.

She murmurs from dry lips, "Risk. Risk." Then she says, "You have considered the birds?"

Yes, I have. I know God cares for all of us. I know He supplies wisdom to those who ask. And, dear Grandmother, the wisdom I have been given is, how can I leave you at a time like this? All I say is, "I have."

"Good. Because God came down here and talked to me last night."

Tentatively I ask, "He did?"

"Yes, yes." She motions toward the water pitcher, and I pour her a drink in a paper cup. After taking a few sips, she runs her tongue over her lips. "He said you were asking for wisdom and that I was to tell you something."

"What?"

She closes her eyes and in a few minutes, I hear faint snoring. I guess I will never know what God told Ducee when He came down to talk to her last night.

Ducee's mouth moves. At first I hear nothing but the sound of her lips brushing the air. Then ever so clearly her words pierce the silence. "Don't miss the adventure."

I watch her breathing as she sleeps. The rise and fall of her chest gives me hope.

As I leave her room, a doctor I've never seen before meets me at the door. He asks a nurse who is standing nearby for Mrs. Dubois's chart.

She finds it in a pile at the nurses' station.

He flips it open, studies it for a second, and then his eyes meet mine. "She is going to be just fine."

Do I see a twinkle in those eyes? I walk down the hall wondering just who is he talking about.

Ducee?

Or me?

———

ALICE J. WISLER

At home I take my new clothes out of the shopping bags and carefully cut off the price tags and labels. I fold the new pair of Levi's jeans, the green-and-black sundress, and two T-shirts and arrange them in my Samsonite suitcase. I feel the softness of the suede belt and remember how nice it looked in the belt loops of the new jeans when I stood in front of the mirror in Julianne's dressing room.

As I toss a small load of underwear and socks into the washing machine, my mind repeats itself like Flannigan the macaw. *Is going to Japan the right thing to do?* I dump in a capful of liquid detergent, and then another. *Is going to Japan the right thing to do?* Before I let a third capful dribble into the machine, I catch myself. What am I going to do, overload the machine with detergent so bubbles will ooze out of every crevice?

I really, really want to go to Japan.

Turning the washer on, I close the lid, stare at a pair of tennis shoes, and realize I don't know whether to take them or not. Maybe just a pair of sandals and a pair of low-heeled black pumps. No, leave the pumps behind. They give me blisters after a few hours. They make my legs look nice, though. Fine, I'll take all three pairs of shoes.

On the edge of my bed, I curve my body into a ball and wonder what I'm doing. My grandmother is in the hospital. She had a heart attack.

And I am going to Japan.

I feed my fish and realize I haven't arranged a caregiver for them while I'm away. Ducee was going to ask Grable if Grable could bring Monet over to do the honors. Grable has a host of problems due to the divorce. Her plate is full. Why would I want to add to it?

252

I sit outside on the step this hot summer night, raise my face to the sky, and scan the glittering darkness for the Big Dipper.

"Mama?" I call out. My voice sounds thick, weary. It would be too much effort to attempt my usual wave.

A soft haze circles the near-full moon. The murkiness of the circle is like a reflection of my mind, boggled with uncertainty.

A howling dog is the only response I hear. The night is lonely; Hilda isn't even in her garage.

Chapter Thirty-Six

I fill my bathtub with hot water and sprinkle in a cup of lilac bath salts, the ones Ducee gave me. As I soak in the water and breathe in the scent, calmness settles upon my head and inside the marrow of my bones. Solace penetrates each pore. Closing my eyes and leaning back in the tub, I want to call my grandmother and tell her she's right, as usual—lilac is the scent of peace.

Harrison says one of the pleasures of the *ofuro* is that the water temperature never cools. Heated by gas, the water in the Japanese tub remains hot no matter how much time passes. I think what a good concept that is as I leave my chilly bathtub and dry off with a striped towel.

I hear the phone and race into the kitchen, my towel falling down around my knees. I never learned the fine art of tying a towel above my chest, just under my armpits. It is one of those things that I'm sure Mama would have taught me if she had lived.

With panic in my veins, and a tremble I try to shake off, I pick up the receiver and say, "Hello?"

A raspy voice on the other end. "Nicki?"

Yes, Iva, you know it's me. "Yes. What's wrong?"

Then there is silence, some muffled tones, a few words spoken in the distance and soon Ducee is on the line. In a weak voice, barely audible, she says my name.

Hot tears form in my eyes. "Yes?"

"Will you be sure to bring me back some tea? Green would be appropriate, don't you think?"

The phone goes dead and while at first I am puzzled, I finally figure it out. My grandmother won't disclose more because Iva is there in her room and Ducee's still trying to keep my trip to Japan a secret.

"We can drink it together," I say, even though I know Ducee is no longer on the line. I just stand in my kitchen like a stone.

In my room, I fall onto my bed in a heap. I feel like Monet, sad, hurt, afraid. I wait for the inevitable—tears, streams of them.

They don't come.

I smell the lilac on my skin and let its perfume soak my lungs. Clutching Sazae, I pray, "Oh, dear God, what have you asked of me? I'm afraid of flying." After repeating this over and over, I decide I'd better find some other words. "Help," I say.

———

When my eyes snap open, the clock lets me know I've been asleep for an hour. I turn over on my side to face Sazae. "Sazae," I say, "do you want to go back home to Japan for a while?"

My stomach grumbles, and before Sazae can answer, I've pulled on some clothes and made my way to the kitchen. It's been hours since Iva and I ate turkey sandwiches for lunch in the noisy hospital cafeteria.

I make a bowl of grits, add a few tablespoons of butter, swirl the mixture with a spoon, and eat. I will always be grateful for grits. But grits will soon be replaced with Japanese food. My stomach doesn't know what to do with that information. You once ate eel, I tell it.

I wander around the house like I'm lost. I sit in Aunt Lucy's chair, stand, go to my fish tank, step outside to view the sky, come inside to the cool house again, and chew a nail. It's a fact; I don't know what one is to do the day before embarking on an adventure.

Do I shake myself and say, look at you, look, do you know what tomorrow brings? Tomorrow is the first of July, the day you're to get on a plane, take Dramamine, and start your journey to Japan. Are you ready?

Tomorrow is going to arrive whether I'm ready or not.

My overnight kit, a square floral cloth bag, contains shampoo, conditioner, brush, comb, toothbrush, toothpaste, new nail polish, perfume, and lipstick. My plan is to take this on the plane as a carry-on, never letting it leave my sight. I can fit a magazine in, just under where the bag zips. There are some blank notebook pages inside the magazine cover in case I'm able to pause from motion sickness and compose my August column for the Pretty Fishy site. A week ago I sent my July column, six-hundred twenty-two words on the best kinds of gravel and rocks for a marine tank. It's to be posted in three days.

I squeeze in a pair of underpants and a T-shirt. The addition of the clothing to my kit is in case my suitcase ends up in Mongolia and I end up in Madrid. At least I will be able to brush my teeth and change my underwear while waiting to be reunited with my belongings. I heard that these things can happen. Iva reads about them in the newspaper all the time.

"Japan," I say to my fish. The word doesn't make my spine chill or nerves shake as it once did.

I close both the overnight kit and the Samsonite and am assured that at least my possessions are ready for this trip. From my closet I take out the Mount Olive T-shirt with a drawing of a jar of pickles on the front pocket. It's hard to believe that in less than forty-eight hours I'll be giving this shirt to Harrison. Handing it to him while my feet stand on Japanese ground— ground where Mama once stood. Could it be that as I look into his blue eyes as he comes to meet me, something will trigger from the past? Perhaps when I see him, some repressed memories will start to find their way out, like the early shoots from daffodil bulbs.

Am I diving off the deep end? Of course nothing will trigger. I was two years old.

There is a gift for Watanabe-san, too. I'll carry it in my purse, attended by me at all times, because I can't bear to think of this gift being tossed around in my suitcase. It's in a pint-sized glass mason jar. I sure hope this sweet yellow delicacy will taste as good to her as she remembers it did. Back when Mama stood in her kitchen in Kyoto, back when she brought the Gospel and pineapple chutney to Japan.

I carry my suitcase, overnight kit, purse, and passport to the hall. I set the passport on top of the suitcase.

What will two weeks away be like?

Then I feel my stomach drop.

I need to call Grable about feeding my fish. What if she says no? And who is going to make the Mount Olive centerpiece for the reunion? And how am I going to get to the airport?

Airport. I see a huge building with dozens of revolving doors, all covered in flames, Panic sets in. I must have had a nightmare about an airport, for I've been to Raleigh-Durham International to pick up the Wyoming relatives and don't recall fiery revolving doors. Who can drive me to RDU tomorrow? Great-Uncle Clive comes to mind, but he's out of commission with his arm in a cast. Of course I didn't call him immediately after seeing the Check Engine light come on the first time. I waited until the car started to rumble and rock when I shifted gears on the way home from the hospital. Clive told me he'd be by to take a look at it, but he hasn't come yet. "Don't drive any more than you have to" was his warning. "You could damage the transmission." That scared me because I know from past experience the high cost of service to transmissions.

A sigh lifts from my lungs and circles the dining room. The secret keeping is going to have to end earlier than Ducee and I planned. I'll have to call someone and ask for a ride. It's almost two hours to the Raleigh-Durham airport. That's a long round-trip drive. Who would question me the least about where I am headed and why?

I could call a cab. A cab driver wouldn't care to know what I was up to. As long as I paid him. I cringe at that cost, calculating whether or not I have enough cash in my wallet for a cab. I lift the snow globe on my dresser. I used to keep a few dollar bills under it, but only a penny sits there now, mocking me.

And then the doorbell rings and I open it to see a smiling Salvador and a giggling Kristine, both in motorcycle helmets that gleam in the early summer moonlight.

Chapter Thirty-Seven

"We brought you back a gift from the beach!" says Kristine, wearing a jewel-studded pink tank top and a pair of tiny white shorts. She holds a striped orange-and-teal paper bag in her hand. Her tanned skin is now almost identical to Salvador's.

Salvador, dressed in jeans and a white T-shirt, takes off his helmet, exposing a head of thick hair. His smile shows rows of pearly teeth and a tiny dimple in his left cheek. "Kristine wanted to bring you a souvenir."

I figure the proper southern etiquette thing to do is to invite them inside.

We stand in the cool hallway as Kristine hands me the bag. She then lifts her helmet from her head and swings her hair, spilling the scent of peach. I open the bag to find a metal wall plaque in the shape of a clownfish. The stripes on it are painted orange and white. The two eyes are tiny bleached-white seashells. "Thank you," I say.

Kristine gushes, "Isn't it cute? I know how much you love fish. Your students tell me that all the time in science class, you know."

I had no idea. I figured my students wanted nothing to

do with me once I was away from them. Out of sight, out of mind.

"We found the fish at a cute little store where we had lunch on the way home from Emerald Isle." Kristine's jade earrings jingle as she speaks. "We ate the best chicken and dumplings. Salvador had never eaten that before." She squeezes his arm.

Salvador looks as if he isn't sure they were the *best*.

I wish I could gush in the style of Kristine, going on and on about this gift they've brought me. Tell them it was thoughtful and kind. But the more I look at the bleached seashell eyes, the less I can find to say.

Salvador looks at my suitcase arrangement, picks up the passport, and asks, "Where are you going?"

"Oh . . ." What do I tell them?

"Overseas?" asks Salvador.

Kristine giggles. "How fun!"

"Well," I murmur. "Yeah."

"Where to?" asks Salvador.

I take a breath. I guess telling them isn't really exposing the secret. They aren't family; they won't tell anyone expected at the reunion. "Japan."

"Way cool! When?" Kristine flashes a smile.

"I'm supposed to leave tomorrow."

"Are you going by yourself?"

By myself. I feel like a little kid sitting at the big people's table. "Yeah."

Kristine giggles. "There must be a guy involved. Someone you're going to meet once you get there."

She says it like a statement, not posed as a question, so I don't feel I have to answer.

"Japan." Salvador says with a wide smile. "There's a potter

there named Miyako." He nudges Kristine. "Some of his pottery was for sale at that shop in Asheville we went to, remember?"

Kristine does remember the shop they found during their trip to the mountains over Easter. With a frown, she recalls the teacups costing over two hundred dollars each. "Except for that toothpick holder. It was thirty dollars, but it was so small."

"It was a *sake* cup," her boyfriend reminds her. "It's really nice stuff," he adds. *"Bizen."*

I have no idea what *bizen* means but can tell he'd like to be able to afford one of this Miyako's pieces, even if it is only the tiny *sake* cup.

"Is the boy cute?" Kristine asks as Salvador returns my passport to the top of my suitcase.

I want to say, "I knew you'd ask. I knew all along if I told you about Harrison, you would want that question answered above any other." I take them over to my computer and soon they are looking at a photo of Harrison on my screen. Harrison seated beside his outdoor pond. So many times I have wondered what it will feel like to be seated right next to him on that stone bench, the summer sun in my eyes and the smell of the koi pond beside me.

Kristine bends closer to get a better look. "He is cute. Nice eyes."

Cute? I want to shout. He's traffic-stopping gorgeous. He has become simply one of the most handsome men I have—

Salvador interrupts my thoughts. "So when are you leaving?"

"I have a flight from RDU tomorrow . . . but . . ." I hesitate and stick a finger in my mouth. "Well . . ."

"What's wrong?" asks Salvador.

"My grandmother was going to take me to the airport, but she's in the hospital."

"Is she okay?" asks Kristine.

Such a good question. Is she? "I could drive to the airport and leave my car in the parking lot while I'm gone." I add, "But my car is acting up. I don't think it's safe to drive that far."

"Salvador," says Kristine, tapping his arm, "you could take her to the airport."

He nods, runs fingers over his chin, and asks, "What time tomorrow?"

"My flight's in the afternoon. Two-twenty." I've memorized the departure time for all my flights, including the length of time for each layover. Harrison says there is bound to be some delay or change of airlines along the way; never has he flown across the ocean without at least one, what he calls, glitch.

"I can pick you up at ten-thirty or eleven," Salvador says. "That should get you to the airport by one. Will that be enough time?"

I realize I am smiling ear to ear.

But the relief leaves when Kristine says, "You'll love riding on his motorcycle."

Motorcycle?

In the hallway, Salvador takes another look at my luggage. Running a hand through his dark hair, he notes, "This suitcase is too big to carry on the back. My luggage rack won't hold it. Do you have a different type of bag?"

I don't. My attic holds a gigantic green suitcase with a broken handle and a straw beach bag with a frog on it, and that's it for luggage.

He turns to Kristine. "Do you have something?"

"Besides a suitcase?" She twists a lock of hair. "I don't think so."

The three of us cross the lawn to Hilda's. She's in her lit garage, as usual. I'm convinced the woman lives inside it. She looks up from a box of plastic insects to greet us. Spiders, grass-hoppers, crickets, and worms sit motionless inside the cardboard. I know people donate all kinds of things, but who would donate a box of toy insects?

I ask if she has something I can borrow for a trip. Something to carry my clothes in that's more flexible and compact than a suitcase.

Hilda stands and adjusts one of her pink hair curlers. "Let me see . . ."

We all stand in her garage, waiting as she thinks. The air in the garage is stuffy and thick, with a mixture of odors—from old shoes to insect spray.

Hilda takes her hands from her hips and then points to a large row of metal shelves to her left. On the very top is a silver-colored duffle bag. "Is that what you had in mind?"

Salvador stands on a crate and pulls it off the shelf.

"Will that work?" Hilda asks.

Salvador examines the bag. He nods. "This should fit on the cycle. We can strap it on the back along with that other small bag you have." He looks at me for approval.

In the warm night, I feel a chill rise up to my neck. Am I really going to ride on a motorcycle? And get on an airplane? And go to Japan? Lord, my faith is only a seed in the ground. . . .

I thank Hilda. "I'll bring it back in about two weeks."

"You can have it," says my neighbor. "A woman from Hick-ory donated it. It's in good shape. The china dishes, silverware, and linens she also brought by a month ago are in those boxes over there." Hilda waves a hand at a stack of brown boxes in a corner of her garage.

"She donated a lot," says Kristine.

Hilda brushes her nose against her sleeve. "She did. She has breast cancer and doesn't think she'll be around much longer. Ah, they say you can't take it with you. . . ."

As Hilda's voice trails off, we just stand there looking at each other.

"I'll go see her soon," Hilda continues as she sniffs. "I'll stop along the way at a group home in Winston-Salem to deliver some blankets and jackets." She fingers a plastic green caterpillar. "Maybe they'll like these things."

"What are they?" Kristine exclaims.

Hilda lifts a spider and squeezes it. "Fun," she cries. "Silliness. We all need more of it, wouldn't you agree?"

You are a saint, Hilda. You are a saint.

Kristine eyes the plastic creatures inside the box and exclaims that they look too real for her to think about *fun*.

I express my thanks again and then follow Salvador and Kristine back to my driveway. My driveway where the Harley sits, shiny and scary.

"See you tomorrow," says Salvador, handing me the silver duffle bag. He places his helmet back on his head and smiles. I see his dimple in the moonlight.

"You are gonna love riding on the Harley," Kristine tells me as she buckles her helmet's strap under her chin. "After the first thirty or so miles, your heart won't beat as fast."

I run my teeth over a thumbnail and clear my throat. I can't smile; I don't even bother to try.

Sure as the sun, tomorrow is going to arrive, whether I'm ready or not.

Removing my thumbnail from my mouth, I take a long look at the moon. Tonight it is a moon of flickering shadows.

Perhaps I will get to see if a rabbit is visible inside.

Harrison says the Japanese don't see only a still rabbit. Oh no. There is more. The rabbit is pounding rice into *mochi*. For them, that is what lives in the moon.

Clutching my new possession, the duffle bag, I head up the brick steps and into my house. The next time I enter this house I will have seen Japan. Again.

———

In my dining room, I watch my fish swim peacefully, wishing my stomach would quit spinning. What a long way I have come, I think, as I study the pagoda at the bottom of the tank, the gift Aaron gave me years ago. I kept the pagoda because it was a gift given in kindness, even though Aaron held the hope it would make me want to connect to my past. All these years I managed to deny the Japan part of my life. Now I am ready to accept it.

These thoughts make my stomach spin into a knot.

Rubbing my scar, I make a cup of Earl Grey to calm me.

At midnight I repack the items from the Samsonite into the lady-with-cancer's duffle bag. I spend a few minutes debating about what to wear tomorrow. I choose a green cotton shirt and a pair of khaki pants instead of a sundress because I can't see myself on the back of a red Harley in a dress. Face it, I can't picture myself on the back of any color motorcycle in any kind of clothes.

As I stroke the velvet of Aunt Lucy's chair, I think of Ducee dreaming of heaven in her hospital bed, Clive out of commission with his arm in a cast and anger boiling inside him, and Grable exhausted from another day of being the sole caregiver to a child with high needs. It is as though an Irish ballad is playing beside my thoughts, a soft melancholy tune.

Then I think of Father.

I wish he would call.

Strange as it may sound, I want him to give me his blessing for this trip across the sea. Ducee wants me to go. Why can't he just relent and tell me I have his permission to go?

Closing my eyes and sinking into the chair, I pretend I hear him say, "Nicole, it's okay to go. I am just afraid you'll be too overwhelmed. But you are not me. You don't have the guilt I live with. You didn't leave a pregnant wife and toddler to go to a conference. Nicole, don't blame yourself. You walk a different path, so Japan won't be the frightful demon of my nightmares for you. Go child. You want my blessing; I give it. Go to Japan with my blessing."

It's a little peculiar and hard to explain, but somewhere in my heart I do believe he could say those words. He never will say them to me. But he could. Just like he could get off the sofa and go back to being a respected physician at any hospital of his choice.

Wishful thinking?

Maybe.

I compose a short message to Harrison, my last one before meeting him.

Harrison,

I have been busy. Ducee's in the hospital and I've debated whether or not to even continue on with my travel plans. But she insists I go, and like I've told you before, my grandmother is a tough cookie to fight.

I will see you soon. It will be easy to spot me at the Osaka airport. I will be the redhead with her fingernails all bitten off.

Nicole

Chapter Thirty-Eight

The shiny red Electra Glide Ultra scares me so much that at first I don't know how to move my legs to actually get on it. Salvador turns the engine off and says I can practice a bit, get used to it without the electrifying noise. After a few minutes, I feel foolish seated on the back of a silent motorcycle, like a child pretending to drive in a parked car. I hope my neighbors aren't peering out their windows, observing me in my driveway.

Salvador holds a black helmet in his hand and asks, "Are you ready?"

Are you ready to see the big wide world?

I take the helmet from him, reluctantly strap it on under my chin, finally buckle it after three tries, and swallow. "I will be," I say. "I will." Sweat forms on my forehead, trickling down my scar. All I can think of is that it's going to be a long, hot, petrifying ride to the Raleigh-Durham airport. Perhaps I should take my first Dramamine now.

Salvador isn't bothered. He hums as he secures my duffle bag, purse, and overnight kit in the compartment behind the seat.

"You will be fine," he reassures me. "Kristine was scared the first time she rode. In a minute, you will be smiling."

Kristine is not me, I think. She holds no fear. She's dated ex-cons.

Salvador hops onto the motorcycle and starts the engine.

I close my eyes as tightly as they can shut and swing my shaky arms around his waist. He guns the engine, we begin to move, and I stop breathing for at least ten minutes, I'm sure.

Then we are sailing down Carved Oak Place, or I think that's what we are doing—my eyes are still closed. I feel wind in my face and on my back, cooling my perspiring body. When Salvador turns a corner, I am sure my helmet is going to slip off and bounce onto the pavement. But that doesn't happen.

At a stoplight, Salvador tilts his head back to ask, "How is it going?"

"Great," I say, certain the fear I'm trying to mask is evident. Then, to show just how comfortable I've become, I open my eyes and release one arm from my grip around him to brush strands of hair from my mouth. But when the light changes to green, both arms are once more plastered to him. Cautiously, I open my eyes to watch houses, trees, and people drift past. I still haven't smiled, and I most likely won't. I pray none of my students see me. Let this be the day they are out of Mount Olive, at Grandma's in Brevard or Charlotte.

When Salvador speeds toward the highway, I feel my stomach rise to my throat.

Ducee always says to think of something peaceful when faced with the unpleasant. I recall an autumn trip to the mountains of Brevard with Ducee and Grandpa Luke back when I was ten. We stopped at a farm that belonged to someone Grandpa knew, and picked Scuppernong grapes. I thought we owned the world then—to be able to pick grapes for free on a cool autumn day. None of my classmates had ever done this. I remember how tart the green grapes tasted, not at all sweet like red or purple grapes. But the jelly Ducee later made at her house from those Scuppernongs was delicious. Ducee said it was almost as good as pineapple chutney. And for Ducee to admit that must mean she really enjoyed it.

———

Salvador stops the motorcycle at the curb by the Delta terminal and says, "You made it, Nicole."

I let go of his waist, slowly peeling my curled fingers from him. Taxis, cars, buses, and all sorts of busy-looking people surround me. My throat feels as stiff as my fingers.

"Have a good trip. Email Kristine when you get there," Salvador tells me as he unfastens from the chrome tapered luggage rack Hilda's duffle bag, my purse, and overnight kit. As he places them on the curb, I wonder what in the world I'm doing at the airport when I hate to fly.

I stand; my knees don't seem to want to bend to walk.

He takes my helmet off of my head because I'm too dumbfounded to do so. Squeezing my arm, he says, "You rode to the airport on a motorcycle. Flying will be easy now." He gives me a broad smile, one I wish I could return. But my mouth feels like I've eaten packing peanuts, and the wind from the ride has caused my muscles to stiffen.

"Thank you," I say as I take small steps toward my belongings.

In an instant, Salvador hops back on his Electra Glide Ultra, and before I can say "Mount Olive Pickle Company," he is off with a slight sputter and then a fierce roar.

Well, well, I think as I watch him sail down the road, weaving around traffic, and then out of sight, I guess there is no turning back now.

I breathe in and out, raspy breaths, sounding like Iva. The sun glares at me, and I suddenly feel sticky in this heat.

The airport terminal is huge, and I know it must have grown since the last time I was here picking up relatives from the West for a family reunion. On TV it never looks this big.

After I enter through the sliding glass door—no flames, thank goodness—I find an unoccupied place by a window and just stand. My duffle bag is slung over one shoulder and the other shoulder holds my purse and overnight bag. I feel like a coat rack, immobile. Smiling families in T-shirts and shorts headed for vacations, and businessmen and women talking on cell phones stand before me in lines to check in.

I continue to stand like a statue and wonder if there's anyone going on a trip like I'm about to embark on. Is anyone as nervous? Is anyone going to a place they vowed never to return to ever again? And one more question, is there anyone who would be willing to give me some sips of cold water when I get sick on the plane?

I feel a bit better knowing Sazae is stuffed inside my duffle bag. It's tempting to take her out and hold her for comfort. That might cause some people to suddenly pay attention to me. Instead, I decide to pretend. I pretend that Sazae has to get to Japan. I envision a doctor—perhaps the one with the white mustache—writing out a prescription for Sazae Michelin. "It is imperative that you get your doll to Japan as soon as possible. One trip to Japan for her health. To be taken immediately. Without water." Which is good, because Sazae has never had any water in her cotton life.

Panic consumes me when I think that perhaps I've stood here daydreaming too long and missed my flight. Quickly, I edge my way to the Delta ticket counter line with one hand gripped to the handle of the duffle bag and the other clutching my purse and overnight kit. I'm in line along with everyone else who is sharing this day of travel with me. Strangers—all kinds of faces, all sorts of eyes, all with pasts, and destinations.

———

After I reluctantly check my duffle bag onto the plane, hoping that Sazae and I will be reunited in Osaka and that she won't be rerouted to Madrid, I purchase a Sprite at a kiosk. Once I spend five minutes making sure I'm at the correct gate, I find a seat in the lobby and take a sip of my drink. I heard Sprite is good for an upset stomach. I pray it'll calm my nerves, but even after three sips, I'm still too jittery to read my *Redbook*.

Salvador said the plane ride shouldn't be as scary since I've been on his motorcycle. But Salvador doesn't know me. Of course, I wonder if I know myself anymore. How did I just ride ninety miles to the airport on the back of a motorcycle?

Inhaling and exhaling, I listen to the conversations of others as they discuss people and cities I've never heard of. One girl, looking to be no more than sixteen, keeps talking about how she can't wait to get to Alice Springs. I wonder where that is—is it in America, or in another country, or just the name of a spa with a Jacuzzi? I have never been fond of geography.

Then a young man in his twenties, wearing khakis and a splashy Hawaiian shirt, bends toward me from his seat, asking if I know the time.

"I don't have a watch. Well, I mean I do, but it's at home."

He doesn't seem to care. He tells me he's from Mebane and

is on his way to Argentina. At least I know that Mebane is just down the road from Greensboro, where I went to college, and that Argentina is somewhere in South America. His girlfriend is in Buenos Aires. She owns a salon and makes "good money" cutting the hair of tourists who have "lots of money to burn." He visited her at Christmas and is now making another trip. "This time," he says as his eyes shine as bright as his shirt, "I'm giving her a ring."

He continues on, even as my mind wanders to Ducee. When he pauses to take a breath, I ask if he knows where a pay phone is.

"You need to call someone?"

Well, I think, that is usually the reason people want to know where a phone is.

"I need to call Mount Olive."

And even though we are at an airport in North Carolina, and he claims he's from Mebane, he has no idea where Mount Olive is. "Israel?"

His geography is worse than mine. "No, no," I tell him without sounding like a teacher. "North Carolina."

"Oh, sure." He hands over his Motorola cell phone and then shows me how to use it.

I dial the number from memory and listen as the phone rings once, twice, three times.

"Hello?"

"Iva." Have I ever been this grateful to hear my aunt's raspy voice? "Is Ducee there?"

"Not for much longer," Iva says, clearing her throat.

"What?" Anxiety grips me.

"She is being discharged."

"Really? Really?" And that is when I start to laugh. Discharged!

How did she finagle that? Last I heard, Ducee was to be in the hospital under observation for at least two more days.

"Yes, she's telling me to hurry up. I'll call you later." Aunt Iva coughs and hangs up.

I give the cell phone back to the young man and laugh.

"Must have been funny," he says.

The thought of Ducee in her white tennis shoes with the green laces, heading out the door of her hospital room, Iva lagging behind and calling, "Wait up! Don't you want to take these flowers home with you?" causes me to continue laughing. I imagine my grandmother running to get out of there, to get back home to her ginger tea brewing in her bone china teapot, to her beloved Maggie McCormick, to her maroon-covered Bible and her chair where she can fall asleep with ease during episodes of *Columbo*.

Funny. "Yeah, yeah, it is," I reply, trying to absorb the impact the conversation with Iva has had on me. I produce a smile for the young man. "Thanks for letting me use your phone."

Settling against the black chair in the airport terminal, I take a moment to let relief filter over me. Yes, yes, Ducee might live to see the year 2000, after all. Unless, of course, Iva's computer blowup fear comes true.

A twinge of loneliness surfaces as I realize that I won't receive any phone calls from Aunt Iva for a full two weeks. Upon my return, Iva will just have to call every hour to catch me up on all the Mount Olive gossip I've missed. And I am sure she will.

From the large window across the room, I watch a plane land. How do those tiny wheels keep it steady? It seems airplanes, like people, should have feet in proportion to their size.

Someone—it sounds like a child—says, "That's our plane!"

Nausea wells up in me and I know I need a Dramamine so

that by the time the flight takes off, I will be relaxed. From my purse, I take out a pill and down it with the last of my Sprite.

Right at that moment, a woman announces that the flight to Atlanta will be delayed. Passengers groan, as though on cue.

The young man from Mebane turns to me and continues where he left off. "The last time I was in Argentina I rode a bull." There is pride in his voice. "I stayed on for about three seconds and then was knocked off. That bull started rushing toward my head and I don't know how, but someone picked me up and got me out of there."

I really don't know what to say. I chew a nail as my nervous stomach rumbles.

When he leaves to find a restroom, I'm relieved. Closing my eyes, I take Ducee's advice again and think of one of the most pleasant aspects of my life—my fish. I picture them swimming joyfully in their salty water. I wonder if Monet has fed them yet today. Last night after Kristine and Salvador left my house, Grable called. She apologized for the late hour of her call and said she'd decided that after the reunion she and Monet were going on a trip.

"Costa Rica?" I guessed and she said, yes, that was where they were going.

"The travel brochure looks nice," she told me. "I hear the weather is great there in January."

I wanted to say, "See, Grable, your life isn't over yet. You're going to get your dream of going somewhere. You'll see the palm trees you've been eyeing in the brochure. Dennis just won't be accompanying you."

But, strangely, I felt sadness mixed in with the joy for her. Both emotions were wrapped up like a giant burrito and yet the sorrow was seeping through the flour tortilla, sorrow that couldn't be contained.

"Monet will enjoy it," she told me.

And, I let myself think, Costa Rica will never be the same after a visit from the wild one.

When she said that Monet wanted to come visit my fish, I asked, "How would she like to come every day for two weeks?"

Grable was all for the plan. I told her I'd leave a key to the house with Hilda. I could tell my cousin was distraught over Dennis, though. You don't get over an unfaithful spouse in one afternoon. The trip to Costa Rica would do her good, but she still had a lot to deal with.

Quickly, before asking to speak with Monet, I added, "Don't tell anyone, but I'm on my way to Japan. Only Ducee knows."

She said that even though her mother and grandmother were unable to keep secrets, she could.

Soon Monet took over the receiver—she only dropped it once—and I chatted with the wild child.

"Nicccc houuussss?"

"Yes, yes."

"Nicccc fissssszz!" Monet shouted so loudly I had to keep the phone at a distance.

"Yes, but feed them only a little. Okay?"

"Okaaaaa!" Then she screamed, "Dolll!"

"You like your new doll?"

"Yeessss." I heard her laughing. "Thannn yooooo."

"You're welcome."

"Nicccc." She breathed heavily into my ear. "My doooolll izzzz Nicccc!" Then she squealed, dropped the phone, and I listened as she asked her mother for a hooot dooo.

She didn't return to the phone.

I guess the anticipated hot dog with the tiny pool of ketchup on the side took precedence over me.

I hung up and shortly after that got ready for bed.

Now, I sit upright, look in all directions around me, and gulp. Was I sleeping? Snoring even? I can't fall asleep here before getting on the plane. What if the plane takes off without me?

The guy from Mebane is back. Standing in front of me with worry in his eyes, he asks, "Is everything all right?"

I was resting my head on my overnight bag while thinking about my fish and Monet and recalling the conversation with Grable and, goodness, I must have dozed off. I blink. None of that would mean anything to him because he knows nothing about me. I just reply, "I'm a little sleepy."

He wanders off. Minutes later, when I'm turning the pages of my magazine, he comes back with two cups of coffee. "You look like you need coffee," he tells me, thrusting one of the cups in my direction.

I wonder just how bad one who needs coffee looks. "Thank you."

"Cream or sugar?" he asks, waving paper packets of each.

Since I'm not a coffee drinker, I'm not sure what to do, so I add a packet of sugar and one of cream. I stir the beverage with the wooden stick he provides. I sip the coffee, burn my tongue, and after a few swallows, realize my aching tongue and I are now fully awake.

———

A perky voice announces that the flight to Atlanta is ready for boarding. Smiles break out on the faces around me—faces I've grown quite familiar with over the past hours. Bags are lifted; other people snap shut laptops. An elderly couple ambles toward a forming line.

The man from Mebane says, "Aren't you getting on this flight?"

"Oh." I take hold of the situation by changing my tone from bewildered to assured. "Well, it will be good to get on board at last."

I heard sometimes if you proclaim something in a positive way, you can actually convince yourself to be positive.

I stand on wobbly legs and swing my overnight kit and my purse—both so heavy with the jar of chutney and other items for that re-routed flight to Morocco or Mozambique—over my shoulder. Then I smile nervously at no one in particular and moisten my lips. I can do this. I can do this. It's all working out. So far, so good.

And then, since the creek has not risen and the Good Lord is willing, I step onto the plane headed to Atlanta.

An airline attendant looks at my boarding pass and directs me to my aisle seat.

The guy from Mebane secures my overnight kit in the compartment above my seat.

I look around the cabin as I'm bumped by a few passengers making their way past me, and then decide the only thing left to do is to sit down.

Chapter Thirty-Nine

"First time flying?"

I wonder why this seatmate, seated in the right window seat, is asking. I've glanced at her—a woman in her late forties, dressed in a gray business suit, with mauve lipstick and eyes hidden by a pair of gold-rimmed glasses. She holds a slick briefcase on her lap, takes a paperback from it, and then sets the briefcase near her shiny black leather shoes. Her nails are painted scarlet. True, she could be a hand model.

How can she tell? I pry my hands from the armrests where they've been glued. My feet are two blocks, stuck to the floor. My smile is forced and weak. I want to say yes, it is my first flight, but that's not true. There was that time I threw up when Father and I returned from Japan.

The need to say anything leaves me as the plane picks up speed down the runway.

My seatmate looks out the tiny window. Then she opens her paperback novel and lets it absorb her.

How can she calmly read at a time like this?

My eyes automatically shut, and I hope the second Dramamine tablet I took will kick in quick.

This flight is only to Atlanta, I keep telling myself. This is cake compared to the thirteen-hour nonstop ride to Osaka yet to come.

The skin over my knuckles stretches tightly as the plane races faster and faster along the runway. I know for sure now that we are all going to die. There is no way that this plane is going to glide into the air like a bird. It's about to collide with a wall and everyone will splatter like eggs in a hot pan.

I am unable to swallow. It's humanly impossible to do so when I'm plastered against my seat and sure that soon my life— all thirty-one years of it—is ready to flash before me in a brief second. This is it.

But instead of my life, I see the faces of Ducee, Clive, Monet, and Iva. Then like a puff of smoke, their faces dissolve and I see the smile belonging to Salvador. Salvador, my new motorcycle hero. I will have to find some *bizen* in Kyoto to bring back to him as a souvenir.

I moisten my lips and consider biting a nail, and then wait to catch my breath. There's a significant bump and then the plane is soaring, no longer on the ground, but suspended in the air, just like a bird.

I look around the cabin and see the heads of other passengers seated in front of me. Everyone's still attached—arms to shoulders, knees to legs—and in the seats to my left, a couple is even laughing. Suddenly, without any notice, the aircraft coasts into the clouds, as smooth as a fish with fins gliding through water.

There, right outside the window, if I look over my seatmate, who has not bothered to lift her head from her paperback, is the most fantastic sight.

The sky is a canvas of orange threaded with wisps of pink

clouds. The orange looks like the belly of a goldfish and the pink clouds, like ocean coral. Who would have thought the sky could hold similarities to the ocean? Who would have thought?

The Fasten Seatbelt light disappears, but I keep my belt secured around my waist.

Passengers are standing now, some heading to the restroom, others smiling, reading, talking. A few have headsets on, listening to music.

Like this is just another day. Like they fly all the time. No big deal.

I feel sleep fill my eyes, but I'm not ready to succumb to it. Outside, the sky is an array of orange clouds, a sea of the bellies of hundreds of goldfish, all crowded together so all I see are the shimmering orange undersides. It is as though the fish have taken over the sky, swimming in this sea-sky of tranquility.

Ducee's words flow through my mind. The words she said to me that night when I asked, "How does the duck know she can swim in the pond?"

She doesn't. But there is a good chance she can.

Am I swimming now?

I make a conscious effort to relax my arms and cross them against my stomach. I glance at my salmon-colored nails I painted last night after Kristine and Salvador left my house. I smudged one while waiting for the polish to dry and one got chipped when I placed my duffle bag on the scale at the check-in counter, but other than that, if I do say so myself, my nails look rather nice.

Did anyone ever tell you that you have hands like your mother?

"Pretty," my seatmate says, looking over the edge of her book and out the window. As she starts to yawn, she covers her mouth with an elegant hand, returns her eyes to the novel, turns a page, and continues to read.

My ears pop, so I swallow hard. Harrison gave me this tidbit of advice. He also wrote that chewing gum helps ease the popping sensation that comes from being at a higher altitude. So I bought three packs of spearmint and two packs of cinnamon.

The captain of the plane welcomes everyone aboard with a cheery voice, as though he just ate a plate of pancakes covered in whipped cream and the sugar has him electrified. "Folks," he says, "if you need anything, anything at all, don't hesitate to ask our flight crew. We thank you for flying Delta, and we hope you'll enjoy the flight." And for the third time this afternoon, he adds, "Once again, ladies and gentlemen, we apologize for the delay. We'll try to get you safely to Atlanta as soon as we can."

Soon, two flight attendants push a metal cart loaded with canned soft drinks, bottled water, cups, ice, and peanuts.

I think I'll ask for a Pepsi. Then I can tell my great-uncle that I drank his favorite soft drink at an altitude so high that I don't even care to hear what it is.

Maybe I'm not going to throw up. Maybe I'll be okay, able to enjoy a drink.

I tilt my head against the headrest and close my eyes.

Ducee should be home now, Iva by her side. Maggie McCormick will be braying so loudly with pleasure that I bet she'll be heard all the way in Havelock. What will they do about preparing all the food for the reunion? Surely Ducee won't have the energy to cook. And no one else has the time. What will happen? Will they bring in food from Howie's sub shop?

I guess I'll just have to wait to find out. After all, there is nothing I can do about it. I'm sort of suspended in the sky right now.

It gives me a jolt of amusement to think of the email message I plan to send from Harrison's computer to the group gathered this week at the family reunion. I'll send it to Aaron, of course. No one else has a computer.

I only wish I could see the expression on his face as he reads my words from thousands of miles across the ocean: "Arrived safely in Kyoto. Wish you were here." And I might even add, just for his sake, "Decided it was finally time to get to know the Japan side of me."

I picture them all around the new picnic tables, framed by the oak trees, cucumber and egg salad sandwiches before them, asking Ducee, "Where is Nicole?" They will make some comment that I wasn't there for the Friday night dessert time, and that was unusual; however, not everyone makes it to the Friday night part of the reunion. But Saturday at Ducee's. No one misses this event.

And then, just then, at the perfect moment, just like in the movies, the message will appear on the screen of Aaron's laptop.

"Oh," my cousin will say, "I just got a message from Nicole."

Ducee's lips will certainly be sealed with a grin, as family members look at her with bewildered eyes, wanting to grasp how Emma's daughter could have something else to do and let it be important enough to take her away from this anticipated family reunion weekend.

Ducee will tell them, yes, she encouraged Nicole to make the trip. She will say, "Yes, yes, it was to be."

Will they understand?

And if they don't?

Actually, they should be amazed, and for two very good

reasons. One, that I'm traveling to Japan and on a plane when I hate to fly, and two, that three of our relatives were able to successfully keep a secret from the rest of them. That's something for the front page of the *Mount Olive Tribune*!

I rub my scar and then my neck, trying to ease the pressure in my ears. Opening a pack of spearmint gum, I chew a piece. I wiggle the toes on my left foot and then the ones on the right. If I can wiggle my toes on an airplane in flight, how bad can flying be?

The golden sky is perfect; I know we can't be far from heaven.

Mama. Oh, Mama. Your little girl is daring, isn't she? She is going to see the big wide world. She may not be ready, but are any of us humans ever ready? We'd like to think we are brave, capable, and strong. But the minute we lose our luggage or are delayed, we've been known to break into pieces.

I'm going to give it my best shot. Certainly, future generations will equate me right up there with bold Lizzy McCormick.

I breathe in an aura of reverence, "God, you have always been with me."

And then, sure as the sun, I feel it. God's hand, steady and tight, around my shoulder. It feels like warm fingers, warmer than even the ocean waters of my dreams, circling my whole being. It's as real to me as my very feet, feet that are wiggling, no longer blocks of concrete. Feet eager to step onto Japanese soil.

My reflection in the plane's small window is of a woman with confidence. Confidence that matches every one of her bitten polished nails.

My smile is as wide as the sun over the Carolina coast on a brilliant summer morning.

Chapter Forty

Just like Harrison wrote, Watanabe-san's room at the Katsura nursing home has a small bulletin board crammed with pictures. In the center is a color photo of her, taken when she was much younger and more limber, dressed in pants, cap, and an orange fleece jacket, climbing a snowy mountain. In another, a black-and-white, she smiles while holding a little girl with frizzy hair. I look closely and my heart melts. "It's me," I whisper to Harrison.

He peers toward the photo to get a better view. "I remember you that way," he says. His voice is deep, rich, and over the past days, one I love to hear—one reason being, it speaks a language I understand.

There are two black-and-white photos of Mama I've never seen before today. In one she has her arm around Father. Youth fills each of their joyful faces. The other is of Mama standing in the kitchen. On the burner beside her elbow sits a large metal pot.

I point to it, asking Harrison what Mama was cooking. He asks Watanabe-san in Japanese.

Still clutching the jar of chutney I earlier presented to her, Watanabe-san, seated in a wheelchair, rattles off a few lines.

"Pineapple chutney," Harrison tells me. "That particular day your mother made it for a group of women she taught at a Bible study."

How many times have I heard Ducee repeat that Mama brought pineapple chutney and the Gospel to Japan? Yet somehow hearing today and in this place that Mama did make chutney and teach the Bible makes it more real—much more real than hearing the tale in little ol' Mount Olive, far from where it took place. Of course, I'd never let Ducee know this sentiment.

"You also helped," Harrison continues to translate. "You liked to stand on a chair and mix the chutney with a large wooden spoon as your mother held on to you."

"Did we wear aprons?" I think of how Ducee, Iva, and I always don our Mount Olive aprons when we cook up a batch of the delicacy.

The answer comes back. "Yes, green ones from your mother's hometown."

Some things never change, I think, and the thought makes me smile.

"She doesn't have it on in the picture," Watanabe-san explains in Japanese. "She took the apron off because she spilled pineapple juice all over the front."

So Mama was clumsy like I am, I think. I guess the apple doesn't fall far from the tree.

The photo in the middle of the board is the same one I have in the silver frame at home. Mama, Sazae, and me, all in kimono, looking much more international in this Japanese setting than we look on my bedside table in Mount Olive.

Harrison stands next to me, studying all the pictures. He

claims he spent much time looking over every photo during his past visits to meet my former maid at this nursing home. "I've often thought this one of you and your mom is cute," he observes now with a grin.

"With Sazae," I say. I turn to look at the real Sazae. My cotton doll is seated in the wheelchair with Watanabe-san this afternoon. Last night as the bullfrogs and crickets sang under a crescent moon, Harrison and I sat by his koi pond planning this visit to the home. I asked whether or not to bring the doll.

"Of course," he told me. "She'll be thrilled." Then he gave me a few lessons on how to correctly pronounce my companion's name.

I tried to say Sazae, enunciating every syllable like he taught me. Finally I concluded with, "I don't know. All these years she's answered to the way I've said her name. If I change, she might not know it's her."

"She answers when you call her?" Harrison looked at me with wide eyes, as if I had six heads.

He thinks I'm crazy, I thought, or badly affected by jet lag. I then tried to come up with some response.

Before I could say another word, he asked, "So does she answer in English?"

"Always."

He grinned and I thought it was nice of him to play along with me. Really nice.

And Watanabe-san was thrilled. Tears welled in her worn eyes as she took my cotton doll and murmured a few words. My eyes filled, too. We took tissues Harrison handed us from a box on Watanabe-san's bedside table.

"You are so beautiful and so grown-up," Watanabe-san said between light sobs. "I remember brushing all that red hair."

With one hand over her heart, she repeated a number of times, "And you really are alive."

As Harrison translated, a lump formed in my throat. Here I am, Mama. Did I ever think this day would come? I only hope it's not a dream, that I am really standing in my former maid's room, this woman who knew a part of you I am so eager to learn about. I'm not in a sea with fish, and Harrison looks human, so perhaps this is reality.

When I tried to answer Watanabe-san, no words came. Gently, Harrison placed his arm around my shoulders—the first time he'd touched me since hugging me upon my arrival at the airport three days ago. I felt my heart flutter and then I knew if it could, it would have turned a complete cartwheel, one of those spontaneous ones children do with sheer agility.

Now Harrison and I move together from the bulletin board to sit in chairs beside the older woman. She is still holding on to the chutney and Sazae. As we sit, she carefully secures the objects in her chair against one of her thighs. Pushing her wheelchair close to me, she reaches for my right hand, taking it, painted bitten nails and all, between her scarred palms. They are a dull purplish red, looking ugly, like bruises. These hands of hers— God used them to save me. And they cost her. I have never seen such beauty.

Observing that I am studying her scars, she speaks.

Harrison translates. "These wounds are superficial. The real longing has been in my torn heart. Oh, to see your mother again. She was such a kind woman."

I note Watanabe-san's wrinkled face, her gray head of hair pulled back into a bun, and imagine what it must have been like to have been rocked by her as an infant as Mama and Father smiled at each other. I breathe in talcum powder and a faint aroma of cold cream.

As much as I'm grateful to Harrison for being the interpreter, I only wish I knew the language to get the real gist of what Watanabe-san is conveying to me.

Yesterday at a hole-in-the-wall restaurant over a lunch of *unagi*, which is absolutely fabulous, Harrison explained something to me that makes sense. He said that even if I can't speak the native tongue, my body language as well as the tone of my words in English will bridge the sea of the language barrier. "People know you are sincere and happy to be with them and be here. That's what translates well."

Sitting here with Watanabe-san, Harrison says, "She knows you have more questions about the past. Perhaps you want to know about that night. She says your father was a brilliant man. He loved your mom and you very much."

I smile. I want to stop the conversation here, put a period at the end of her sentence, and not venture any farther. But I know there's more.

So far this afternoon, we've talked about the house we lived in—what it looked like, the neighborhood with the market and the playground where I fell off the swing. I asked about the hospital where I was born and where Mama and Father worked. I learned Mama would affectionately kiss the top of my head each night at bedtime, just as I've seen other mothers do. She enjoyed watching children's programs with me on the black-and-white TV in the living room. We'd both sit barefoot on the sofa with a quilt covering us as we watched the shows.

But yes, I did come here to hear more.

I listen as Harrison and the woman converse. Then my body tenses as Harrison translates again. "Your father became a shadow of his former self once your mother died." Solemnly Harrison adds, "Apparently he and your mother got into a fight the day he left for the meeting in Tokyo."

My skin feels clammy, and I have to take my hand away from Watanabe-san's hold as she continues with the story. I stick a finger in my mouth, remove it, and then clamp my hands tightly in my lap.

Harrison explains, "The house was cold. There was no central heating, and earlier that day your dad had gone out to buy a kerosene heater. The oil stove in the living room only heated a portion of the house. After he returned with the heater, your mother asked him to stay and not go to the conference in Tokyo. She wasn't feeling well. She had the flu and, as you know, was pregnant. She'd told few people about the pregnancy. She'd had a miscarriage the year before and wasn't sure this baby would stay. Your father said, 'I got you this heater, what do you mean I don't do enough for you?' He purchased the heater secondhand. I will always wish he'd spent the money for a reliable new one." Here Harrison pauses, nods to Watanabe-san.

She continues in halted sentences. "Your father left in spite of the argument. He called a cab that took him to the airport. Poor thing, last time he saw her alive she was sad, coughing, and crying. He never got to apologize. But she would have forgiven him; he needs to know that."

Harrison's translation of the rest of the incident comes slowly. "The heater had a leak, and the firemen that came later said that was the cause of the fire. While your mother slept, the kerosene leaked and caught the rug and the curtains in her bedroom on fire. She woke and tried to get out of the room, but she had already breathed in too much smoke. Your mother died from the very heater your father thought would keep her warm."

My throat feels as if someone has stuffed a towel inside it. I try to breathe, speak, swallow. In my mind I see Mama's youthful body motionless on her bedroom floor. Mama, my poor mama. Harrison notices my struggle and places his hand on my arm. My eyes are clouding over again. I sniff, hoping to hold back more tears.

The old woman's weathered cheeks are moist.

I reach out to squeeze her hand, and as I do, that place in my heart for Father starts to ache. "Sometimes," Ducee has said to me over the years, "those who survive have the hardest burden. Survivor's guilt is a weary load." He bought a heater that killed her. As if that guilt—his heavy shackle—of not being at the house to protect her that night wasn't enough. The thoughts make my head sting, along with my eyes. I rub my scar, as though the motion will ease my pain.

When my eyes meet Harrison's, I note his deep-set blue eyes are watering, too.

He has to clear his throat before being able to translate Watanabe-san's next statement. "I can die now, is what she says. I can die now a happy woman. God in heaven has answered my prayers. You are here."

Suddenly, there is a knock on the door and an attendant in a white uniform quietly enters the room. She's the same one who ushered us into Watanabe-san's room an hour ago, rounding up extra chairs for us to sit on.

The attendant and my former maid talk as Harrison gently runs his fingers against my bare arm. "Are you ready to go?" he asks me. "We can come back another day."

Before I can answer, Watanabe-san has shifted from her

mellowness and is rapidly ordering the attendant to get some-thing. The attendant bows, cries, "Hai!" and bolts out of the room.

I look at Harrison, questioning.

He translates. "Watanabe-san said it's time for tea. You've come all the way across the world to see her and she has yet to serve you tea. What a terrible hostess she's been."

I start to laugh. The sound of my laughter is like a cascad-ing waterfall—robust and full of life. *Just throw your head back and let it out.*

Harrison joins me. I like the way his mouth curves upward and his eyes light like a warm, starry night. Sincere eyes, kind eyes. Eyes that have even glossed over when told a sad story.

Watanabe-san glances at us for a moment, as though she doesn't know what to make of us. Or perhaps she is remember-ing those years, decades ago, when Harrison and I were both small and walked on narrow streets to the neighborhood park. She chuckles in her tender way.

After a moment she asks if I still sing.

"Sing?"

"The rain song," Harrison interprets. "About the falling rain and the mother coming to pick up the child with an old Japanese-style umbrella."

The song I sang that helped this woman know where I was so that she could follow my voice through the smoky house and rescue me. I wish I knew the words.

Watanabe-san's face softens. "It is somewhere still inside you—the words." She sounds like Ducee whenever I'd say I recalled nothing about my mother. *She is you. You are her.*

When the *ocha* is served—steamy green tea in round pink cups painted with pale cherry blossoms—I taste more than I can imagine. It is the past and present all melding into one. It is understanding, truth, hope. I briefly close my eyes, trying to absorb it all.

And when I open them, through wet eyelashes, I smile at Harrison drinking his tea.

As he smiles back, I think that maybe I see the future.

I hear Ducee's voice as clear as if she's seated right next to me, nodding in the way she often does, eager to voice her familiar phrase. *Yes, that's it, yes.*

The McCormick Family Recipe

PINEAPPLE CHUTNEY

1 fresh pineapple
1 cup water
salt to taste
1 cup brown sugar
4–6 whole cloves
2 cinnamon sticks
2 tablespoons lemon juice
1 teaspoon powdered cinnamon
3 tablespoons vinegar

Peel the pineapple and slice into bite-sized pieces. Cook over low heat in 1 cup of water with salt. Bring to boil. Let boil for three to four minutes. Add sugar, cloves, and cinnamon sticks. Stir constantly and simmer for ten minutes. Remove from stove and add lemon juice, powdered cinnamon, and vinegar. Let cool and then spoon into mason jars.
Seal tightly.

Recipe can be doubled for any family reunion.

Acknowledgments

No work is ever accomplished without the critique and guidance of others. For spending long Tuesday nights with my chapters, I want to thank the Six Serious Scribes—Julie, Martha, Catherine, Dianne, Katharine, and Kim. For believing in me so that my feet can enter the door to the novel publishing club, my gratitude goes to my agent, Kristin Lindstrom, and my editor, Charlene Patterson. And to the woman who gave me a pedicure at the spa years ago, thank you for encouraging me not to give up.

About the Author

Alice J. Wisler, daughter of missionary parents, was born and raised in Japan. Since graduating with a B.S. in social work, she has worked in a group home in Pennsylvania and taught English-as-a-Second Language at a refugee camp in the Philippines and a church school in Japan. In 1997, after the death of her son, Daniel, she founded Daniel's House Publications, an organization to help other bereaved parents and siblings. She gives workshops across the country on Writing the Heartache, believing that writing through pain is an essential tool to healing. She lives in Durham, North Carolina, with her three children. *Rain Song* is her first novel.

QUESTIONS FOR CONVERSATION

1. All her life Nicole has pushed away anything to do with Japan. Why does Nicole fear Japan so much? Is her fear justified? Is there any place you particularly dislike because of something that happened there?

2. Nicole's feelings about Monet change the more she gets to know the little girl. Have you ever found beauty in someone you once thought irritating? Has a child ever surprised you with his/her talent or intelligence? Have you ever dealt with a hard-to-diagnose condition?

3. Do you have a family member you never got to meet due to his/her death that you wish you had been able to know? What has captivated you about this relative?

4. Nicole has to come to terms with her past so she can welcome her future. Have you ever had to do this? Do you think Nicole handled it well? Do you think Nicole's life will be different now that she knows more about her family history?

5. Do you attend family reunions or get-togethers? What do you like and not like about them? Do you consider family togetherness important?

6. What are some traditions that keep your family united?

7. What does Nicole value in her life? What do you value in your life?

8. Nicole's father is prone to alcohol abuse and depression, and often disappoints Nicole. Why do you think he has never been able to get over Nicole's mother's death? How do you handle those in your family who are hard to deal with?

9. Nicole heads to the beach to consider Harrison's request to come to Japan. When you have a problem to ponder, do you have a special place you go to think? What do you like about this place? If you could visit one country you've never been to, which one would it be?

10. What do you think of Ducee's Southern Truths? What bits of wisdom have other people given you? Do you have any of your own "Southern Truths"?

11. Do you see a future for Harrison and Nicole? Why or why not?

Looking for More Good Books to Read?

You can find out what is new and exciting with
previews, descriptions, and reviews by signing up for
Bethany House newsletters at

www.bethanynewsletters.com

We will send you updates for as many authors or
categories as you desire so you get only the
information you really want.

Sign up today!